Natasha realized that the brightly lit entrance she was being hustled through was completely unfamiliar to her.

"What is this?" she demanded huskily. "Where am I? Tell me at once."

Silent, impassive, the men halted in front of a pair of double doors and knocked. The doors opened noiselessly.

They didn't push her in. It wasn't quite as crude as that. But somehow she was stepping forward, and they were moving backward, and the doors were closing again behind her. Leaving her standing there, alone.

Except that she was not alone.

It was a very big room, but all Natasha noticed was the bed, lit on either side by tall lamps, like a stage set. Illumining, she realized dazedly, the man who was sitting in that bed, leaning back against a mound of snowy pillows, naked down to the sheet discreetly draped across his hips, and probably beyond, as he worked on the laptop computer open in front of him.

He unhurriedly completed whatever task he was engaged in, then Alex Mandrakis closed the lid, put the laptop on the adjacent table and looked at her.

"Ah," he said softly. "The beauty I was promised, here at last."

Dear Reader,

Welcome to the March 2010 collection of fabulous Presents stories for you to unwind with.

Don't miss the last installment from bestselling author Lynne Graham's PREGNANT BRIDES trilogy, *Greek Tycoon, Inexperienced Mistress.* When ordinary Lindy goes from mistress to pregnant, shipping tycoon Atreus Drakos will have no choice but to make her his bride!

We have another sizzling installment in the SELF-MADE MILLIONAIRES miniseries. Author Sarah Morgan brings us *Bought: Destitute yet Defiant,* where unashamedly sexy Sicilian Silvio Brianza has plans for the disobedient Jessie!

Why not relax with a powerful story of seduction, blackmail and glamour in Sara Craven's *The Innocent's Surrender,* and go from humble housekeeper to mistress for a month in Trish Morey's *His Mistress for a Million.*

Cassie's life changes altogether when her new boss turns out to be none other than the notorious Alessandro Marchese, the father to her twins, in *Marchese's Forgotten Bride* by Michelle Reid. And when Eva finds herself married to the notorious Sheikh Karim, she discovers that her husband is having a startling effect on her in Kim Lawrence's *The Sheikh's Impatient Virgin.*

Don't forget to look out for more tantalizing installments of our new miniseries during the year, kicking off with DARK-HEARTED DESERT MEN in April! The glamour, the excitement, the intensity just keep on getting better.

Sara Craven

THE INNOCENT'S SURRENDER

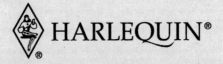

HARLEQUIN®

TORONTO • NEW YORK • LONDON
AMSTERDAM • PARIS • SYDNEY • HAMBURG
STOCKHOLM • ATHENS • TOKYO • MILAN • MADRID
PRAGUE • WARSAW • BUDAPEST • AUCKLAND

Recycling programs
for this product may
not exist in your area.

ISBN-13: 978-0-373-12903-4

THE INNOCENT'S SURRENDER

First North American Publication 2010.

www.eHarlequin.com

Printed in U.S.A.

All about the author...
Sara Craven

SARA CRAVEN was born in South Devon and grew up in a house full of books. She worked as a local journalist, covering everything from flower shows to murders, and started writing for Mills and Boon in 1975. When not writing, she enjoys films, music, theater, cooking and eating in good restaurants. She now lives near her family in Warwickshire. Sara has appeared as a contestant on the former Channel Four game show *Fifteen to One,* and in 1997 was the U.K. television *Mastermind* champion. In 2005 she was a member of the Romantic Novelists' team on *University Challenge: the Professionals.*

CHAPTER ONE

'SO,' NATASHA KIRBY said, glancing round the lamplit table, her gaze steady, her voice cool and even. 'Is someone going to tell me what's going on? What I'm doing here? Or do I have to guess?'

There was an awkward silence, then Andonis leaned forward, his smile cajoling. 'Why, sister, it is only that it has been some time—too long—since you paid us a visit. *Po,po,po*, does there have to be a problem before we invite you here, for a little family party?'

'No,' Natasha agreed levelly. 'But I usually come in the spring and early autumn in order to see your mother. Invitations at other times are rarely so last-minute—or so pressing,' she added drily. 'And if this is a party, I certainly don't see many signs of celebration.'

On the contrary, she thought, the atmosphere at the house was more reminiscent of a wake. Her antennae had picked up on it as soon as she'd arrived. Although it was hardly surprising in view of recent events.

And while the meal itself had been splendid—her favourite lamb dish, she'd noted cynically, oven-baked with tomatoes, garlic and oregano until it melted off the bone—the conversation round the dinner table had been strained, almost muted.

Even Irini, the youngest of the late Basilis Papadimos's three children, had been quieter than usual, as if she was deliberately reining back her normal overt hostility to her English foster sister. Which should, Natasha recognised, have been a relief. Yet, somehow, wasn't...

There was another uncomfortable pause, while she watched Andonis look at his older brother, his shoulder lifting in a shrug that was almost resigned.

And Natasha sat back in her chair, sighing under her breath, as she thought, *Oh God, there's trouble. I knew it.*

The problem was she did know. Because she knew them all—much too well. And had done since her childhood, she thought wryly.

Since the moment, in fact, when Basilis, that great, loud bear of a man who'd been her father's friend, had swooped down in those bleak, traumatic days after Stephen Kirby's sudden death and carried her off to his palatial home outside Athens, ignoring all the protests from the child-support agencies in London.

'I am her godfather,' he had rumbled, his eyes fierce under the heavy eyebrows, daring anyone to oppose him. 'And, to a Greek, that bestows a lifetime of responsibility. Stephanos knew this, always. Knew I would happily accept his daughter as my own. There is no more to be said.'

And when the millionaire owner of the Arianna shipping line spoke with such finality, it was generally better to obey.

She had been welcomed gently by Madame Papadimos, who told her that she must call her Thia Theodosia, then smoothed her soft fair hair with caressing fingers, and gave her a handkerchief scented with sandalwood when the inevitable, bewildered tears began to rain down her white face.

The sons of the house, Stavros and Andonis, greeted her more exuberantly, clearly seeing in her another female victim, alongside their younger sister, Irini, for their teasing and practical jokes.

But being a joint target had not created any kind of bond between Natasha and the Greek girl, only two years older than herself. From the start, Irini had never exhibited even an atom of the *philoxenia*—the love of strangers—that was the heart of Greek hospitality. On the contrary…

Even though she was grieving, Natasha had soon realised that Irini had resented her from the first step she'd taken over the Papadimoses' family threshold, and that little had happened since to change that in any way. That to the other girl she would always be the outsider—the interloper that her father had imposed upon them.

And sadly the attitude of Basilis himself had not helped the situation. Young as she was, Natasha became uncomfortably aware that Irini's life was already one long, painful contest for her father's attention. A contest that she seemed not to be winning.

Because where his only daughter was concerned, Basilis was kind enough but invariably remote in a way he never was with the boys. Or, Natasha had to admit, with herself, whom he treated with wholehearted affection.

And whether Irini behaved like an angel, or turned into a whining, spiteful, needy devil, as she could do at the drop of a hat, it made no noticeable difference. So, without any real incentive to be good, she usually chose the other option, with nerve-shattering results.

'And to think her name means peace,' Stavros had commented sourly one day, after a particularly spectacular row with screaming and door-slamming. 'She should have been named Hecate of the Three Heads, because she whines like a dog, bites like a snake and looks like a horse.'

He'd been punished for his unkindness, but Natasha knew that he and Andonis had still used the name on the quiet to torment their sister.

And for all she knew, they might be doing so to this day, which could be why the other girl's mouth had thinned into a line of ill-natured grievance, and her dark eyes snapped at the world with un-disguised suspicion.

As she'd got older and more perceptive, Natasha had often won-dered why Thia Theodosia, who must have realised the reason for Irini's tears, tantrums and sheer bad temper, didn't intervene—point out to her husband the damaging disparities in his treatment of his children.

But perhaps it was because Madame Papadimos had her own per-sonal battle to fight. She had always seemed frail, a shadow to her husband's larger-than-life vibrancy, but now, since Basilis had died suddenly of a heart attack two years ago, she seemed to be slowly but deliberately fading out of the family picture, apparently content to live quietly in her own wing of the villa with Hara, her devoted nurse-companion, in close attendance.

Nor had she joined tonight's dinner party, which Natasha felt was a bad sign in more ways than one, as neither Stavros nor Andonis ever willingly discussed business matters in front of their mother. If this had been a purely social occasion, she would have been there.

Their wives, of course, were a different matter. Both Maria and Christina Papadimos were present—and both clearly on edge, their smiles too forced, their bursts of laughter far too shrill.

I suppose, Natasha thought, sighing inwardly, it's up to me to get the ball rolling, or we'll be here all night and tomorrow, too, and I need to get back to London, and my real life.

She looked round the table. 'So, let's drop the social niceties and have the truth—shall we? I presume that I've been summoned to discuss the recent well-publicised problems of the Arianna line.'

'There is nothing to discuss.' Irini might not have said much so far, but the familiar basilisk glare was suddenly back in full working order. 'Decisions have already been made. You are only expected to agree. To sign where you are bidden. No more than that.'

Natasha bit her lip. This, she knew, had always been a bone of contention—that Basilis had decreed in his will that she, the foster child, should have a place on the Papadimos board, with full voting rights and the same level of salary as the rest of the family.

She had waived the salary, and rarely attended any of the board meetings, but, in view of the stories that had been appearing in the newspapers over the past months, she realised ruefully that this might have been a big mistake.

Because the Arianna line had been stalked by disaster of late. The *Arianna Queen* had suffered a serious outbreak of food poisoning, affecting almost two thirds of her passengers. The *Princess* had been detained at Malta when the crew had gone on strike in a dispute over late payment of their wages, and two of the smaller boats had experienced engine faults, resulting in their cruises being curtailed. And the *Empress*, their new flagship, had been deluged with complaints after the maiden voyage, about poor workmanship in the staterooms and bathrooms that didn't work properly.

And that, she thought, was only the passenger line. The cargo vessels that comprised the Leander fleet had experienced problems, too, with an oil tanker running aground and the inevitable spillage, and a fire on board another ship.

Natasha had read all these horror stories, appalled, knowing that none of these things would have happened when Basilis was alive and in charge, because he was a man with a nose for trouble.

In fact, just before his heart attack, he had been talking about instituting a mass refit on the whole fleet of cruise ships, particularly the galleys, which were showing their age, and the engine rooms.

She could only assume that after his death, in an act of blatant unwisdom, these eminently sensible—indeed necessary—plans had gone quietly into abeyance. Certainly she'd never been consulted about any cancellation or postponement to the modernisation of the Arianna line, or she'd have fought tooth and nail for Basilis's wishes to be adhered to.

It was the only course of action that made economic sense. How could the brothers not have seen it?

Not that Stavros and Andonis often listened to advice, especially from women. And in this, she was forced to admit, they resembled their father, who took the unenlightened view that the female of the species was of more use in the bedroom than the boardroom. And who had shocked Natasha rigid on her eighteenth birthday by summoning her to his study to outline his plans for her own forthcoming marriage.

Apparently, she'd learned with horror, her pale blonde hair, creamy skin and wide, long-lashed green eyes had found favour among a number of the susceptible young men in the wealthy social circles that the Papadimos clan moved in. The question of whether or not she had a brain had not come under consideration by any of her would-be suitors.

She was regarded solely by them all as a trophy bride.

But, Basilis had announced magnanimously, she would be permitted to make her own choice among them. Nor would she go to her husband penniless, the sum of money which her father's will had left in trust for her having multiplied in value under his stewardship. All this, she must understand, in addition to the dowry that he would settle on her himself.

Which, in his assumption, made everything all fine and dandy.

My God, Natasha had thought, trying to suppress the appalled bubble of laughter welling up inside her, looks and money. I've suddenly become the catch of the season, if not the year.

It had taken, she recalled, hours of patient persuasion to convince Basilis that his plans for her were doomed. That she had her own vision of her future, that clashed fundamentally with his on a number of points, and that marriage didn't feature—or not for some years, anyway. And any future husband would be expected to respect her intelligence and her need for independence.

Hours of standing her ground against his roared disapproval and voluble reproaches. Hours, too, of resisting the more subtle emotional blackmail he used as a last resort, when anger and pleading had clearly failed.

And hours of assuring him with perfect truth that she loved him dearly, and that she would be eternally grateful for his care of her while she was growing up. That she owed him more than she could ever repay.

But that she was now in charge of her own destiny, which she was sure rested in England rather than her country of adoption. And that it was there that she would try to carve out a life for herself.

Also she had been very careful not to hint, as she might have done, that it was Irini who could be in need of his matchmaking abilities, as no queue of hopefuls appeared to be lining up to woo her.

Now, she looked away from the other girl's glare and said quietly, 'I see. And may I ask what exactly is on this dotted line that's been prepared for me?'

Stavros reached over with the wine bottle. 'It is merely a small matter of negotiation,' he said soothingly. 'A delaying tactic. No more than that.'

Natasha moved her glass out of range, regarding him stonily. 'Indeed?' she queried drily. 'Well, if it's so trivial, why bring me all this way? Why not just send the papers to my solicitors in London— as we agreed last time I was here?' She paused. 'I do have a business to run, you know.'

Without surprise, she heard a contemptuous snort from Irini, followed by Stavros and Andonis explaining in unison that it was not *quite* that simple. That it was a family matter, and therefore better dealt with on a personal basis, without lawyers being troubled.

'Oh, God,' Natasha muttered under her breath, watching Christina chewing at her lip, and Maria tugging at the gold chains that festooned her plump neck as they exchanged frankly uneasy glances. Things must be much worse than I thought.

Eventually the full story began to emerge, her foster brothers taking the narration in turns, rather like a Greek chorus from some ancient drama. Strophe, she thought wryly, and antistrophe—as Basilis had painstakingly explained to her on their visits to the theatre to watch the plays of Aeschylus and Sophocles.

Only it was a very different tragedy she was hearing this time. A tragedy of mismanagement, greed and stupidity on a fairly grand scale, with disaster right there, waiting in the wings. Because now there were big questions being asked by their insurers, and the shareholders were running scared, which, for the first time, made Basilis's once-powerful empire seem vulnerable. Something she had never thought could happen.

And where, she asked herself as disbelief warred inside her with something very like hysteria, where was the god in the machine, so beloved in classical drama, who would descend to save the day?

'But we are taking steps to regulate the situation,' Stavros announced grandly. 'To begin with, we plan a major refit of all the passenger accommodation on the Arianna line,' he added, as if it were suddenly all his own idea, and Natasha found she was biting her lip again—hard.

'Well,' she said. 'That's—good.' *And certainly better late than never.*

'Except that the necessary finance is proving more difficult to obtain than we thought,' Andonis added.

But there'd been money set aside, Natasha recalled, startled. So what had happened to that? Better, she thought, not to ask, perhaps.

But if they'd asked her here hoping for a loan, then they'd be seriously disappointed. Helping Out, the small business she'd started with the inheritance from her father, was established now, and doing well enough for her to have taken on a partner, and be thinking about expansion.

Because there were always emergencies, large and small, in people's lives. They might simply need their dogs walking, or their children collecting from school or nursery, or someone to house-sit while they were on vacation. Or there could be elderly relatives to be visited, or taken shopping.

And, in the worst-case scenario of accident, illness or bereavement, they wanted someone calm and trustworthy to step in and take over. To make sure that meals were cooked, laundry was done and life went on with an element of stability until matters settled down.

And it was infinitely satisfying to know that Helping Out had an excellent name for reliability, and that most of her clientele came on personal recommendation, even if they were a little surprised to find that both she and Molly Blake were only just past their twenty-first birthdays.

The business provided Molly and herself with a decent living, because, while their fees were not extortionate, they did not sell the services of their staff cheaply. They employed good people, and made sure they were paid accordingly, and were not afraid to pitch in themselves when required.

But at the moment, there wasn't a lot of financial slack.

'Of course, we are exploring every avenue,' Stavros continued. 'And we hope that the necessary loan will be available to us very soon.' He paused. 'But while the details are being finalised, we have to deal with another problem.'

A kind of shiver went round the table—as if a chill breeze had suddenly rippled across a cornfield.

'Unfortunately, news of our difficulties has reached other people.' Andonis took up the tale of woe. 'And if there is blood in the water, there will always be sharks circling. It was rumoured that some of our rivals were considering a hostile takeover, which was quite bad enough.'

'Until two weeks ago.' Stavros spoke with gritted teeth. 'When we received an offer to buy outright a half-share in both the Arianna line and the cargo fleet.'

There was a silence, then Natasha said carefully, 'And you regard this as a problem, instead of a possible solution?'

Andonis banged his fist on the table. 'It was an insult.'

'You mean, they were offering peanuts?' Natasha mused aloud. 'Well, that often happens with an initial bid.'

'No,' Stavros said harshly. 'The money could be considered fair.'

'And could always improve,' she suggested tentatively. 'If, as you say, there's room for negotiation, it might be the answer.'

And if I were in your situation, she added silently, I'd take the cash, while it's there, because this might be as good as it gets. And, although the thought of an outside partner has always been anathema up to now, maybe beggars can't be choosers.

'That is not possible,' Andonis said, glancing at his brother, their brooding anger almost tangible. 'Not when it comes from such a source.'

And Natasha drew a ragged breath as suddenly realisation dawned. Oh, God, she thought. Not that again. Not another episode in this eternal family feud. Please—*please*—don't let it be that.

Knowing all the time that her prayer would not be answered.

She said quietly, 'In other words—the Mandrakis Corporation.' And watched the general recoil, as if she'd uttered some disgusting obscenity. She made an attempt at reason. 'But surely that's all behind us now that Thio Basilis is dead and Petros Mandrakis has retired.'

'Then you are a fool to think so,' Irini said with contempt. 'Because in his place sits his son, Alexandros.' She spat the name.

'Alex Mandrakis?' Natasha questioned incredulously. 'The playboy of the western universe, and darling of the gossip columns? Oh, give me a break here.' She snorted. 'Judging by his reputation, he's far more interested in making love than war.

'Besides,' she added brusquely, 'he probably thinks the Arianna line is a string of polo ponies.'

Andonis pulled a wry face. 'Perhaps that is how he was. But he is now the head of the Mandrakis empire, and he is making everyone aware of the fact.'

'But for how long?' Natasha queried drily. 'Until the *après-ski* beckons from the Alps, or the *Floating Harem* starts its summer cruise of the Med?' She was referring to the tabloid Press's nickname for the Mandrakis yacht, *Selene*, but regretted it when she saw Irini's outraged expression.

She shook her head. 'Leopards don't change their spots, brother, and he'll soon get bored with being the latest tycoon, and revert to his former way of life.'

'I wish we could think so,' Andonis admitted. 'But our information says that it is not so. That he is indeed his father's son, and has therefore become a force to take account of. So we need to be wary.'

'His father's son,' Natasha repeated silently. She stifled a sigh. If only the same could be said of either of you two, she thought without pleasure.

'Because he is as much our enemy as his father ever was, or more.' Irini was speaking again. 'And he will not be content, that one, until the whole Papadimos family is finished—starving in the gutter.'

Natasha's lips tightened. 'A little extreme surely,' she said. 'Stavros has just admitted that he's offered a fair price for a share in both lines.'

'Because he knows it will not be accepted,' Andonis said. 'That we would rather die first.'

Unlikely, Natasha thought drily. Not if push actually comes to shove.

'However,' Stavros said with faint triumph, 'we have let his interest become known among the bankers we have approached, and have said that we are giving the matter our serious consideration.'

She frowned. 'Why would you want to do that?'

'Because having Alex Mandrakis as a business partner,' Andonis said, 'would be considered excellent security for any loan. A licence to print money, in fact.

'Already attitudes to our request for refinancing are changing.'

Stavros nodded. 'In fact, an offer in principle was made almost as soon as we had explained our own terms for this partnership. Terms that appear to bind our mutual interests together like hoops of steel, and which we have already submitted to Alex Mandrakis.'

There was a note in his voice that was almost gloating. 'The delaying tactic I spoke of, little sister. Because he, of course, will eventually refuse these terms. We count on it. But not immediately, because he is clearly intrigued, and has even asked for certain…assurances from us, which we are prepared to give him, although, again, not immediately.'

'We wish, you understand, to string him along,' Andonis explained kindly. 'To make him believe these negotiations might even be genuine. That we are prepared, as you say, to let bygones be— bygones.' His eyes flashed. 'But we are not, Natasha *mou*, and by the time he discovers this we will already have our loan, and he will no longer be necessary to our requirements. You understand.'

Only too well, thought Natasha. My God, is this their idea of being wary?

Aloud, she said slowly, 'Far be it from me to rain on your parade, but it may not be as simple as that. What if your bank demands his signature as an essential part of any deal? If they want to make sure that Mandrakis is definitely on side before they reach their decision?'

'That is unlikely,' said Stavros. 'Because the nature of this new agreement is a matter of extreme delicacy, and the bank will hesitate to exert pressure on either party.'

He was being altogether too smug, and on the shakiest of foundations, Natasha thought, annoyed and concerned at the same time.

She said coolly, 'I didn't think banks were particularly delicate— not when enormous sums of money are involved. And, while the Mandrakis Corporation may be fireproof, because of, or in spite of, their new chairman, the Papadimos track record over the past year or so is not that great,' she added, ignoring a choking sound from Irini. 'They'd be taking a big risk.'

'But they will not see it in that way,' said Stavros. 'Not if they believe that our families will soon be joined by more than a business agreement.'

Natasha stared at him. 'I'm sorry,' she said slowly. 'I think you've lost me.'

'We have suggested a different kind of partnership,' said Andonis, and smiled. 'A marriage with our family, no less. And that is what he is even now considering.'

Natasha's gaze swung automatically to Irini.

No wonder she's in such a foul temper again, she thought. And this time, I can actually feel sorry for her. Whether they mean it or not, it's pretty ghastly finding yourself offered to someone like Alex Mandrakis, knowing you'll be turned down, whether you want him or not.

Although being accepted would undoubtedly be a whole lot worse. Because who in their right mind would want to be married off, as part of a business deal, to a man who didn't know the meaning of the word *fidelity*? And who changed his women as often as his elegant suits?

Most of her knowledge of him, admittedly, had been garnered from the gossip columns and glossy magazines in which he featured with such prominent regularity.

But she had seen him once in person at a reception in Athens which she'd attended with her friend Lindsay Wharton, whose father was attached to the embassy.

'Oh, wow,' Lin had whispered joyously. 'Don't look now, but one of the wonders of the world has just walked in, accompanied, of course, by the usual size-zero model. Oh, why didn't I go on with that diet?'

'What are you talking about?' Natasha demanded, intrigued.

'Alex Mandrakis,' Lin sighed. 'Sex on a stick, and loaded with it.'

Mandrakis, Natasha thought with a start. Now, there was a name to conjure up trouble within the Papadimos household. Basilis would never have let her come tonight if he'd known his arch-enemy's son was going to be present.

All the same, she'd risked a glance, knowing that their paths were unlikely to cross ever again, so this might be her sole opportunity to see what all the fuss was about.

Even without Lin's description, he was unmissable, being taller than anyone else around him, and all lean elegance in his evening clothes.

And he had a face that you wouldn't forget in a hurry, either, she thought, her breath catching, his olive-skinned features strongly marked from his frank beak of a nose to the deep cleft in his chin, via a mouth that could best be described as sinful.

She hadn't meant to linger on her appraisal, even though everyone else in the room seemed to be gawping at him too, but suddenly, as if alerted by some invisible antenna, he'd turned his head and those midnight-dark eyes under the straight black brows had looked right back at her, that astonishing mouth curving in a smile as his gaze swept over her in an assessment as candid as it was total.

Undressing her, some instinct had told her, with his eyes.

Natasha had felt a wave of warm blood wash from her toes to her hairline, as she prayed for the floor to split apart and swallow her into some fathomless depths forever.

But it hadn't happened, and she'd had to be content with merely turning her back instead. Pretending he didn't exist.

Now, as the memory stung her again, she said harshly, 'If he has been suddenly transformed into Mr Shrewd, then he'll know this is a set-up. After all, Irini has hardly been discreet over her views of the Mandrakis family as a whole, and Alex in particular.'

There was an odd silence. Once more the brothers exchanged glances, but this time they were both smiling broadly. Almost gleeful, in fact.

And if I were a child again, Natasha thought, I'd be searching my bed for lizards.

'Irini?' Stavros shook his head, enjoying the moment. 'Even if she allowed it, we would not be so foolish. No, my little one, the bride we have offered Alex Mandrakis is yourself, Natasha *mou*.'

His satisfied beam widened. 'So, what do you think of that? It is clever, *ne*?'

CHAPTER TWO

'CLEVER?' Natasha's voice rose. '*Clever?* It's the most ridiculous idea I've ever heard in my life. The pair of you must have taken leave of your senses.'

Her condemnation was received in frosty silence, and she saw Maria and Christina exchange affronted glances at this lack of respect to their husbands.

'But, Natasha, this is such a simple thing we ask you to do for us.' Andonis leaned forward. 'You have only to sign a letter which we shall send to Mandrakis, telling him you are willing to become his wife in accordance with our offer. Is that really such a difficulty?'

'Because I promise you that he will never agree to this proposal. He has no wish to marry anyone.' He shrugged. 'Why should he tie himself to one, when so many beautiful girls are willing to share his bed without honour?'

Ignoring the shocked squeals from Maria and Christina, he went on, 'His age is, what? Thirty? In ten—fifteen years, perhaps—he will take a wife, in order to breed himself a son, if he can find a woman to have him.

'Until then, Natasha *mou*, he will do just as he pleases.'

'But do not worry,' Irini broke in scathingly. 'You are not likely to please him, with your pale hair and your white skin. A creature who looks as if no blood runs in her veins.' She laughed scornfully. 'How could you be wanted by any man? With Mandrakis, you will be quite safe.'

Natasha was jarred once again by the memory of amused dark eyes coolly scanning her seventeen-year-old body, and of Lin's excited murmur, 'They say he can make love in four languages. Isn't he to die for?' And to her vexation, she now found herself flushing at the thought.

There were a number of pithy retorts she could have made to Irini, she thought, including the information that she was currently dating a man in London who clearly didn't find her in the least undesirable, but she controlled herself with an effort.

She could also understand why Madame Papadimos was absent. Thia Theodosia will know nothing about this nightmare, she thought. Nothing…

She said tautly, 'Safe doesn't actually enter the equation. I refuse to be even marginally involved with this crazy scheme. Please let that be clearly understood.'

There was a silence, then Stavros said heavily, 'I will be honest. I am saddened, sister, by this lack of gratitude—this failure in your duty to the family that raised you.

'This letter,' he added reproachfully, 'is a formality—no more. So, is it really so much to ask? Especially when he will be expecting to receive it from us. And when so much depends upon it.'

'I thought you wanted to drag things out,' Natasha returned curtly. 'To keep him waiting.'

'We have done so,' said Andonis. 'But now some gesture is needed. A little…propitiation to keep him interested.' He chuckled. 'And to keep him sweet.'

'I don't think *sweet* and *Alex Mandrakis* are words that belong in the same sentence.' Restlessly, Natasha pushed her chair back and rose, walking over to the tall glass doors which opened into the garden. 'You shouldn't have brought me into this business,' she said, staring into the warm darkness. 'Not without asking me first. You had no right—no right at all.'

'But where is the harm?' Andonis demanded. 'There will be no marriage between you and Mandrakis. We swear it. You have only to say you accept the terms we are offering. Give him something to think about.'

He looked at her appealingly. 'The fact that a girl he has never seen is offering herself to him will appeal to his vanity and his arrogance. In the short term, it may cloud his judgement, and create a delay that is vital to us, and to the continued prosperity of the Papadimos family—in which you share, Natasha *mou*.'

He paused. 'Perhaps you should remember that. Also how my father rescued you and treated you as his own,' he added significantly. 'Maybe it is time you repaid the memory of his kindness, with a little generosity of your own.'

She said coldly and clearly, 'Your father wouldn't have touched a deal like this, and you know it. He hated the Mandrakis family far too much to offer even a bogus olive branch.'

And Alex Mandrakis has seen me, even though he won't remember it...

'That is true,' Stavros agreed. 'But think what a fool this Alexandros will appear when we obtain our money, and his offer is brushed aside with our contempt. He will lose face with his shareholders, his board, and most of all, with his father. Old Petros will not easily forgive him for walking into our little trap.

'And he has made other enemies. Once we have demonstrated that he is not fireproof, they too may move against him.' He sighed gustily. 'Our ultimate victory may be greater than we could hope for. And that is something our father would relish indeed. As you well know, sister.'

Yes, Natasha thought bitterly. Only too well. Where the Mandrakis family was concerned, Basilis too had seemed to abandon all logic and reason. He would never have forgone an opportunity to do them a serious mischief, if it had lain in his power.

But did it never occur to either Stavros or Andonis that what they had in mind might prove to be a double-edged sword, and that Alex Mandrakis might well have some similar plan?

Or did they believe they were the ones who were fireproof?

If so, she thought fatalistically, God help us all.

She said abruptly, 'Very well. If there's really no other way, give me the letter, and, for your father's sake, I'll sign.'

She paused. 'But I still think it's a truly terrible idea, and I hope it with all my heart that it won't all end in tears.'

It wasn't just that one letter, of course, she reflected later, as she lay in bed, listening to the soft swoosh of the ceiling fan above her. When it came down to it, there'd been a whole sheaf of documents relating to the refinancing that also required her signature, and she'd obeyed wearily, sitting at Basilis's old desk in his former study, with Stavros and Andonis like twin sentinels fussily directing her pen.

Afterwards they'd been barely able to conceal their triumph at her capitulation, and she'd had no difficulty in refusing their offer to join them in the *saloni* for a celebratory drink, on the grounds that she had an early flight the next day and needed to get her rest.

Except that she couldn't sleep, she thought, turning over and giving her inoffensive pillow a thump, as if that might improve the situation.

But her failure to relax had nothing to do with her physical surroundings. It was the nagging conviction that she'd just made a hideous mistake that was keeping her awake.

She wished with all her heart that she could go down to the study, retrieve the letter to Alex Mandrakis and destroy it. But it was locked away in the safe, along with the other documents, and she didn't have the combination.

And telling the Papadimos brothers over breakfast that she'd changed her mind would make not an atom of difference, she thought bitterly. It was too late, and there was no way back.

What a pity, she thought wryly, that I can't share Maria and Christina's unswerving faith in their husbands' perspicacity. In their belief that this ludicrous swindle has some outside chance of success.

She'd been almost tempted to confide in Thia Theodosia when she'd visited her on her way to bed. But she'd found the older woman lying on a couch, a book neglected in her lap, and gazing into space with eyes that seemed to see nothing but sadness, and she'd known at once that she could not add to her troubles.

So she'd sat with her for a while, bringing a smile to her lips with stories of some of Helping Out's more eccentric clients, and then, as she'd always done, asking for her foster mother's parting blessing.

But this time, she'd had an odd feeling that her request was prompted by more than mere convention. That, after the evening's events, she needed all the protection she could get.

She felt almost as if she'd stepped through some barrier into an alternative universe, she told herself wryly, consoling herself that things would seem altogether better once she was back in England, and out of harm's way, her debt to the Papadimos family finally paid.

London was her real world, she thought gratefully. The flat she shared with Molly while the latter's fiancé was overseas, the company they were steadily building together, and now, of course, Neil.

Closing her eyes, she let herself reflect pleasurably and deliberately on Neil.

They'd met six weeks ago at a book-launch party for an author whose domestic life had been thrown into chaos when his pregnant wife had been taken into hospital with persistent high blood pressure, leaving him with two demanding older children, a total lack of catering skills and a fast-approaching deadline.

Natasha had moved in, restored order with a firm hand, and given the author the space he needed to finish his book, along with three meals a day. She'd also stayed on to help when the mother-to-be was eventually allowed home with strict orders to rest, and joined in the general rejoicings when seven-and-a-half-pound Nathan—'The nearest we could get to Natasha for a boy'—had been safely born.

Neil was an executive with the PR company used by the publishers.

He was tall, distinctly attractive, effortlessly charming, and he'd made an unashamed beeline for her when she'd made a hesitant appearance in the doorway of the crowded room, looking round for James and Fiona.

He hadn't haunted her side all evening, because he had work to do, but he'd sought her out again as she was leaving, asked for her card, and suggested they should have dinner some time.

Some time had proved to be the following night, she recalled, smiling into the darkness, and they'd been seeing each other regularly ever since.

'So, is he the one?' Molly had enquired teasingly only a few nights ago when Neil had brought Natasha home from the theatre, drunk the offered coffee as always, then taken his leave with the usual ruefulness. 'Are you finally going to take that leap into the great unknown of sex?'

Natasha had flushed. 'You think I'm mad to have kept him waiting this long, don't you?'

'Not altogether. "Treat 'em mean, keep 'em keen" would seem to be working in this case. And when it happens, he'll know you really mean it.' Molly allowed herself a small reminiscent smile. 'But you're far more hard-hearted than I was with Craig.'

'Blame my sheltered upbringing,' Natasha said lightly. 'According to my Aunt Theodosia, sex before marriage does not exist. A girl's innocence belongs to her husband, and no one else. Because any slips on the path of righteousness would only lead to misery, shame and despair.'

'But the bride's tough luck if she found out too late that the husband was lousy in bed,' said Molly cynically.

Natasha shrugged. 'How would she know?' Her eyes danced. 'Besides, Greek men are all fabulous lovers. Another belief I was taught in my formative years.'

'Well, there's a comfort,' Molly said affably. 'All the same, were you never tempted to test that interesting theory?'

'No,' Natasha returned with unnecessary emphasis as she carried the used cups into the kitchen. 'Not even once.'

The sheet suddenly seemed to be tangling round her, and she pushed it away, sighing irritably, and got up from the bed. Her window was already slightly open in an attempt to capture some stray current of cool air, and she slid it back to its fullest extent, pushed open the shutters, and went out onto the balcony.

There wasn't a breath of wind, however. The warmth of the night lay like a blanket across the city, and even the ceaseless noise of the Athenian traffic seemed muted as it warred against the rasp of the crickets in the garden below.

The moon was full, hanging in the sky like a great silver globe, almost close enough to touch, its radiance catching the cool shimmer of the swimming pool.

She looked down at it with sudden longing, feeling hot, sticky and frazzled. Each of the rooms in this part of the house had its own flight of steps to the pool area, but no one else had been drawn out into the open air. In fact, the shutters on each window were closed, and there wasn't a glimmer of light showing, indicating that all the occupants were peacefully asleep.

Stelios, the security man whose task it was to patrol the perimeter wall, had gone past some fifteen minutes before, because she'd heard his soft footsteps and the subdued whine of his dog. He'd be safely back in his room now, drinking endless coffee, and keeping half an eye on the screens showing the film from the cameras positioned at each entrance, and at intervals round the outside of the wall.

The rest of his attention would be devoted to whatever international sport was being shown on satellite TV.

Anyway, there was no camera covering the pool area. Maria and Christina had protested vociferously about any such thing, claiming it would be an intrusion into their sunbathing privacy. And Basilis had reluctantly given way.

So if she wanted to relax with a swim, there was nothing to prevent her.

Her mind made up, she fetched a towel from her shower-room, and made her way quietly down the marble steps and through the thickly encircling bushes and shrubs to the pool.

She dropped her towel onto its tiled surround, sent her nightgown to join it and stood naked for a moment, dipping an experimental foot into the water. Then, with a little sigh of pleasure, she slipped down into the cool depths, and swam a couple of slow, easy lengths before turning on her back and floating for a while, letting the stress of the evening ripple away in the moonlight that surrounded her.

Heaven, she thought, sighing softly as she swam back to the side, lifting herself out of the pool in one lithe movement. She twisted her hair into a thick rope, wringing the water from it, then shook it loose again before reaching for her towel and beginning to blot the moisture from her skin.

As she did so, it occurred to her that the noise from the city had become appreciably louder, and that was because the crickets were suddenly silent.

My fault probably, she thought, smiling to herself. I must have put them off their stroke.

And at the same moment, a first, faint breeze whispered through the tall, crowding shrubs, rustling their leaves and making her shiver as she pulled on her nightgown again.

She picked up her damp towel, and went swiftly and silently back to her room. The bed received her, and within minutes Natasha was deeply and dreamlessly asleep.

'I'm sorry,' Neil said. 'I thought a weekend away together might be the next step for us, but I've clearly got things terribly wrong.'

'No.' Natasha reached across the table and put a placatory hand on his. 'It's not you—really it's not. It's me.'

'Oh, God,' he said, wincing. 'Not that excuse, please.' He looked at her broodingly. 'Tasha, you haven't been the same since you got back from that flying visit to Greece three weeks ago. You've been quiet—evasive, even. I haven't been able to get near you. I thought that maybe some time away together, completely on our own, might get us back on track.'

'It could. It will.' She took a deep breath. 'But you must know that I have…family problems. Serious ones.'

'Shipping millionaires don't have problems,' he said. 'They just buy another fleet of tankers.'

'Unfortunately,' Natasha said quietly, 'in this case, the fleet being bought happens to be ours.'

She saw his brows lift, and nodded jerkily. 'I've been reading hints in the business news for days now, and praying they weren't true,' she went on. 'But this morning there was an unconfirmed report from Athens that a refinancing bid by the Papadimos brothers had failed, and both the Arianna line and the cargo ships have been acquired by an outfit called Bucephalus Holdings for some rock-bottom price.'

She groaned. 'Oh, God, I knew it wouldn't work. They thought they were being so clever, yet now they're in a total mess, free-falling to nowhere. Their father must be turning in his grave. And why on earth didn't they tell me what was happening instead of letting me read it in the papers?'

'Probably too busy trying to save something from the wreckage,' Neil suggested reasonably, then paused, frowning. 'Bucephalus? Wasn't that a famous horse?'

'Yes,' she said. She reached for her glass and took a substantial sip of wine. 'It belonged to Alexander the Great.'

'Who's been dead for several thousand years,' Neil pointed out. 'His horse too. So hardly a threat.'

'Unless he has a present-day counterpart,' Natasha said grimly. 'Or someone who thinks he is.'

'Even so.' He looked faintly puzzled. 'Why should that affect you? I mean, I'm sorry your family's suffered this awful loss, but you've always given the impression you never really wanted to be that involved in their business affairs anyway.'

'I didn't,' she said shortly. 'And now I won't be, except, I suppose, for another trip to Athens for more damned paperwork. Although I can't just turn my back and walk away, even then, because the only one who really concerns me in all this is Thia Theodosia. She's going to be absolutely devastated. I've been trying to call the house today, but there's no answer.'

'Phone unplugged?' Neil suggested. 'Keeping the world at bay? You can hardly blame them.'

'Don't you believe it,' said Natasha bitterly, and sighed. 'Ah, well, there's nothing that can be done now. It's over.'

'Not quite—if you have to go back to Greece at some point.' He paused, adding gently, 'But when that's done, maybe we'll have some time for each other.'

She realised how considerate he was trying to be, and how aloof she must have seemed recently, and made a conscious effort to shake away the troubling thoughts which had been crowding in on her—oppressing her—for weeks. Some of which she hadn't dared consider too closely.

'You can count on it,' she said softly, and smiled at him.

The e-mail summoning her arrived a week later. It came from a firm of lawyers she'd never heard of, and advised her that her presence was required in Athens in order for the transaction with Bucephalus Holdings to be completed. It added that, on receipt of her flight details, she would be met at the airport.

Well, that was short and to the point, Natasha thought wryly, and quite unlike the other e-mails she'd been receiving from Stavros and Andonis, which were barrages of recrimination, accusation and self-justification. It took every scrap of patience she possessed to read them, let alone reply to them.

Everyone else's fault, as usual, she thought wearily as she pressed the delete button on the most recent outpouring.

It was not lost on her either that her anxious queries about their mother were being totally ignored.

But when I'm there, she thought, I'll be able to see for myself how she is.

'I'm sorry to leave you in the lurch like this when we're so busy,' she apologised to Molly as she filled her overnight bag. 'But it won't happen again. Any future visits will be solely to see Thia Theodosia, and I'll be able to schedule those during my normal holidays. That's why I've booked evening flights, so I'll only be away for a day.'

'It's all right, so stop fussing,' Molly ordained severely. 'We can cope without you for twenty-four hours, no worries, so go and do what you have to.' She paused. 'I just hope it won't be too awful.'

Natasha shook her head. 'Bound to be,' she said wearily. 'I—I just can't believe it's all collapsed so quickly. And what's going to happen to the workforce? It's a generational thing. Whole families are involved.' Her voice was suddenly husky. 'Thio Basilis was always so proud of that.'

'Surely the new owners will keep them on,' Molly suggested. 'After all, the ships need to go on sailing.'

'But not necessarily with Papadimos crews.' Natasha zipped up her case. 'Oh, God, why couldn't those idiots make peace not war for once with Alex bloody Mandrakis? If they'd accepted his original offer, at least they'd have been left with something. But, no. They had to try and get the better of him.'

'There was a picture of him in the paper the other day,' Molly said idly. 'Attending some film premiere with his latest squeeze. Admittedly gorgeous, but not someone I'd choose to mess with.'

'You have wisdom beyond your years,' Natasha said bitterly. 'But—he's done his worst, and all we can do now is try and pick up whatever pieces remain.' She reached for the dark grey jacket that matched her skirt, and slipped it on over her crisp white shirt. Business clothes, she thought, for a business meeting, and sighed imperceptibly.

She added, 'I almost feel sorry for Maria and Christina. They never bargained for this at those lavish weddings a few years ago.' A note of mischief entered her voice. 'But I bet they're not treating their husbands with quite such doting devotion these days. In fact, with any luck, they're giving them hell.'

And on that upbeat note, she grabbed her bag, and left for the airport.

Neil had offered to see her off, but she'd refused on the grounds that parking would be a nightmare and that, anyway, it was no big deal.

'I'll be back before you know it,' she'd promised.

'And I'll be counting the hours,' he'd returned, and taken her in his arms, his parting kiss displaying an unaccustomed hunger.

Something, she realised, that she'd found disturbing, and not al-together for the right reasons.

In effect, she thought as she sipped at the orange juice she'd or-dered from the drinks trolley, it had been a candid reminder that, on her return, he was confidently expecting that they would be moving their relationship on a stage and becoming lovers. That she'd pretty much promised him that would happen.

'Oh, God,' she groaned under her breath. Don't chicken out. Not again. Not this time.

You really like Neil. You may even be starting to fall in love with him. But how will you ever know—be sure—until you commit yourself, even in this most basic way?

The problem was she hadn't been joking when she'd told Molly about the strictness of her upbringing. And it was difficult to shake off that kind of conditioning, even if you believed you might have met the right man.

For Thia Theodosia, Mr Right came with a wedding ring in his pocket, and treated you with total respect, knowing that your vir-ginity was part of the dowry you brought him, until the ring was on your finger and the priest had pronounced you man and wife.

For her, it was that simple, and that iron-clad, and she would be distressed beyond measure if she thought that Natasha would ever consider a breach of that strict moral code.

And the fact that Natasha had begun to regard herself as some kind of curious anachronism would be no valid excuse.

But was it only the tradition in which she'd been raised that had held her back since she'd left Greece to live an independent life? Or was it more that she'd never been seriously tempted to break that unwritten sexual law?

And was she deeply tempted now—with Neil?

I wonder, she thought unhappily. I really wonder.

She considered Molly and Craig, who'd met at a party, fallen into bed together within twenty-four hours, become engaged a few weeks later and were waiting impatiently for Craig's contract in Seattle to end so they could be married.

No one or nothing could have kept them out of each other's arms, she acknowledged, their temporary separation being marked by letters, e-mails and nightly phone calls.

But perhaps I'm a different temperament, she thought. The slow, steady type as opposed to Molly's headlong certainty about what she wants from life, and how to get it. Maybe that's why we've been friends since school, and why we work so well together now.

So far Neil had seemed content to play by her rules, but that was not going to last much longer. She'd reached the same stage before, with other boyfriends, who'd got fed up when she kept backing off and had walked away.

She could read the signs. He wanted them to be like the other couples they knew. And when Molly and Craig were married, he'd expect her to live with him.

He had no idea, of course, how totally inexperienced she was.

And that could well be a major factor here, she realised. Perhaps she was just scared of the unknown. Simply lacked the courage to discover whether or not she'd be 'good in bed'.

After all, wasn't that the criteria by which everyone was judged these days?

He can make love in four languages...

She sat up, gasping, as Lin's wistful words came back into her mind. And what had prompted that, for God's sake?

Apart from the fact that Alex Mandrakis had engineered her brothers' downfall, of course, she reminded herself wryly, and that was why she was on this plane at this moment. So it was going to be impossible to dismiss him totally from her thinking, however hard she might try.

His name was bound to crop up at some point, she thought, her mouth twisting. Probably more than once.

But at least he wouldn't be around in person to administer the death blow. Some minion would do that for him.

As people said—this was business, not personal, which was something to be thankful for. She had no wish to set eyes on him ever again.

And now she would just have to relegate her heart-searchings about her love life with Neil until a more appropriate moment, she told herself firmly as the seat-belt light came on for the descent into Athens.

Because the next twenty-four hours would require a very different kind of courage from her, and nothing could be allowed to deflect her from that.

Nothing—and no one.

CHAPTER THREE

NATASHA'S arrival in Athens occurred in the middle of a thunder-storm, but was otherwise painless. She had no baggage to reclaim, and a placard with her name on it was the first thing she saw when she emerged from Customs.

It was carried by a heavily built man in a pale linen suit who greeted her with unsmiling politeness, took her bag, and led her to a waiting limousine complete with uniformed chauffeur.

The air was like a hot, wet blanket smothering her and she was glad she'd decided on the cooler option of pinning her hair up into a loose knot on top of her head, rather than wearing it down.

She found herself being ushered into the rear of the car, occupy-ing its luxurious seating in solitary splendour while her escort sat in silence beside the driver.

She leaned back, listening to the distant growl of thunder, and watching the rain pour down the windows, as she relished the rich scent of expensive leather.

No doubt the cost of this transfer would go on the lawyers' bill, she thought with an inward grimace. It would have been far cheaper to get a cab, although, admittedly, not nearly as comfortable. And was it really necessary to send two people to collect her? After all, she was hardly likely to come all this way just to do a runner.

It was too dark to see anything, even without the distortion of the rain on the glass turning street lights and approaching traffic into a blur, so she closed her eyes and let her thoughts drift.

She had almost dozed off when she realised that the car was slowing down, then coming to a complete halt.

Now to face the family, she thought without pleasure. She sat up hurriedly, pulling her skirt over her knees, as the passenger door opened. Another man was standing there, holding a large umbrella, and for a moment, she assumed it was Manolis, the Papadimoses' major-domo, and was just about to greet him when she saw that he was also a stranger. Realised too, that the brightly lit entrance she was being hustled towards was also completely unfamiliar to her.

She tried to hang back. 'No,' she said in Greek. 'There has been some mistake. I should be at the Villa Demeter.'

'No mistake, *thespinis*. This is the right place.' The pair of them were on either side of her now, their hands implacably under her elbows as they urged her forward into a vast hall dominated by the wide sweep of an imposing marble staircase.

Natasha hardly gave her surroundings a second look. She was too angry for that, trying desperately to remember the name of the lawyer who'd sent them, because he'd be someone to complain to—and about—when this muddle was eventually sorted.

In the meantime, in spite of her efforts to pull free, she was being taken up those curving stairs to a galleried landing.

'What is this?' she demanded huskily. 'Where am I? Tell me at once.'

Silent, impassive, they halted in front of a pair of double doors, and knocked. The man from the airport reached down to the ornate handles and the doors opened noiselessly.

They didn't push her in. It wasn't quite as crude as that, but somehow she was stepping forward, and they were moving backwards, and the doors were closing again behind her. Leaving her standing there, alone.

Except that she was not alone.

It was a very big room, but all Natasha noticed was the bed, lit on either side by tall lamps, like a stage set. Illumining, she realised dazedly, the man who was sitting in that bed, leaning back against a mound of snowy pillows, and naked down to the sheet discreetly draped across his hips, and probably beyond, as he worked in the laptop computer open in front of him.

He unhurriedly completed whatever task he was engaged on, then Alex Mandrakis closed the lid, put the laptop on the adjacent table and looked at her.

'Ah,' he said softly. 'The beauty I was promised, here at last.'

His voice was cool. His English spoken with only a faint accent. *He can make love in four languages...*

Her throat closed as, for the second time in her life, his dark gaze swept her from the silk of her blonde hair down to the neat black pumps on her feet. But this time, the expression of frank appreciation in his eyes was mixed with something altogether more disturbing.

Involuntarily, Natasha took a step backwards, and saw him smile. She said hoarsely, 'What's happening? Why am I here?'

'You offered yourself to me,' he said. 'In writing.' He shrugged a bare, muscular shoulder. 'I am therefore accepting your offer. It is perfectly simple.'

'No.' This time Natasha stood her ground, and glared at him. 'It's total nonsense, and you know it as well as I do. So don't pretend you were fooled even for a moment by my agreement to marry you.'

She turned and walked to the door, with an assumption of calm she was far from feeling. 'However, the joke's worn thin for me now, so I'm out of here.'

She grasped the door handles, twisted them one way then the other, but the heavy panels they controlled did not move an inch.

'You are wasting your time.' His voice was tinged with amusement. 'The door is locked and will remain so until morning.'

She swung round. 'But you can't do this,' she said thickly. 'You can't shut me in—stop me leaving. I—I don't know what game you think you're playing here, Kyrios Mandrakis, but please believe I have no intention of becoming your wife. Now or ever.'

'Then we are at least in agreement about that,' he drawled. 'Because there is indeed no question of marriage between us, Natasha *mou*. And you are the one playing games, not I.'

He paused. 'You must understand that I am referring to your second letter, which was couched in very different terms from the first, and which promised me a range of intimate delights that few unmarried girls would dare admit they knew, let alone suggest to any potential husband.' He added mockingly, 'And least of all to a man they had never met.'

Her lips parted in shock. *'Second letter?'* she repeated helplessly. 'There was no second letter. I only signed the first under duress. You must be raving mad.'

'And you are a hypocrite, which I find a disappointment,' he told her coolly. 'I had expected that a girl who spoke with such mesmerising frankness of her sexual desires and fantasies would at least have the courage of her convictions, when finally confronted with the focus of her…longings.'

'You're the focus of nothing, Kyrios Mandrakis, except my dislike and disgust,' Natasha said curtly. 'I thought my brothers had cornered the market in arrogance and conceit, but you beat them—hands down.'

'And I shall continue to do so, Kyria Kirby,' Alex Mandrakis retorted, 'in every way that occurs to me, therefore your ludicrous assessment of my character does not concern me.

'You may well regret your candour in writing to me, *agapi mou*,' he added, the firm mouth twisting. 'But I do not. And, while I may never have believed in you as a future wife, I look forward with eagerness to enjoying your versatility as my mistress.

'Which is why you are here with me tonight, as you must know by now. To begin your new career in my bed.'

The breath seemed to choke in her lungs. She stared at him incredulously, her startled eyes taking fresh stock of his state of undress and its devastating implications.

The formal evening dress he'd worn at their first encounter had concealed broad shoulders, and a sculpted chest shadowed by body hair tapering down towards his flat stomach and lean hips. His tanned skin was almost shockingly dark against the white bedlinen.

She didn't want to imagine how the rest of him might appear.

Her voice seemed to come from a great distance.

'I'd rather die!'

His brows lifted cynically. 'When it was your own idea?' he challenged. 'I hardly think so.'

'But I keep trying to tell you,' she protested, hating the edge of growing desperation she could hear in her own voice. 'There was never any second letter. Oh, why won't you believe me?'

'Because I have the evidence which makes a liar of you.' His tone was almost casual. 'In which, of course, you are no different from the rest of the Papadimos clan. Liars and cheats all of you, and, like most of your persuasion, only sorry when you are found out.

'But your foster brothers will have even more to regret,' he went on. 'They will have to endure the shame of knowing you belong to me as my *eromeni*—my pillow friend—and that when I tire of you they will have you returned to them—used, and discarded.' He paused. 'Maybe…even pregnant.

'A final blow to their family honour from which they can never recover,' he added harshly as Natasha caught her breath.

'You can't do such a thing.' Her voice was ragged. 'No one could. It's barbaric—vile. And do you imagine that I'll let you get away with it? That I won't have you arrested for kidnap and—and rape, no matter how powerful you may think you are?'

'Kidnap?' Alex Mandrakis repeated musingly, and shook his head. 'When you responded willingly to my invitation, and allowed my driver to bring you here? He reported no scene at the airport. No screams or struggles.

'As for rape, I doubt whether such an accusation could possibly succeed. Not when your letter is made public, as it would have to be. No court would convict me for taking advantage of the services you volunteered of your own free will.'

She flung back her head. 'I say you're the one who's lying, Kyrios Mandrakis. I don't believe this letter even exists.'

He sighed, then leaned across to open a drawer in the bedside table.

The sheet slipped a fraction, and Natasha hastily looked away.

When Alex Mandrakis straightened, she saw with a sinking heart that he was holding a file. He extracted two sheets of paper.

'The first,' he said, holding it up. 'Your agreement to become my wife as part of this mythical deal between our families. You accept that exists?'

'Yes,' she said. 'I admit that.'

He paused, his mouth curling sardonically. 'And this is the second letter, which outlines your alternative proposals for our future union. The signatures on both documents are identical, as you see.'

Yes, Natasha thought numbly as she looked at them. She did see.

She said in a voice she hardly recognised, 'I don't understand.'

'Shall I refresh your memory—of the third paragraph, perhaps, which seems particularly inventive?'

He began to read it aloud, his tone almost impersonal, but before he'd uttered more than the first couple of sentences, Natasha was whispering, 'Oh, God, stop—please stop,' her whole body burning with shame, her hands pressed to her ears.

'Ah,' he said. 'So you do remember.' He replaced the papers in the file and returned it to the drawer, which he closed.

She stared at him, hugging herself with her arms. When she could speak, she asked, 'you think that I could think about such things, let alone write them down? Degrade myself in such a way?'

He shrugged again. 'Why not?' he countered. 'When you swim naked at night, careless of who might see you.'

She began, 'But I don't…' Then stopped, the hot colour deepening in her face as she recalled the one occasion when she'd succumbed to the temptation of cool water against the entire surface of her skin.

She said with a gasp, 'You mean that—even then—you were having me watched?'

'No,' he said. 'I mean, I came to see you for myself.'

'But why?'

'In case, by some remote chance, your brothers were serious about a marriage between us. I wished to refresh my memory of what was on offer, so I arranged a brief visit to your room while you were asleep.' He saw the look of horror on her face, and flung up a hand, laughing. 'No, *agapi mou*, nothing more. Not then.

'But even that became unnecessary,' he added softly. 'Because suddenly you were there, and I had only to stand in the shadows and look at you in the moonlight.'

'That's not possible,' Natasha said sharply. 'You couldn't get into the garden. We have cameras—a security patrol.'

'Cameras can be switched off,' he said. 'And poorly paid men can be bribed. When I was informed you had been sent for, I made my plans accordingly.' He smiled reminiscently. 'And I was… infinitely rewarded.'

There was a silence while Natasha struggled to compose herself. To tell herself that this wasn't happening. To pray that she was asleep and enduring the worst nightmare of her life. Was it only a couple of hours ago that she'd been sitting on that plane, debating the comparative morality of sleeping with Neil? Complacently considering her choices in their relationship as if they were all that mattered.

And now she was faced with this—*this*…

She was still aware of the snarl of the storm overhead, and found herself praying ridiculously that the house would be struck by a thunderbolt if nothing else could save her from this—horror.

Eventually she said, not looking at him, 'Whatever you saw on your spying mission, *kyrie*, I still did not write those things to you. I—I couldn't.

'And you don't really want me,' she went on in a low voice. 'If you...do what you've threatened, it will only be another form of revenge against my family. You've said as much.

'But I—I have a life in England. A man I could love. And you—you're seeing someone too. You...don't need to do this. So, I'm begging you now to unlock that door and let me go.'

She took a deep breath. 'I'll tell my brothers my plane was delayed, and I won't say a word about what's happened here tonight. I swear it. No one will ever know except the two of us.' She added, 'And I'll thank you every day of my life.'

'Your brothers are expecting you to arrive tomorrow, just in time for the meeting,' he told her softly. 'And I want them to know about us, Natasha *mou*. Also to imagine what they cannot know.'

She said, 'I am not your Natasha.'

'But you will be,' he said. 'And your life will belong to me—until I decide otherwise. Did I not make that clear to you?'

He smiled at her. 'However, you plead with passion, *agapi mou*. I hope you will bring the same intensity to the pleasure we shall soon share, when I prove beyond any doubt that I do indeed want you, and not just for revenge.'

He paused. 'My attentions may even console you for the English lover you have lost.'

He took two of the pillows from behind him, and placed them beside him on the bed. 'But we have talked enough. Now, my lovely one, it is time you came to me. So, take off your clothes.'

She took a step backward. 'No,' she said fiercely. 'I won't do it.'

His brows lifted. 'Would you prefer my men to help you?' he enquired pleasantly. 'I have only to summon them.'

'Oh, God.' Her voice cracked. 'Do you possess even a scrap of decency?'

'When it is required.' He shrugged. 'To judge from your letter, none is needed in your case. To find yourself being stripped by strangers might even have appealed to you. But no matter. Now, do not keep me waiting any longer,' he added. 'A pretence of coyness is hardly appropriate.'

Pretence? she thought. When I've never knowingly undressed in front of anyone in my life. When I've never actually seen a man naked either, apart from paintings and statuary.

The door was locked, but the window might not be, she told herself desperately. If there was a balcony outside, she might be able to jump…

And stopped right there, knowing that a broken arm or leg might be the least harm she could do to herself.

She was trapped—caught between Scylla and Charybdis, the monster and the whirlpool, in the story of 'The Odyssey' that Thia Theodosia used to read to her.

She touched dry lips with the tip of her tongue. 'Will you at least—turn off the lights?'

'No,' he said. 'And I am becoming impatient.' The dark eyes scanned her again more slowly. 'You may begin by taking down your hair. I prefer to see it loose.'

Instinct warned her that she had nowhere else to go. That tears—the only option she had left—wouldn't move him any more than her protests had done, her pleading.

She had abased herself for nothing, and she would not do so again, she told herself with cold determination. From now on, she would concentrate on survival alone.

She had never understood or been part of this feud between the two families, and had always found it faintly ludicrous that grown men should so implacably pursue each other's downfall.

But all that had changed forever when she'd entered this room, and found him waiting for her. Because Alex Mandrakis was now her enemy too, and someday, somehow, he would pay for tonight.

I'll make him sorry that he was ever born, she vowed silently as she took the clips from her hair and shook the long, silky strands free over her shoulders.

He said softly, 'Like a cloud of gold. Now, continue.'

She took off her jacket, and let it drop. Stepped out of her shoes.

He can't touch the real me, and he never will, she told herself. Whatever he does, however he treats me, I won't let him reach me in any way.

She would simply, endure until it was over, and he let her go. Because, although it might seem an eternity, in reality her time with him was unlikely to last very long.

It couldn't, she thought, as she began to unbutton her shirt, forcing her trembling fingers to obey her. Not once he discovered that she would never in a million years meet the sophistication of his demands on her. That she had no sexual enticements, as her current lacklustre performance must be demonstrating.

My God, she thought, sliding the shirt off her shoulders. I don't even know how to be a woman, and I certainly won't be learning with him.

And when it was finally over, and she had made him suffer as she was doing now, she would manage, somehow, to put all the shame, all the betrayal behind her, and rebuild a life for herself back in England.

It wouldn't be the same, of course. She couldn't imagine Neil wanting to be a part of it any more once he discovered what had happened. And if Alex Mandrakis made good his threat to parade her publicly as his mistress, and, clearly, he did not threaten lightly, then Neil was bound to find out, and be hurt.

One day, she would grieve about that. About the might-have-beens that he would always represent, which were all being systematically destroyed by the man in the bed, silently watching her undress.

And the way to deal with that, she told herself as she unzipped her skirt, was to pretend that Alex Mandrakis did not exist. That she was actually alone in her room at the London flat, getting ready for bed. Just a night like any other.

If I don't look at him, she thought as her skirt joined her other garments on the floor, I won't know that he's looking at me. I can make that my first line of defence.

And there would be others.

She couldn't fight him off physically, because she would lose. Every line of his lean, toned body told her that.

Besides, he was probably decadent enough to enjoy subjugating her, and she would do nothing that might give him any kind of pleasure.

It would be far safer to bore him, she thought. To adopt a policy of passive resistance. Obedient, but unresponsive, with never a kiss or a touch given of her own free will. And the complete opposite of the reaction he was expecting.

In spite of this resolution, it took every scrap of courage she possessed to remove her underwear, and bare herself completely to his gaze. She tried to tell herself as she unhooked her bra, and slid down her briefs, that he'd seen her naked before, even if she'd been unaware of it, and therefore, this time, it didn't matter. It mustn't be allowed to matter.

Except that somehow it did—quite terribly.

She had to fight, too, not to cover herself with her hands but keep them, in a show of her indifference to his scrutiny, at her sides, as she waited for him to say something. Anything.

But when he spoke, her startled senses reacted as if his hand had touched her quivering flesh.

'The moonlight did not lie, Natasha *mou*,' he said quietly. 'Your body is indeed exquisite.' He threw back the sheet, indicating with an imperative gesture that she should go to him.

Natasha crossed slowly to the bed, aware that he was lying on his side, propped on one elbow, waiting for her. She supposed that in some shrinking corner of her mind she'd gone on hoping against hope that he might decide he'd humiliated her enough, and call a halt.

But he was not going to relent, she thought, her heart thudding in panic at the prospect of what awaited her. Her one small consolation was that it would be on her terms, not his. And that one day his own life would lie in ruins too.

However, he'd said he was running out of patience, so it might all be over very quickly. In fact, if he was sufficiently disappointed in her lack of response, this might not be just an initial encounter, but also the last one.

But that made the immediate future no easier to contemplate as she lay beside him, staring rigidly at the ceiling. It shouldn't be like this, she thought as tension knotted inside her. Not her first time. She should be with someone who'd treat her with tenderness and consideration.

Instead, she was about to be possessed by her family's enemy, a man who despised her and would make no allowances for an innocence he didn't believe existed.

She sank her teeth into the inner softness of her lower lip as she remembered the things he'd read to her from that vile letter. Was that what he'd want from her, and, if so, how could she bear it?

Then, just as her taut nerves approached snapping point, Alex Mandrakis touched her at last, his fingers hardly more than a whisper on her skin as he pushed her hair back from her forehead, before winding one silken strand round his hand, and lifting it to his face as if to inhale its fragrance.

It was the last thing she'd anticipated, and, in spite of herself, she turned, startled, to look at him, and saw his smile, crooked, almost rueful.

Then he bent, putting his mouth very precisely on hers and caressing it softly, coaxing her silently and with insidious gentleness to part her lips and allow him the deeper intimacy he sought.

This was not the brutality she'd expected to defy, but deliberate temptation.

And for an instant, as his lips moved on hers, Natasha was aware of an odd, tingling warmth deep in the pit of her stomach, and realised just how much on her guard she would need to be.

She closed her eyes, staying motionless, her mouth tightly compressed against him, forbidding any closer access. At the same time, she was unable to prevent him moving ever closer, so that the warmth of him seemed to be permeating the chill of her own flesh, while the musky scent of his skin filled her consciousness like an intoxicant.

Eventually, the insistent sensuous pressure on her mouth halted and she was aware that he'd lifted his head. He said, 'Look at me.'

Slowly she raised reluctant lids, staring up into his dark face with cool antagonism.

'You do not include kissing in your repertoire?' He sounded little more than mildly curious.

'Perhaps I merely have no wish to kiss *you*, Kyrios Mandrakis.'

'The possibility had crossed my mind,' he murmured. 'And are you also unwilling to call me by my given name?' His hand cupped her breast, his fingertip teasing the nipple, rousing it to a proud, aching life that she realised with horror she could not control. 'Although such formality in the circumstances is strangely erotic,' he added with faint amusement.

'Circumstances that are not of my making.' To her chagrin, her own voice sounded slightly breathless.

'And that you are trying to ignore.' The amusement was open now, his hand still moving on her in devastating purpose. 'Your mind may have decided you no longer harbour your former overwhelming desire for me, Natasha *mou*, but your body seems to have other ideas.' He added softly, 'Instead of a certainty, you have become an intriguing challenge.'

Natasha turned her head away. She said bitterly, 'Have you no shame?'

'I could ask you the same question, my little cheat,' Alex Mandrakis retorted. 'After all, you were my would-be wife—the one making all the promises that were supposed to blind me to your family's real purpose.

'No doubt they guaranteed you would never have to keep any of them,' he added scornfully. 'Well, now you know you are wrong, and they will know it too.'

He altered his position slightly, significantly, making her suddenly, shockingly aware of the heated potency of male arousal against her thigh, then bent his head and put his mouth to the scented mound of her breast, his tongue stroking its taut, rosy peak with lingering appreciation.

Sensation, sudden and unwanted, lanced through her. She pushed at his shoulders. 'Don't…'

He raised his head and looked at her, his gaze quizzical. 'It is not easy to please you, *agapi mou*.'

'Then don't try,' she flung at him, stormily. 'Just—let me go.'

'Having taken all this trouble to acquire you?' he mocked. 'I don't think so. Not yet.'

'But for how long?' she asked in a stifled voice. 'You have to tell me.'

He was silent for a moment. 'Perhaps—until you no longer wish to leave, Natasha *mou*. But for now….'

His hand slid down her body with slow, insolent mastery, caressing the flat plane of her stomach, and the delicate inner hollow of her hip, before moving down to the silky triangle at the junction of her thighs.

Natasha set her teeth, her skin burning with embarrassment as he parted her legs, and she felt the glide of his fingers exploring her moist inner heat, setting off another chain of unwanted response that almost verged on excitement.

She was bitterly, angrily aware that her breathing had quickened even more, in spite of herself, and that there was an unfamiliar ache somewhere deep within her.

But she wouldn't let herself think about that, or its inevitable implications. She would focus instead on disgust. On hating her body's scalding, slippery reaction to this new intimacy almost as much as she loathed the man who was creating it with such casual expertise.

Then, as if he recognised her mental struggles: 'Why don't you stop fighting me, *agapi mou*?' Alex Mandrakis whispered. 'Because the battle is already lost.'

'Not for me,' she managed hoarsely. 'I'll never forgive you for this. Not as long as I live.' *Or as long as you do…*

He shrugged. 'Then I have nothing to lose,' he said, half to himself, as he lifted himself over her. 'But everything to gain,' he added in husky triumph. And entered her with one smooth, unerring thrust.

CHAPTER FOUR

Up to that moment Natasha had only really thought about the outrage to her feelings, and the nightmare effect on her life of this unbearable, shameful indignity that was being inflicted on her. It had not occurred to her that her first experience of sex might cause her actual physical pain.

Her taut muscles shocked into resistance, she wanted to cry out to him that he was hurting her, and beg him to stop. To give her unaccustomed body at least a little time to adjust to the stark reality of his penetration of her.

Yet she did nothing, said nothing, determined not to grant him the satisfaction of knowing that anything he did could affect her in any way—pleasure or pain.

For a moment she felt him pause, heard him say her name harshly, almost questioningly, then, when she still did not offer any kind of response, push forward in the final surge of conquest, sheathing himself in her completely.

Natasha stayed totally, rigidly motionless, only her hands moving as they clenched into tight fists at her sides.

It will be over soon, she thought as tiny sparks danced behind her tightly closed eyelids, and repeated the words like a mantra—over soon—over soon…

She caught her bottom lip between her teeth, deliberately emptying her mind, and shutting off all thought and emotion, as Alex Mandrakis began to move, driving into her slowly and rhythmically, furthering his possession with an exquisite sensual precision that in itself seemed a kind of insult.

Even though her eyes were shut, she knew instinctively that he was watching her, waiting presumably for some kind of reaction. But he would learn nothing, she thought, from a face that she was taking care to keep as blank and expressionless as a mask.

But it wasn't easy. To her dismay, and in spite of the slight discomfort that still lingered, she soon discovered she was not totally immune to the alien, bewildering sensations being provoked by the compelling motion of his body inside hers.

She'd expected to fight him, she thought, alarmed, but she had not bargained for having to fight herself too. But she could not let this happen, she resolved, her throat tightening in mingled shame and panic. She could not allow herself such weakness when she needed to be strong.

Yet how could she have known, she asked herself in bewilderment, how, in spite of everything, he might make her feel? How her body might act against the strength of her will—her anger—tempting her to surrender.

Then, as she found she was actually beginning to struggle to maintain her self-control, she heard his breathing change, and was aware of his pace quickening, until suddenly he cried out, his voice harsh, almost agonised, and she felt the pulsating heat of him deep within her, before he slumped forward, his sweat-dampened face against her breasts.

Natasha waited for a few moments, but he did not stir, so slowly and carefully she began to ease herself away from him.

Immediately, his arms tightened around her. 'So the statue comes to life at last,' he said huskily. 'Now, when it is over.'

Over, she thought with thankfulness. Over—exactly as she'd wanted it to be, and she'd given him nothing. So it was ludicrous to feel so…bereft. Mortifying, too, to know that, for the briefest instant, she'd actually been tempted to cradle his head between her hands, and stroke his hair.

She said in a small, wooden voice, 'You're heavy.'

'Forgive me.' His voice was softly ironic. 'Treat it as just one more inconvenience among so many others, Natasha *mou*.'

He lifted himself off her and lay back against his pillows, staring in front of him as he steadied his breathing.

After a while, she spoke again. 'Please, may I use your bathroom? I'd like to have a shower.'

'Later,' he said. 'After we have talked a little.'

'I don't think there's anything left to say.' As she tried to turn away his hand snaked out and captured her chin, making her face him.

'Then you would be wrong,' he told her. 'As a beginning, tell me about your English lover.'

'He's warm, kind and decent,' Natasha said shortly. 'Your exact opposite, in fact, Kyrios Mandrakis. What else do you want to know?'

'When you are in bed with him, do you come?'

She gasped, and colour flooded her face. 'Yes,' she said jerkily, pushing his hand away from her. 'Yes, of course.'

'And before him,' the quiet voice went on. 'How many other men were there?'

'Dozens,' she said defiantly.

Alex Mandrakis sighed. 'If I teach you one thing in our time to-gether, Natasha,' he remarked tersely, 'it will be to tell me the truth. Until I took you a little while ago, you were a virgin, so do not bother to deny it. Or did you think I would not know?'

'I—I wasn't sure,' she muttered, aware that her flush had deepened.

'Yet you did not think to tell me,' he said. 'Why not?'

'Because you'd already made up your mind what I was,' she said. 'Thanks to that revolting letter. So you wouldn't have believed me, whatever I'd said.' She paused. 'Besides, even if you had known, would it have made any difference to—to what you were planning for me?'

'No,' he said. 'Except that I would have made sure that your body was rather more receptive to such an initiation.' His mouth twisted wryly. 'I hurt you, Natasha *mou*, but by the time I realised the truth, it was too late, and I regret that.'

He paused. 'My only excuse is that I wanted you very badly.'

'Well, please don't let it weigh on what passes for your con-science,' she said tautly. 'In the broad scheme of things, it's hardly the worst injury you'll make me suffer, I'm sure.'

He said slowly, 'It does not have to be like that.'

Her eyes flew to his. She said hoarsely, 'Do you mean you're willing to let me go after all?'

'No,' he said, 'I am not, so do not even hope.'

'But why?' She swallowed. 'You've got what you wanted, so you don't need to keep me around any longer. There's no point.'

'There is the pleasure of your company,' he corrected silkily.

'You can say that when you know I hate you?' Natasha shook her head. 'When you must realise that I wouldn't voluntarily choose to spend five minutes with you?'

'Perhaps, Natasha *mou*, you will discover that I improve on acquaintance.' His voice was solemn, but, to her fury, amusement was dancing in the dark eyes. 'And to prove that I too can be kind on occasion, we will take that shower you mentioned.'

We...? Alarm bells sounded in her head as Alex tossed away the covers and swung himself off the bed.

She clutched at the sheet. 'I—I can wait...' she said, trying, even at this juncture, not to look at him.

'Why—when there is no need?' He was laughing openly now. 'Believe me, my lovely one, you have nothing to fear. You will never be safer from my attentions than you are now.' He held out a hand. 'Come with me.'

He waited, and when she still hesitated he sighed briefly and impatiently, twitched the sheet from her grasp and scooped her up from the bed, carrying her in his arms across the room to a door standing ajar, and shouldering it open.

Natasha received a fleeting impression of creamy tiles marbled in blue and gold, and mirrors everywhere, as Alex walked with her to a shower cabinet almost as large as the entire bathroom at her flat. He set her on her feet directly under the shower head and joined her, switching on the water to full power.

As the force of it hit her, she gasped, and Alex's arm went round her, steadying her. After a moment, he adjusted the flow, and reached for the shower gel. He tipped some into his hand, turning her so that her back was towards him, and began to apply the scented lather to her skin, beginning with her shoulders and working downwards in small circular movements, his fingertips firm and very sure.

She wanted to tell him to stop—that she could manage for herself—but her voice didn't seem to be working properly, and it was important for him, somehow, not to know that.

As his fingers moved down over the curves of her buttocks to her slender thighs she could feel her resistance draining away, to be re-placed by a disturbing inner trembling. Every nerve-ending seemed to be tingling as her body came reluctantly, unexpectedly alive under the leisurely path of his hands.

He soaped every inch of each slim leg, then turned her to face him and began his ministrations all over again, moving up from her ankle to her knee then slowly edging higher.

His hands lingered on her thighs, brushing gently across the soft mound at their apex, making the breath catch in her throat as she waited, on a knife-edge, torn between panic and excitement, for him to touch her again there—*there*.

Only he did not. Instead, his fingers moved unhurriedly upwards, across her abdomen to her breasts, where he paused, anointing each swollen peak with as much tantalising care as if he'd been stroking the petals of a flower.

And she stood before him, hollow, helpless, with her legs shaking under her, every touch, every caress burning into her mind. Suggesting possibilities—dangers she refused even to contemplate.

Alex stepped back, studying her, his face absorbed and intent, as if judging his own handiwork, then took a further handful of gel and applied it briskly and thoroughly to his own body, before turning the water back to its full flow and rinsing the lather from them both.

Turning the shower off, he lifted her out, wrapping her in a fluffy bath sheet, then took a towel and began to dry her wet hair, combing the damp strands with his fingers.

This task also completed to his apparent satisfaction, he took the edges of her bath sheet in both hands, drew her forward and kissed her slowly and gently on the mouth, his lips barely moving on hers, demanding no real response.

When at last he lifted his head, he said quietly, 'Next time we make love, it will be better for you, I promise. But for now, I think we should return to bed, and get some rest.'

She stared at him, mind and body in total confusion. She thought, I don't dare be in bed with him again—not feeling like this. Not wanting…

She brought that line of thought to an abrupt and very necessary halt. Found her voice at last, and let scorn mask any unsteadiness in her tone.

'Nothing you do will ever make things better between us, *kyrie*. I just want to be rid of you. And I have no intention of sleeping with you, either.'

His brows lifted. 'Most people who share a bed sleep at some point, *pedhi mou*.'

'I am not your little one,' she denied curtly.

'Then do not behave like a child.'

She set her lips mutinously. 'And I prefer to sleep alone.'

He shrugged. 'In future, you will heed my preferences. Did I not make that clear also?' He paused. 'Now, will you go with me willingly, or must I carry you a second time?' His smile did not reach his eyes. 'I have no objection, you understand, except it might prompt me to test my powers of recovery sooner than you may wish.'

She was in no doubt as to his meaning. She bent her head defeatedly. 'I—I'll walk.'

'You are learning,' Alex approved softly.

She hesitated. 'But if—if there was just something I could wear. I'm just not used to being without my clothes—in front of people.'

'Your modesty is laudable, but unnecessary, Natasha *mou*. Because I am not merely people. I am your lover, and your body is a delight to me, so I wait impatiently for the moment when you will be as joyously naked with me as you once were, alone in the moonlight.

'And I do not share your inhibitions, *agapi mou*,' he added lightly. 'So you must accustom yourself to seeing me without my clothes. However, for you, I am already prepared to make a concession.'

He led her back into the bedroom, before opening another door adjacent to the bathroom and walking into what Natasha realised must be his dressing room.

He returned a moment later with a length of silver satin draped over his arm, which he handed to her.

It was a robe, she realised, admittedly without buttons or a zip, but better than nothing. And certainly better than a damp bath sheet, she told herself as she emerged discreetly from the folds of towelling, and slipped it on.

'Designed to fit all sizes, I presume,' she said coolly, as she wound the long sash securely round her waist.

'Bought yesterday for you, and no one else.' His correction was immediate and curt. 'Do you wish to see the receipt?'

She bit her lip. 'No,' adding stiltedly. 'It's—beautiful. *Efharisto*.'

'*Parakalo*,' he returned politely. He walked to the bed, straightening the sheets and putting the pillows back in place with casual efficiency.

'Feel free to join me as soon as you wish,' he told her, yawning, as he slid under the covers. 'Tomorrow will be a very long day.'

The satin whispered around her as she obeyed. It seemed he was quite serious about his intention to rest, because he was already turning on his side, his back towards her. Which presumably entitled her to do the same, she decided as she climbed into the other side of the bed, tucking the robe more firmly round her.

But, long after he was asleep, Natasha was still awake, unable to find oblivion so easily.

She tried to tell herself that it was anger and disgust holding her captive. That it was impossible for her to relax when the man who had used her so despicably for the sake of some shallow revenge was lying beside her.

At the same time she was aware that, if she was honest, it was only part of the truth. That her greatest struggle was against the edgy restlessness of her own body, which seemed determined to allow her no peace.

And for that, she realised, she could blame that endless, languorous time with him in the shower, which, for the first time in her life, had left her aroused in a way she'd never dreamed of.

Something for which she would never be able to forgive herself, she thought grimly. Especially as she suspected he'd done it quite deliberately to punish her for her earlier display of indifference.

But, whatever his motivation, and Alex Mandrakis was clearly a law unto himself, Natasha could neither explain nor excuse the way he'd made her feel. She only knew that she was shamed to her soul by the effect he'd had on her—and with so little effort too.

But that, of course, was how he'd earned his reputation. And it was her own small tragedy that her first experience of real desire should have been sparked by someone as worthless as he was.

Neil, she thought with sadness and regret, had never made her body ache with yearning in a way that kept her from sleep. And, if she'd slept with him, would it have been through passion or might it have been more from curiosity—a need to make discoveries about her untried sexuality, without necessarily making a lifetime commitment, but with a man she regarded as safe?

Something, she acknowledged bitterly, that could never be said about Alex Mandrakis. While loathsome and despicable didn't even come close, either.

Not that Stavros and Andonis had emerged with any honour from the situation, either. She supposed that they'd slipped that second letter in amongst all the other papers requiring her signature.

Oh, God, she thought, fighting the sudden tears she could taste in her throat. Why didn't I obey my instinct and refuse to have anything to do with their stupid deception? Then I'd have been spared this at least.

She had to accept that Neil now belonged very definitely to her past, and that what she had to concentrate on was the present—and the immediate future. And escaping permanently from the control of the enemy sleeping next to her had to be her number one priority.

And she needed to go quickly before he could fulfil his other threat—to make her pregnant.

Unless it had happened already, she thought with swift alarm, her hand going swiftly and protectively to her abdomen. But she wouldn't believe that she could be that unlucky.

So, somehow, she had to persuade him that there was nothing to be gained by bringing another unwanted child into a world which held too many of them already. Or by continuing to deny her freedom.

Because there's no reason for him to be doing this, she thought. Not any more. The feud has to be over, now that he's taken—everything. The fact that I've spent tonight with him is quite enough to bring dishonour to the family. There's no need for anything else.

And he can't have found his encounter with a statue particularly rewarding, not when his world is full of willing girls, so why would he want to keep me around any longer anyway?

He must see that, she told herself passionately. I have to make him see it.

Because I belong back in London. I'm needed there. I have my share of the rent on the flat to pay, quite apart from the business. And it's not just Molly to be considered—there's the rest of the Helping Out staff.

He's a businessman. Surely he'll understand that at least.

Although his advance planning had been pretty thorough, even to sending out some secretary to buy her a dressing gown, she thought uneasily, feeling the brush of the satin against her skin. That in itself was a fair amount of trouble for a strictly short-term arrangement, let alone a one-night stand.

But she was particularly disturbed by his admission that he'd paid that secret night-time visit to the Villa Demeter. The thought of him standing there, watching her, made her whole body clench in embarrassment.

Although that sudden silence of the cicadas should probably have warned her that there was something wrong.

She wondered if Stelios, the security guard who'd sold them out, was still on the Papadimos payroll, because, if so, she'd make sure he was fired by the end of the day, even if it meant admitting that she been caught skinny-dipping.

Thia Theodosia would be shocked, of course, but that hardly mattered. She could only imagine her foster mother's horror when—if— she learned what had happened here, in this room, tonight to the girl she'd always protected with such care.

And if Alex Mandrakis really intended to flaunt her publicly as his mistress as he'd threatened, there was no way Thia Theodosia could be guarded from the unpalatable truth.

She remembered, with a pang, that he'd said he would make her stay with him until she no longer wished to leave.

But that had just been words, surely, she thought. A meaningless boast that he could transform her into an ardent and willing partner.

Something that would never happen, she told herself with renewed vehemence. No matter what he did.

She found herself wondering how long it would take before he realised he was wasting his time and gave up on her. And, until then, how many nights she might be forced to spend lying in bed beside him, trying to sleep, and praying that he wouldn't wake.

And, stifling a small, bitter sigh, Natasha turned her face into the pillow and closed her eyes.

In spite of herself, she slept eventually, and woke to a hand touching her shoulder.

Natasha shot bolt upright with a stifled cry to meet the startled gaze of a middle-aged woman in a dark dress and snow-white apron who was standing beside the bed.

'There is something wrong, *thespinis?*'

I could compile a very long list, thought Natasha, drawing a deep and calming breath. Aloud, she said, 'I'm sorry, I—I must have been dreaming.'

An ongoing nightmare where the hand touching me belonged to Alex Mandrakis....

Who had apparently vanished, she realised with a thankful heart, because the bed at her side was empty.

It occurred to her that she had not heard him leave, but no doubt one of his skills was an ability to extricate himself from a situation that had served its purpose.

So, maybe last night's difficult heart-searchings had been unnecessary, after all, she thought, a flicker of hope stirring inside her.

Perhaps his night's rest had prompted some second thoughts, bringing Alex Mandrakis to the same conclusion as herself—that there was no need to prolong their encounter any further—and she would therefore be allowed to leave without argument.

The woman said placidly. 'I am Baraskevi to wait on you, *thespinis.* If you wish a bath, I will prepare it for you. And I have brought your clothes,' she added.

Natasha's eyes widened as she realised that the shirt and underwear now folded on the bed had been freshly laundered, by some magical means, while her travel-creased suit was on a hanger, neatly pressed.

The kind of service honed to perfection by long practice, she thought. Finding a strange girl in her master's bed was nothing new for Baraskevi, but something she'd learned to take in her stride.

But how did the girls feel when they woke in the unshadowed light of day to find themselves alone? Natasha wondered.

Even discreetly covered by the satin robe, she felt desperately awkward and self-conscious, as she realised how many people in the household must know of her presence—and why she'd been brought there.

On the positive side, however, she saw with a leap of the heart that her bag and overnight case had also reappeared.

Which had to be tacit permission to depart, she thought, saving them both another confrontation. Better and better.

And was very glad she hadn't yielded to a momentary temptation to ask Baraskevi where he was.

'Thank you,' she said stiltedly. 'And a bath would be good.'

It might even make her feel clean again, she thought, her throat tightening, as she watched the older woman vanish into the bathroom.

She was still aware that she ached slightly—a potent and inescapable reminder of everything that had happened. But the real bruising was to her pride, and to the sense of independence she'd fought so hard to achieve.

I might as well have let Thio Basilis line up the most eligible males—and let me pick one at random, she thought. At least Alex Mandrakis wouldn't have been among them.

She pushed back the covers and swung her feet to the floor, re-fastening the sash of her robe as she did so. Before wakening her, Baraskevi had drawn back the curtains and opened the shutters, allowing the untrammelled sunlight to pour into the room, together with a welcome freshness in the air.

One storm may well have passed, she told herself wryly. But the next is about to begin. That's inevitable. Except it may not leave quite as much devastation in its wake as I feared.

She unzipped her case and retrieved her toiletries, then quickly checked the contents of her handbag to make sure that her passport and wallet were still safely inside, and that she could just…walk away. Not unscathed. There were some memories that would haunt her for a very long time.

But not forever. Because there would come a day she would belong to herself alone again, and this would appear nothing but a bad dream.

I swear it, she told herself, and went to take her bath.

The warm water, scented with sandalwood, turned out to be precisely what she needed, although she could have done without having to put on last night's discarded clothes again afterwards.

At the first opportunity, she thought as her face warmed, I shall burn every damned stitch. I need no reminder of how I was once made to take them off.

Dressed, with her hair twisted back into its knot, she went to pick up her bags, then paused. Maybe there was one more memento she could take and burn, she thought. That letter.

She walked round the bed and opened the drawer in the night

table, but the file had gone, along, she realised, with his laptop, which had been on the floor.

She sighed with frustration, then went back across the room, flinging open the unlocked door. Only to walk into the human equivalent of a brick wall.

As she recoiled, she realised it was the man who'd met her at the airport last night.

'*Kalimera, thespinis.*' His greeting was just as expressionless as it had been then. 'Breakfast is waiting for you on the terrace. I will take you there.'

'Thank you, but I'm not hungry,' Natasha returned coldly. Actually, she was ravenous, but she wasn't going to admit it. 'And I would prefer to leave at once.'

'That is something you must discuss with Kyrios Alexandros, *thespinis,*' he said, detaching her bags from her grasp with implacable firmness. 'He is waiting for you. Go with me, please.'

She almost said, And if I don't? but decided she didn't really want to hear the answer.

If, after all, she was to be forced into another encounter with the enemy, she reasoned, she'd rather walk there than be carried under someone's arm, perhaps, with her feet ignominiously dangling.

Maybe she could even salvage some vestige of dignity at their final meeting.

The terrace in question was at the rear of the house, and a table had been set at the far end in a pergola shaded by bougainvillea.

Alex Mandrakis was sitting there, reading a newspaper, the top button of his immaculate white shirt unfastened and his silk tie pulled loose.

At her approach, he rose courteously, indicating that she should take the seat opposite that her bodyguard was placing for her.

When they were alone, she said coldly, 'Is your watchdog really necessary?'

'I think so.' He picked up a jug of chilled orange juice and poured some into a glass for her. 'Until I am sure I can trust you, Natasha *mou.*'

That did not sound like goodbye, and it jolted her, her earlier optimism fading fast.

Her mind working feverishly, she took one of the hot rolls from the napkin-lined basket he proffered to her, and spooned cherry jam onto her plate.

'There is coffee.' He gestured towards the tall pot waiting in the middle of the table. 'But there can be tea, if you prefer.'

'Please don't put your staff to any more trouble on my account.' Her dry mouth relished the coolness of the freshly squeezed oranges.

'Nevertheless, you must let them know about any requirements you may have,' he said. 'I wish you to be comfortable.'

'In that case,' she said, 'perhaps you'll get your chauffeur to drive me home. That is all I find necessary.'

'Then you will be disappointed,' he said, shrugging. 'Because your home is now with me, until I decide otherwise.' He paused. 'And the sooner you accept that, *agapi mou*, the better it will be for you. So, please believe that, and let us enjoy breakfast together.

'The first of many, I hope,' he added softly, and smiled at her.

CHAPTER FIVE

NATASHA stared at him for a long moment, her green eyes narrowing dangerously.

'Lost for words, *agapi mou*?' he gibed. 'Perhaps you should have some tea, after all.'

'My God,' she said. 'You're unbelievable, do you know that? You're destroying my life, and here you are, chatting about my choice of beverage.'

He shrugged. 'I gather it is good for shock.'

'I'm not shocked.' She kept her denial cool and crisp, in spite of her inner turmoil. 'How could I be? The events of last night showed me what a worthless individual you are, Kyrios Mandrakis. So I suppose I was a fool to imagine you might feel any belated remorse for your disgusting behaviour, or attempt some kind of amend, however inadequate.'

'But I have every intention of making amends to you, *agapi mou*,' he said, silkily. 'But in my own time, and in my own way.'

Her throat tightened. 'Then maybe I should make it clear right now that I shall not be meekly submitting to any more of the degradation you've subjected me to.'

'I hope not,' he returned coolly. 'Meekness has no appeal for me. I want you warm and eager in my arms, Natasha *mou*, not submissive.'

'Then you're going to be seriously disappointed.' Her voice thickened. 'I may not have kicked and screamed last night—although my chief regret is that I didn't leave you permanently damaged—but that doesn't mean I accept the situation you forced on me, or that I ever will do.

'After all,' she went on, 'even you can't keep me locked up forever, or trailed by your gorilla. At some point today my signature will be genuinely needed in order for you to take over the Papadimos assets.

'And you can hardly deliver me to the designated meeting place bound, gagged or chained to your wrist.'

She paused. 'So, this is where it ends, Kyrios Mandrakis. Be content with your new shipping lines, because I don't go with them. This is our first breakfast and it's also our last. Once the papers are signed, I'm out of here, and there's nothing you can do to stop me.'

'No?' He leaned back in his chair. 'I would not be so sure of that.'

'Then think again,' she advised curtly. 'You seem to have overlooked the fact that there'll be lawyers present at the completion of this deal, *kyrie*. Papadimos attorneys, as well as yours. And I shall make it perfectly clear—swear an affidavit if I have to—that you tricked me at the airport into coming here, then forced me to go to bed with you.

'I shall also get Stavros and Andonis to admit that they were the authors of that foul letter, and I knew nothing about it. So I think any abduction charges against you may stick after all—don't you? And believe me, that will only be the beginning.'

He said pleasantly, 'I should have told them to serve you honey this morning, Natasha *mou*. It might have sweetened your temper—and your tongue.'

He paused to refill his cup. 'So, where do you plan to go?' he asked. 'After this dramatic exit? To the Villa Demeter to live once more as one happy family?'

'No way,' she said. 'I'm going to England. Back to the life there you've tried and failed to ruin.'

His mouth curled. 'And to the lover who does not exist?'

'No,' Natasha said. 'Far from it. I run a business, *kyrie*. Small, and meaningless in your scheme of things, of course, but useful—and successful too, and I'm proud of it. I have people relying on me, and I can't—I won't abandon all that on some vindictive whim of yours.'

'Ah, yes.' He gave her a meditative look. 'You call it Helping Out, do you not?'

She swallowed. 'How did you know that?'

'I had enquiries made.' He shrugged. 'But your absence will not be a problem. I can arrange for a temporary replacement to be found for you, until you are able to return.'

'Just like that?' Her voice shook with anger.

'Why not?' His brows rose.

She said defiantly, 'Because I'm not letting some stranger take my place, just so that I can be kept around to…service you. As I thought I'd just explained.'

She lifted her chin. 'I shan't ever forgive you for last night, Kyrios Mandrakis, but, given time, I shall forget. And if there are…consequences, I'll deal with those too,' she added proudly. 'You won't be involved in any way. I intend to treat your incursion into my life as an unwelcome glitch—nothing more.

'Unlike the other women you favour, *kyrie*, I'm not for sale, or for rent. I belong to myself alone, and nothing you can say or do will change that one iota.'

'You sound very determined, *agapi mou*.' Alex Mandrakis drank some more coffee, watching her over the rim of the cup. 'So, tell me a little about your home in London. It is large, with many rooms?'

'No,' she said. 'Why do you ask—as if it's any of your business?'

'Because you will need to find a bigger residence—when it becomes your turn to house your brothers and their families. After all, they will have nowhere else to go, and England may well have its attractions for them, in the circumstances.'

She was very still. Suddenly wary. 'What are you talking about?'

'About the Villa Demeter,' he said. 'The Papadimos palace, which they also used most unwisely as collateral in their quest for money. And which now also belongs to me, Natasha *mou*, along with everything else. Every stick of furniture, every stone in its walls.

'Its memories too,' he added silkily, and watched her colour flare.

'At the moment, your brothers are my tenants,' he went on. 'But who can say how long I will permit this situation to continue? They may already be living on borrowed time.'

He paused. 'And while you may rightly conclude they have only themselves to blame for their present troubles, and refuse to involve yourself further, there is someone else whose well-being may cause you more concern.'

He saw her eyes dilate, and nodded. 'I am told you care deeply for your foster mother, Madame Papadimos. Do you really wish to see a woman of her age, in delicate health, forced out of the house she came to as a bride, and where her children were born?

'What kind of life could she expect, and do you think she could easily withstand such a shock?'

She said unevenly, 'Oh, God, you couldn't. You wouldn't...'

'I mean what I say,' Alex Mandrakis returned. 'As you know to your cost, Natasha *mou*. But I could be persuaded to spare *Madame* this terrible blow—on certain conditions.

'I might even be prepared to negotiate terms on which she, plus her sons and their families, may continue to enjoy the shelter of my roof without interference. And she will not even have the pain of knowing that this has been necessary.'

He smiled at her, his eyes travelling from her parted, trembling lips to the curve of her breast under the prim shirt.

'But that, my moonlight goddess, depends entirely on you.' he continued softly. Inexorably. 'You may either elect to return to England, having made your wrongs public and exacted what retribution you can, although I remain dubious about your success.

'Or, as I have already said, you can remain with me until my desire for you has been fully satisfied, and I let you go. You will probably not have too long to wait,' he added casually, and she felt her hands clench round the arms of her chair.

'However, that is the choice I am offering, Natasha *mou*. And it is the only one. On this point, there will be no negotiation. Let that also be understood between us. Clearly.'

He paused. 'But you need not give me your reply now. When we meet later at the lawyers' offices will be quite soon enough. The answer to such an important question also requires witnesses—don't you think?

'And once I know your final decision, I will make mine.' Briskly, he finished his coffee, pushed back his chair and rose. 'Whatever it happens to be.'

As he passed her, he let his hand drop onto her shoulder. It was only for an instant, but she felt its pressure like a bruise.

'Remember that,' he said. 'And remember it well.'

And he went, leaving Natasha motionless in her chair, staring into space with eyes that saw nothing.

* * *

'So you have decided to join us at last, sister,' was Stavros's sullen greeting that afternoon as Natasha walked reluctantly into the palatial suite of offices which belonged to the lawyers acting for Bucephalus Holdings. 'We had begun to wonder.'

'How strange,' she returned unsmilingly. 'I've spent the past few hours doing exactly the same thing—wondering.' She looked around her. 'Where is everyone else?'

'They have offered us a private room to wait in. I will take you to it.' He sighed heavily as they started down the corridor. 'My poor Christina cannot stop weeping. She will never recover from the shame of what has happened.'

'Really?' Natasha's brows rose with cool irony. 'Now, I'd say she's got off quite lightly. But perhaps I'm biased.'

'How can you say such a thing?' He halted outside a closed door, his voice hoarse with reproach. 'When this man—this Mandrakis has taken everything from us? And now even the roof over our heads is threatened by him.'

He threw his hands to heaven. 'My unfortunate mother—in God's name, how can Andonis and I ever face her after this terrible thing?'

She said bitterly, 'The real question is—how could you and Andonis ever think you could take Alex Mandrakis on and win?'

'It was a good plan,' he said defensively. 'The suggestion that there could be a marriage interested him. Gave us time.'

Time to do what? she wondered bleakly. Make things a thousand times worse?

'Is that why you wrote that other letter?' she asked quietly. 'Because you thought it would keep him even more interested? Give you a bigger window of opportunity to try and trick him?'

He gaped at her, his jaw dropping. In any other circumstances, Natasha might almost have found the combination of guilt and astonishment in his expression amusing. As it was, it made her feel frankly nauseous.

'What other letter?' he managed at last. 'I don't understand.'

She said wearily, 'Of course you do, Stavros, so stop playing games. I've even worked out how you managed to get a spare signature from me.'

'But how did you know?' he demanded. 'How could you have found out? I demand to know.'

'I don't think you're in a position to make demands, brother,' Natasha said quietly. 'Not from me or anyone else. Besides, what does it matter? It's far too late to worry about it now.'

Turning away, she opened the door and entered the room beyond.

The first person she saw was Andonis, looking the picture of misery, head bent under a shrill deluge of sound being aimed at him by his wife, his sister-in-law and Irini.

Behind her, she heard Stavros mutter something that might have been a curse or a prayer.

Her gaze travelled to where Madame Papadimos was seated with quiet composure in a chair by the window, looking down into the street as if quite oblivious to the uproar elsewhere in the room. Although, Natasha knew, that could not possibly be true.

She swung round on Stavros. 'You brought your mother?' she asked incredulously. 'Here—to this?'

He shrugged. 'Her idea, not ours. As God is my judge, Natasha, we tried to shield her, but Hara showed her the newspapers, told her servants' stories, so, when she asked, we had to tell her the truth.'

He shrugged uncomfortably. 'She knows everything, except that Mandrakis can rob her of her home if he pleases. That at least we have kept from her, in case, by some miracle, he decides to be merciful after all.'

She said quietly, 'I don't think mercy features largely in his plans,' and put down her bags.

As she moved towards Madame Papadimos, Maria ran over and seized her arm.

'Sister—we have been waiting for you, Christina and I. Our husbands say this is ruin for us all. But this cannot be. Tell us what we must do.'

'I thought I already did,' Natasha said, wondering how many thousands of pounds' worth of jewellery Maria and Christina were wearing between them. 'Just a few weeks ago. But no one wanted to listen. Now it looks as if the boys will have to find jobs in order to keep you in manicures. It's a tough old world out there.'

'How cruel you are,' Maria said, stifling a sob. 'Anyone would think we were to blame, and not that pig—that brute, Mandrakis.'

'Oh, I think I know exactly where the guilt lies,' Natasha said, and turned away. As she did so, she encountered a look from Irini so venomous that she almost took a step backwards. My God, she thought. Isn't one damaging vendetta enough for this family? Does she have to carry on her hate campaign even now when we should be standing united?

But she recovered herself, and made her way over to Thia Theodosia.

She knelt beside her foster mother's chair, and took a thin hand in hers.

She said softly, 'I'm so terribly sorry, darling. Thank heavens Thio Basilis can't know what is happening.'

'The seeds for this harvest were sown a long time ago, *pedhi mou*, and I always knew its fruit would be bitter.' Madame Papadimos sounded calm but tired. 'Basilis could have stopped it so many times, but he would not do so, even at the last.' She sighed. 'You saw only the good side of him, my child, but he could be cold—cold like ice. Harsh, too, and unforgiving. And as a result our lives, our security have been destroyed.'

Natasha stared up at her with faint shock. She had never heard Madame Papadimos utter a word of criticism about her late husband before. But then, she couldn't remember her foster mother making any overt reference to the feud, either. In fact, she'd always sensed that the older woman found the subject too painful to discuss.

Whereas I, she thought, decided it was just a lot of macho rivalry between two powerful men that had had been allowed to get ludicrously out of control. Something that could be safely ignored.

I certainly never realised how serious it might become—or that I could get caught up in it, and be made to suffer like this as a result.

After Alex Mandrakis had left that morning, she'd simply stayed where she was, sitting on the terrace, too numb to move as her mind circled on the same weary, hopeless treadmill, looking for some means of escape, and failing to find one. Knowing that, unless she co-operated, he would do exactly as he'd said.

Baraskevi, accompanied by a younger girl, had come eventually to clear the breakfast things, both clicking their tongues over how little she had eaten, and anxiously offering other food and fresh coffee, all of which she'd declined before, once she was alone again, sinking back into her bitter reverie.

And most of her mental struggles, she had to admit, had involved the frail woman beside her, who'd shown her nothing but sweetness and affection since her arrival in Athens as a scared, silent child. Someone who did not deserve to have her comfort and peace of mind wrecked in an act of triumphant vengeance by a man who had already taken too much. But who wanted everything.

Looking back, she could see that there had always been an element of sadness about Madame Papadimos, which, with hindsight, might have suggested her marriage was not the easiest of relationships.

But because they both loved me, Natasha thought unhappily, I took the love between them for granted too. Yet it may have been a more complex situation than I ever dreamed.

Now she carried her foster mother's hand gently to her cheek. She'd never had any real choice, she thought, as Alex Mandrakis had known perfectly well when he offered it. Whatever her private thoughts on the rest of the family, there was no way she would allow Thia Theodosia to suffer the ignominy of eviction on top of everything else.

And all she could do now, she told herself, was steel herself to the inevitable—and survive.

'Not everything will be lost,' she said quietly. 'And that's a promise.'

She saw Irini approaching, and rose hastily. She already felt brittle enough to shatter in tiny pieces, and decided that any more petulant hostility from the other girl might just push her over the edge. Something she could not afford in the circumstances.

She needed to be calm and in control of herself and her emotions at all times, particularly if she was to make Alex Mandrakis totally regret this one-sided bargain he'd forced on her.

She needed to ensure that any pleasure he derived from her would be less than minimal, and if that meant retreating back into a shell of bored indifference to resist his advances, then that was exactly what she'd do.

I'm one victory he'll never win, she resolved stonily, moving to the side of the room and looking down with spurious interest at the neatly arrayed newspapers and journals on a table there. I'll make damned certain that he'll be glad to call it a day—or a night—and send me home.

But when, a moment later, a hand touched her arm, she spun round with a little choking cry, only to find herself confronted by a complete stranger—a thin, grey-haired man with glasses.

'Kyria Kirby?' He inclined his head with formal politeness. 'I regret if I startled you. My client, Kyrios Mandrakis, wishes to know whether you have yet come to a decision on the matter he discussed with you earlier. I am to take him your answer.'

She swallowed, steadying her flurried breathing. 'Then you may tell him—yes,' she said huskily. 'That I accept his terms.'

He nodded. 'I will convey that to him, *thespinis*,' he said, and moved away.

Watching him go, Natasha wondered almost hysterically if he had the least idea of the precise nature of the morning's discussion. Whether or not he knew he'd just put an unwilling girl in his client's bed. Or if he'd even care.

Get real, she told herself, scornfully. It won't be the first dubious transaction of this kind that he's been involved with. Not when he works for a man like Alex Mandrakis.

Nor would it be the last.

And suddenly, for no good reason that she could fathom, Natasha found herself sinking her teeth painfully into her lower lip.

The summons to the conference room came a few minutes later. Allowing sufficient time for her message to be delivered, Natasha thought bleakly as she allowed herself to be ushered down the corridor, only Madame Papadimos and her daughters-in-law remaining behind as non-board members.

Drawing a deep breath, she took her seat at the foot of the long polished table, Stavros and Andonis providing a solid bulwark between Irini and herself.

But she could still feel the other's dislike reaching out to her like the first scorching touch of a naked flame.

What's the matter with her? Natasha wondered silently. Surely she can't hold me responsible in any way for what's happened?

The opposing lawyers were lined up on either side of the table, bulging document files open in front of them, maintaining an appearance of civilised professional chat, while secretaries were bustling in with bottled water and trays of thick, sweet coffee.

But nothing could lessen the tingling tension in the room. The oppressive suggestion that some countdown had begun.

Because, at the head of the table, an empty chair was waiting. A throne for the conqueror, she thought bitterly. Whenever he chose to appear in order to stake his claim to his new empire.

And to herself…

It occurred to her uneasily that she should probably have informed her brothers in advance of her reluctant agreement with Alex Mandrakis. Warned them what to expect.

Except that they'd have undoubtedly gone into full explosion mode, she thought with a silent sigh, possibly wrecking the single concession her surrender had achieved in the process. She could not risk that.

But perhaps, too, she was still foolishly hoping—praying—that even now he might have a last-minute change of heart. That he might decide she was not worth the effort, after all, and simply accept her spoken compliance with his wishes instead of the coldly resentful physical capitulation which was the most he could hope for.

If so, there would be no need to say anything at all. And last night, therefore, could be put behind her as if it had never happened.

Unless…

But she wouldn't let herself think about that. Refused to consider the possibility that her first, soulless encounter with a man might, even now, be bearing fruit.

Not that, she thought passionately. I can stand anything but that.

She was not watching the door at the far end of the room, yet she knew the exact moment when Alex Mandrakis finally came in.

It was not necessary for her to look up from her fixed scrutiny of the table, because a faint tremor went through her, as if a lazy fingertip had trailed the length of her spine, even before the scrape of chairs announced that the legal fraternity had risen respectfully to greet him.

Under her shirt, her skin felt damp. She had to resist an impulse to shift restlessly, to lick dry lips and raise a nervous hand to push back a stray tress of hair.

Beside her, she saw Andonis's hands clench on the table until the knuckles turned white, and she placed a hand gently over his taut fist.

'Don't let him see,' she whispered under her breath. 'Never let him see.'

Alex Mandrakis spoke calmly and quietly in his own language, bidding everyone present good afternoon, and welcoming them to the meeting. There was no false note, or audible gloating in his voice.

As if, Natasha thought almost dazedly, this was just another day, with just another deal to be done. As maybe it was—for him. But not for them, or for the distraught women waiting in the other room.

And not for me...

As people resumed their seats, she ventured a swift glance under her lashes. But he was not looking at her, as she'd half expected. His attention was fixed on the sheaf of papers that had been placed in front of him, and which were being delivered to everyone else round the table, herself included. His expression was aloof and even a little stern.

As the man with glasses, who introduced himself as Ari Stanopoulos, rose to outline the main features of the buyout, Stavros and Andonis were leafing through their bundles of documents almost feverishly, their faces strained and dejected as each item of bad news was finally and irrevocably confirmed.

But as he reached the end, Andonis gave a smothered gasp. 'The house,' he muttered behind his hand. 'There is no mention of the house. Perhaps that devil has some atom of humanity, after all.'

But he'd obviously not spoken quietly enough, because all heads turned in their direction, and Alex Mandrakis himself looked down the table at them, his mouth twisting in cynical hauteur.

He said silkily, 'Or perhaps I have decided to trade it for something I prefer, Kyrios Papadimos.'

And for a nanosecond, his gaze flicked to Natasha.

No one else could possibly have noticed, but she was aware of the fleeting caress of his eyes, just as he'd intended she should be, and she felt her body burn suddenly under her clothes. She poured some water into a glass and drank, forcing the cool liquid past the tightening muscles in her throat, as she made herself accept that there would be no reprieve. That he intended to enforce their unholy deal.

There was a pause, then Ari Stanopoulos, with a slight cough, renewed his summary of terms, while Stavros and Andonis exchanged bewildered shrugs.

Natasha let the words brush over her, without even attempting to follow them. Her mind was already reaching ahead to the end of the meeting. To the 'trade', and all its implications.

You do what you have to do, she told herself steadily, as and when he requires, and no more. You don't protest, and you don't plead. You speak only when spoken to. You ask for nothing. You don't look at him unless you have to, you certainly don't smile, and you never cry. That above all.

She realised that Ari Stanopoulos had finished and sat down, allowing the Papadimos lawyers to voice their objections, but it was clear their hearts weren't in it. They'd been defeated long before this meeting had been scheduled, and they knew it.

It's all over bar the shouting, she thought as she took the pen she was handed and silently signed her name where indicated. And the shouting was probably about to begin.

She watched the broad smiles of the Mandrakis team as they shook hands with each other, exuberantly applauding the young man sitting quietly and collectedly at the head of the table.

'Let us go,' Stavros growled, getting to his feet. 'I wish to get out of here, before I choke.'

Alex Mandrakis pushed back his chair, and rose too, the hubbub around him silencing immediately.

He said softly, 'Natasha *mou*,' and held out his hand.

So this was how it was to be done, she thought as her stomach churned. Publicly and irrevocably, just as he'd warned.

Andonis was glaring at him. 'You dare to address our sister by her given name?' he challenged belligerently.

She put a hand on his arm. Her legs were shaking under her, but she kept her voice clear and steady. 'You do not understand, brother. Kyrios Mandrakis has invited me to become his companion for a while, and I—I have accepted.'

She added, 'So there's really no more to be said.'

And, head held high, she walked the length of the hushed room to where Alex waited for her, a faint smile playing about his mouth.

CHAPTER SIX

As Natasha reached him, Alex took her hand and raised it courteously to his lips, only to turn it so that his kiss found, instead, the inside of her wrist, making the startled pulse leap and judder at the swift brush of his mouth.

Something he was no doubt well aware of, she thought, cursing him under her breath as her face warmed helplessly.

'Tramp! Whore!' The stunned silence in the room was suddenly interrupted by the screeched words from Irini, jumping to her feet, her face contorted. She pointed a shaking finger. 'Have I not always said, brothers, that we should not trust this English witch that our father brought to our home? See now how she betrays his memory with her lust for his enemy!'

Natasha moved swiftly—convulsively—her skin not merely warm now but burning, and felt Alex's grasp tighten almost warningly on her fingers.

'Control her.' His instruction was curt, as he looked coldly down the table at Stavros and Andonis. 'Explain to her, some time, how her insults are completely undeserved. How this girl beside me, who has been a sister to you, is the real, the only victim of betrayal. And how it is thanks to her alone that your home still remains to you. Or had you not realised that?'

His condemnatory glance moved to Irini, standing now between the two crestfallen Papadimos men. He added icily, 'Maybe, *thespinis*, you should practise gratitude instead of calling Kyria Natasha names as foul as they are untrue.'

He paused. 'Our business is now concluded, and you are all free to go.' He released Natasha's hand, instead encircling her with his arm, drawing her against him. He said softly, 'Except, of course, for you, my heart's delight. We have a journey to make together.'

She stood in silence, staring down at the floor as the room emptied, acutely conscious of the lithe warmth of his body against hers. Angered by an awareness she seemed unable to control.

When they were finally alone, she said bitterly, 'Why did you bother to defend me against Irini? Isn't that what you wanted her—and everyone else—to think?'

'Originally, yes,' he said. 'Now they will all know, as well as I do myself, that you were a virgin when I took you, and that will be a much deeper wound for their pride, *matia mou*, believe me.'

Something that was almost a pain seemed to twist inside her, but was instantly dismissed. After all, she thought with an inward shrug, what else had she expected him to say? The feud was the only thing that mattered to him, and she was simply an integral part of his victory. He would never forget that, and neither would she.

He reached up a hand and removed the clips from her hair, letting it tumble free to her shoulders.

He said quietly, 'I told you last night. I like to see it loose.'

She was expecting him to pull her fully into his arms and kiss her, to establish his domination if nothing else, and was surprised to find herself released as he moved away to lean back against the edge of the table.

She swallowed. 'May I ask about this trip you're planning? You may have noticed I don't have a great deal of luggage with me.'

'That will not be a problem,' he said, smiling faintly. 'Arrangements have already been made to provide you with a new wardrobe,' he went on softly. 'You will find it waiting for you later.'

She gasped. 'You've bought me clothes?' Her voice rose. 'But that's not possible. You don't even know my correct size in—in anything.'

'I could have guessed,' he said drily, his eyes travelling down her body, 'but I did not have to. A maid that Kyria Irini recently dismissed for clumsiness told me happily all I needed to know.'

Natasha stiffened. 'Was there anyone working at the Villa Demeter who was not in your pay?' she asked.

'The cook,' he said, 'and the gardeners. I decided to discover for myself the food and flowers you favoured.'

'But when it came to clothes, of course, it would never occur to you that I might prefer to choose my own stuff.'

'Stuff is right,' he said thoughtfully, 'if that suit you are wearing is an example of your taste. Believe me, *matia mou*, its only charm is to remind me of how lovely you look without it.'

'And if I refuse to wear the things you've bought for me?' she demanded defiantly.

He shrugged a shoulder. 'Then go naked.' He sounded almost bored. 'Whatever you decide will be no hardship for me, I promise.'

She bit down the cutting remark she longed to fling back at him. She had to stop picking fights she couldn't win, she thought bitterly, and remember only that she'd made a deal with herself to endure whatever he said—whatever he did—and she needed to keep to it. The way he looked at her, the way he touched her could not be allowed to be of any concern to her.

'Very well,' she said, keeping her voice neutral. 'I'll wear what you've provided, if I must.'

'You are gracious indeed,' he said silkily. 'And, as a reward for your reluctant co-operation, I will make you a small gift.'

Jewellery, I presume, Natasha thought, biting her lip. As a symbol of his munificence, I have to be lit up like a Christmas tree.

But the hand that emerged from inside his jacket was not holding the flat leather case she'd expected, but an envelope.

She took it from him, and put it in her own pocket.

'Aren't you curious to know what it contains?' he asked.

'Not unless it's a one-way airline ticket to London,' she said. 'And that I doubt somehow.'

He clicked his tongue reprovingly. 'Your desire to be rid of me is almost wounding, Natasha *mou*.'

'But the cuts are hardly deep, and I'm sure you heal very easily, Kyrios Mandrakis,' she returned tautly. 'Besides, consolation won't be too far away.'

'Not if I choose to seek it, no. But for now, I look forward to my desires being satisfied by you alone, *agapi mou*. Because in the days to come, the journey you make with me will be into pleasure. And you will not find it as difficult as you expect.'

He allowed her to assimilate that, and added, 'But, for now, you

will be free of me for a few hours, as I need to spend some time at
my office. I will join you for dinner later.

'You will go with Iorgos, after Ari Stanopoulos has spoken with
you.'

'Your fixer?' It was difficult to keep her voice steady, with his
words about pleasure still echoing in her head. 'I thought I'd already
had my interview with him.'

'But there are also arrangements to be made in London to cover
your absence, or had you forgotten such a place existed in the pleasure of my company?'

He smiled at her. 'You have rent to pay, *ne*? A partner in business to be reassured and supplied with help also? Ari will deal with
all these concerns on your behalf. You need have no worries.'

'Oh, no,' she said bitterly. 'Life is the proverbial bowl of cherries.
And I suppose in due time Mr Stanopoulos will invent a discreet lie
about my current whereabouts that I can take home with me.

'Or shall I simply say I was abducted by aliens? It doesn't feel
too far from the truth.'

He said gently, 'Then I shall have great joy in demonstrating to
you that I am indeed human—and male. And if I were not awaited
elsewhere I would do so here and now.'

As he moved away from the table Natasha took an involuntary
step backwards, and his smile widened.

'Not so brave, suddenly, *agapi mou*?' he taunted her softly. 'Then
stay that way, and please don't sharpen your tongue on Ari. He is
easily shocked. And play me no tricks, either,' he added as he turned
away. 'Unlike the staff at the Villa Demeter, my people are loyal.
No one will assist you in a daring escape. Besides, you know, I think,
what the consequences would be for your family.'

'Yes,' she said. 'You've made that more than clear.' She paused.
'Have they already left, because I would like to say goodbye?'

Alex swung back. 'After what they have done to you—the things
that have been said?' His tone was frankly sceptical. 'You are very
forgiving.'

She said steadily, 'No, I'm not. I only want to speak to—to
Thia Theodosia. That is, if she's still prepared to have anything
to do with me.'

His voice was suddenly harsh. 'You should not humble yourself, *agape mou*. Please believe that you have no reason to do so.' At the door, he paused, glancing back to where she stood, taut, her hands balled into fists at her sides.

'Nor do you have to be afraid of me,' he said. 'Not again.' And went.

She did not have to ask for Madame Papadimos, because it seemed that Thia Theodosia had already requested to see her, and was waiting to do so.

'She is in my office, Kyria Kirby,' Mr Stanopoulos told her politely. 'You will not be disturbed there.'

The only wall in the room that was not lined with books had a massive leather sofa standing against it instead, and Thia Theodosia, looking small, was seated in one deep corner.

She did not smile and the dark eyes had pain in their depths as Natasha came to sit next to her.

'Is it true, little one?' she asked quietly. 'Have you given yourself to Alexandros Mandrakis? Consented to live with him as his mistress so that the Villa Demeter can remain in our possession?'

There was a silence, then Natasha nodded, jerkily. She said, an open ache in her voice, 'I—I wouldn't let him make you homeless. But I realise what you must be thinking, and I—I'm so sorry.'

'You are sorry?' The older woman spoke with genuine astonishment. 'But how can this be, dear child, when you are to blame for nothing?' She sighed heavily. 'No, *pedhi mou*, this tragedy is my fault, and mine alone. I should have stopped it all a long time ago, but I did not have the courage.

'Now, sadly, the wheel has come full circle, and, like so many other innocents, you are the one to suffer.'

She paused. 'You should not have made such a sacrifice, but even so, it is not too late. You can leave with me now. Let the house go to Mandrakis, if he wants it, and allow my so clever sons to plot themselves a new future—if they can.'

Natasha bent her head. She said quietly, 'I gave my word to Kyrios Mandrakis, and I won't go back on it. I—can't.

'Irini accused me of betraying her father's memory, and that's exactly what I'd be doing if I allowed his home—the house he loved so much, and where he lived with you—to be taken by his enemies, along with everything else. I owe Thio Basilis far too much to let that happen.'

Madame Papadimos said, 'Ah, dear God,' and her eyes closed for a moment.

When she spoke again, her voice was low and sad. 'You should have been married three years ago, Natasha. Become a beloved and cherished wife and, by now, a happy mother. I knew it then, and said so, but I was not listened to, and, to my eternal shame, I failed to insist.'

Natasha stared at her in bewilderment. 'But it was my decision to stay single, and mine alone,' she objected gently. 'Darling, you can't have forgotten that. Thio Basilis tried his best to persuade me, usually at the top of his voice,' she added, forcing a smile. 'But I had my own plans.

'And, in spite of everything that's happened, I'm still sure I was right to stick to my guns, and make my own life.'

Thia Theodosia sighed again. 'But if there had been a man—someone you might have loved and who would have offered you his heart, as well as the protection of his name—what then, my little one?' She spread her hands. 'After all, where is this life you speak of now?'

'It's there—waiting for my return.' Natasha tried to sound buoyant. 'This…arrangement is strictly temporary. To the victor the spoils, and all that.' She lifted her chin. 'But Kyrios Mandrakis will soon be looking for new worlds to conquer like his namesake, and then I'll be free.'

Madame Papadimos looked at her gravely. 'Will you, my child? Can you be so sure that is what you will still want—when the time comes? When you know him better than you do now?'

Natasha gasped. 'I can't believe you've just said that.' Her voice was shaky. 'You, of all people, Thia Theodosia. Do you imagine I could ever forgive him for the way he's treated me? Or that I'd willingly spend an hour longer with him than I have to?'

Thia Theodosia shook her head. 'I do not condone what Alexandros Mandrakis has done, whatever provocation he may have received. Never think that, my dear girl.'

She paused. 'I simply suggest that, perhaps, you should not judge him too harshly. This trouble between our families was none of his making.

'He was a child when it began, forced to take sides. And, maybe, a time will arrive when you might find him…kinder than you believe.'

Natasha's mouth tightened. 'I don't think so,' she said. 'I've already experienced what passes for kindness with Alex Mandrakis, so I know exactly what to expect.'

Nor do you have to be afraid of me…

But that isn't true, because I now have something else to fear, she thought with a pang, fighting the memory of her body's brief, involuntary response to his possession, and the quivering torment of frustration that had succeeded it.

Something which promises to be a thousand times worse.

There was real shock in Theodosia Papadimos's face. 'My child—are you saying that he was brutal? When he must have known you had never been with a man before?'

'No,' Natasha said quietly. 'He didn't know that. In fact, he had good reason to think I'd be…willing, and more. Even so, he wasn't…brutal.'

Now, why did I say that? she asked herself with vexation. I sound as if I'm making excuses for him, when there are none. And suppose she asks me, What good reason? What do I say then? That he believed that life in London had turned me into the kind of girl who gets drunk in Greek bars, strips off and has sex with any man who asks?

It will have to be something like that, she thought, because the contents of that gleefully concocted letter were something she'd rather not share with Madame Papadimos. She hurried on, forcing a smile. 'But—hey—nothing lasts forever. He'll soon get bored and move on. While I—I won't have suffered any lasting damage, except maybe to my pride.

'And one day I'll meet a man I can love, and be happy with him, just as you've always wanted.'

There was another long silence, then Thia Theodosia said gently, 'Then that, *pedhi mou*, is what we must work towards, and pray for, once this present sadness ends.'

And, leaning forward, she kissed Natasha on both cheeks.

It had been a strange conversation, Natasha thought later as she sat returning reluctant answers to Mr Stanopoulos's civil but thorough questions, which seemed to be covering every possible eventuality in the life she led in England. Altogether too wide an area, and too lengthy a timescale, she fretted silently, and possibly revealing that the lawyer believed that his client's preoccupation with his new pillow friend might last weeks and months rather than hours and days as she'd hoped.

And, looking back, it seemed that Thia Theodosia had almost hinted the same thing.

No, she told herself firmly. That's ludicrous. The events of the past twenty-four hours have thrown you completely off balance, that's all, and you're letting your imagination run wild.

But she knew she hadn't imagined the odd exchange between Mr Stanopoulos and Thia Theodosia when they'd met in the passage outside his office.

Natasha's Greek might be a little rusty, but she'd heard her foster mother say, 'So it has come to this. Who could have thought it possible?'

And picked up the lawyer's gravely reserved reply, 'Yes, *kyria*, to my sorrow. But perhaps it may end here too.'

Except it wasn't going to end—or not for the foreseeable future— she acknowledged grimly as the reins of her life were coolly and efficiently detached from her hands.

And knowing that it would all be seamlessly restored to her in due course was small consolation.

She said suddenly, 'Kyrios Stanopoulos, will you tell me something?'

His expression was instantly wary. 'If I can, *thespinis*.'

'This feud between your clients and my family,' she said. 'How did it start? You see, I thought…I was always given the impression that it was simply a business rivalry that had been going on for generations, and had just got nastier. But now I gather it's far more recent than that.'

There was a pause, then he said, 'Who knows how these distressing situations arise? Sadly, I am unable to enlighten you, *thespinis*.'

'And if I was to ask Kyrios Mandrakis—would he tell me?'

'That would be a matter entirely for him, *thespinis*.' He riffled through his papers. 'I believe that is everything.'

'I'm sure it is,' she said, rising. 'My entire life—signed away.'

'Your private and business transactions properly conducted in your absence,' he corrected, and paused, an awkward note entering his voice.

'Please believe, Kyria Kirby, that I wish it could have been otherwise.'

'One view at least that we share,' Natasha said evenly, turning to the door.

'*Ne*,' he said drily, adding, 'if for very different reasons. Good afternoon, *thespinis*. I wish you good fortune.'

She could have walked back to the Villa Demeter blindfold from any point in the city, but the route to the Mandrakis house was still relatively unfamiliar. And it would probably remain so, she thought while she was obliged to travel it in the back of the chauffeured car, with Iorgos the Rottweiler riding shotgun beside the driver once more. Alex Mandrakis was clearly taking no chances with his latest acquisition.

She moved restively, and heard a crackle of paper. It was the envelope that he'd given her, forgotten in the pocket of her jacket.

She retrieved it, and sat for a moment, turning it in her hands. She supposed it must be money—an advance cheque for the services she'd be obliged to render him in bed that night. And, as such, she was sorely tempted to tear it up and fling it out of the car window. Except that it was securely closed because of the air-conditioning.

Besides, a kind of mordant curiosity was stirring her to see precisely how much he thought she was worth.

But there was no cheque. Instead she found just a single sheet of paper, and when she unfolded it and saw the typed lines and her signature at the foot of the page she realised exactly what she'd been given.

For a moment she stared down at it, words and phrases leaping out at her, drying her mouth and setting her stomach churning. Then, with unsteady fingers, she began to tear the paper into strips, reducing each strip in turn to smaller and smaller fragments before cramming them back into the envelope, and pushing it to the bottom of her handbag to be finally disposed of later.

Gone, she told herself, straightening her shoulders. Finished and done with. Although she knew that the memory of its vileness—and the ensuing consequences—could not be so easily dismissed. They would haunt her forever.

She could never be sure when she first realised that the car was not heading for the exclusive residential district where Alex

Mandrakis lived, but out of Athens altogether. Sitting in the rear passenger seat behind the driver, she'd been sitting in silence, staring almost listlessly out of the window until a road sign intruded jarringly into her thoughts.

She sat up swiftly, her attention alerted, then tapped on the glass.

'*Thespinis*?' It was Iorgos who turned almost warily to speak to her.

'You're going the wrong way,' she told him urgently. 'This is the road to Piraeus.'

'Takis is a good driver, *thespinis*.' He sounded almost soothing. 'He knows the route he must take.'

He closed the glass partition and turned back, making a low-voiced comment to the driver, and they both laughed.

Piraeus, Natasha thought feverishly. They were driving to the port.

She sat upright, her hands clenched in her lap, as a desperate suspicion took hold of her.

She banged on the glass again. 'I'll pay you both double your salary,' she said, her voice strained, 'treble, if you'll turn the car round and take me to the airport instead.' She paused. 'You can say that I—I distracted you, and ran off from the car. That you searched, but couldn't find me in the crowd. I swear you can trust me, and that I'll send you the money as soon as I get to England.'

'But we two are also trusted, *thespinis*, by Kyrios Alexandros.' He spoke brusquely. 'We obey his orders and no one else's, and he has told us to bring you to Piraeus and the Pala Marina. And that is what we shall do.'

Her throat muscles tightened uncontrollably.

Dear God, she thought, her heart thudding. She was right. The Pala Marina was where many of the biggest and most luxurious yachts had their moorings, and that would naturally include the Mandrakis boat *Selene*.

The *Floating Harem*, she thought. As a final humiliation, that was where she was being taken, as Concubine of the Month, she thought bitterly, touching the tip of her tongue to her dry lips.

She'd only seen *Selene* in newspaper photographs, generally under some scandalous headline, but she recognised its gleaming white splendour instantly as it rode at anchor in solitary state a short distance from the shore.

And, at the quayside, a sleek and powerful launch was waiting to transport her on board, together with the set of matching luggage in light tan kid which had suddenly appeared from the boot.

As she climbed the metal stairs to the main deck a stocky, fair-haired man, smart in white shorts and a crisp shirt, walked forward to greet her.

'Miss Kirby? Welcome to *Selene*. I'm Mr Mandrakis's skipper, Mac Whitaker.' He beckoned to a small man with eyes like those of a sad monkey and a thick black moustache. 'This is Kostas,' he went on. 'He'll show you to the master suite, and his niece, Josefina, is waiting to unpack for you. Once Alex joins us, we'll be sailing.'

For a moment panic twisted in her stomach, but she clung to her self-command and merely nodded before following Kostas up to the bridge deck.

He threw open a door and motioned her politely to precede him into the room beyond. It was almost as big, she thought shakily, as the drawing room at the Villa Demeter. The walls were lined with shelves, holding books and a sophisticated music system, and there were bowls of fresh flowers everywhere.

At one side, an alcove held a circular table and chairs for dining. The floor was covered in a thick, off-white carpet, while comfortable chairs and thickly cushioned sofas upholstered in a rich, deep blue were grouped round occasional tables. The viewing windows were curtained in the same colour, and also repeated in the quilted spread and curtains in the spacious bedroom, which could be glimpsed through double doors at the far side of the room.

The room, it seemed, where she would sleep with Alex that night. And all the nights that might follow. The room where so many other girls had shared his bed, she thought, biting her lip almost fiercely.

'You are pleased, *thespinis*? It is all to your liking?' Kostas sounded anxious.

And if I say I hate it, will that get me safely back to shore? Natasha wondered grimly. I doubt that very much.

And, anyway, what's the point of upsetting him? Nothing that's happening here is in any way his fault. He's just obeying his master's orders like everyone else.

She forced a smile. 'It's—beautiful.' Which, she thought, was no more than the truth. And wondered how many times he'd had the same enthralled answer from his former companions.

The arrival of her luggage provided a welcome diversion, and it was closely followed by Josefina, a plump, pretty girl, her dark, glossy braids wound into a coronet on top of her head, with a smile that wavered between shy and friendly.

At her insistence, Natasha reluctantly allowed herself to be ushered into the bedroom, but she was unable to share Josefina's admiration for its splendours. She made polite noises about the fitted wardrobes, with their shoe racks, shelving and drawers, all in the same pale, expensive wood, and tried not to notice that a lot of the space was already occupied by Alex's clothing.

Establishing beyond question, she realised, his intention to enforce the intimacy of their relationship, and banishing any faint hope of privacy she might still have cherished.

He could have pretended that I was just one of his guests, she thought unhappily. Given me a stateroom of my own—a line of retreat when all this becomes more than I can bear.

She didn't even want to glance at the massive bed that he'd shared with her predecessors, and not always one at a time, according to the more salacious Press stories, she recalled, biting her lip again.

And paused, as it occurred to her with heart-stopping suddenness how much she hated the idea of being just one more girl on a long list.

But why, in the light of everything else that had happened, should that trouble her particularly? she asked herself restively. When it had to be the very least of the sins he'd committed against her?

After all, she wasn't the first person Neil had dated by any means, and almost certainly he'd slept with his other girlfriends. It had never occurred to her to speculate or become wound up about his past, even though, at the time, she'd thought Neil might well become a major factor in her life.

Something Alex Mandrakis would never be, so how could anything he might or might not have done possibly matter to her?

Except it tells me loud and clear that I don't matter, either, she thought defensively, and who wants to hear that, whatever the circumstances?

She became aware that Josefina had apparently finished extolling the wonders of the bedroom, and was now proudly leading the way to the bathroom. Sighing silently, she followed.

But the other girl's enthusiasm was entirely justified, she ad-

mitted, looking at the white tiles marbled with gold, plus twin wash-
basins, toilet and bidet, all with gold fittings, and the ultimate in
power showers, housed inside its glass and gilded screens.

Certainly large enough for multiple occupation, Natasha told
herself, trying to be casual about it, and failing, as unwanted memories of the shower she'd taken with him Alex night—the touch of
his hands on her body—came back to haunt her.

As she turned away hurriedly a thought came to her that, rather
like the rest of the suite, every luxurious square inch of the bathroom
seemed totally pristine and glossy, giving the impression that no one
had set foot there before. Which, of course, was nonsense.

But it seemed that Alex Mandrakis had a fastidious streak wholly
at odds with his raffish reputation, she acknowledged reluctantly, and
his housekeeping staff must work their fingers to the bone keeping
his various establishments in this kind of order.

It made her realise too how standards at the Villa Demeter had
slipped since Thio Basilis had died. Neither Christina nor Maria
seemed particularly adept in handling servants, she thought ruefully,
and it showed.

She delighted Josefina by agreeing that everything was wonderful, then made her escape back into the saloon.

She sank down on one of the sofas, curling almost defensively
into its corner.

Maybe she should concentrate on practicalities and get some rest
while she could, working on the assumption that there might not be
much opportunity later on, she told herself.

And she would not think of Alex Mandrakis and the way his
smile lit the darkness of his eyes, or how the treacherous nerve-
endings in her skin reacted to the mere brush of his mouth.

A journey to make together…

Even the memory of the words was enough to make her body
shiver, and press more deeply into the softness of the cushions.

Oh, why couldn't he have been seriously unattractive like—like
Stavros's friend Yannis who had thick lips, fleshy hands and hair
like wire wool?

And one of the young men who'd wanted to marry her three years
ago, she remembered, appalled. Pleasant enough—in his way.
Kind—probably. Rich—certainly. But in every other respect…

Was that the fate Thia Theodosia really wished she'd chosen? she wondered, wincing. Because that really could have been worse than death.

Almost on the same disaster level as her current situation.

Couldn't Alex Mandrakis be satisfied with winning on a commercial level? she thought with bitterness. And not as if he had some personal score to settle? With me?

She should have been on her way back to London by now. That evening, in the ordinary way, she'd be at home, chatting to Molly and probably fixing herself some scrambled eggs, before taking a leisurely bath and falling into bed and dreamless sleep.

But there is no ordinary way, she thought bleakly. Not any more. Not for me. However bravely I may have spoken to Thia Theodosia, I know that nothing in my life will ever be the same again. And that I'll never be truly free, either.

But what really frightens me is—why I am suddenly so sure of that.

And felt a shiver run through her.

CHAPTER SEVEN

NATASHA studied herself in the full-length mirror, then turned away, biting her lip. The cream silk slip of a dress, with its swirl of knee-length skirt and narrow shoulder straps, was certainly attractive and beautifully styled, but its design ruled out the wearing of a bra and the soft cling of the fabric over her breasts made her feel hideously self-conscious.

She hadn't actually intended to change for dinner, or make any kind of effort, but Josefina had other ideas.

Or, more accurately, she was under orders. And the charcoal suit had been their first target.

'Kyrios Alexandros wishes not to see it again,' she'd announced, spreading her hands in apology. 'So, I take, if you please, *thespinis.*' She gestured towards the rail of dresses and casual wear in the wardrobe. 'So much loveliness from which to choose,' she added temptingly.

Natasha's lips parted to deliver a stormy dismissal of all Alex Mandrakis's wishes, past, present and still to come, but bit them back, unuttered.

Picking a fight over a coat and skirt was hardly in line with her plan for coldly indifferent obedience, she reminded herself wearily. Especially when she would be glad to rid herself of them, and their memories.

'Fine.' She'd forced a smile, managed a shrug. 'You can collect the suit while I have a shower.'

Josefina rummaged in a different part of the wardrobe, and with almost a flourish produced the silver robe, which, to Natasha's astonishment, seemed to have been washed and ironed by some anonymous and hard-working soul since she'd taken it off that morning.

'Some career choice,' she muttered under her breath. 'Personal laundress to Alex Mandrakis's women.'

On the other hand, she supposed it was steady work, and unlikely to slacken off in the long term.

Left to herself, she discovered the wardrobe drawers were a treasure chest of exquisite lingerie, all handmade in silk and lace, and, to her surprise, pretty rather than overtly erotic.

While in the bathroom, she was unnerved to find an array of toiletries—perfume sprays, creams and lotions—all in her favourite scent.

The helpful maid again, no doubt, she thought bitterly. And I can't bear that he's been able to find out so much about me when, until last night, he was a total stranger, as far as I was concerned. Someone I'd seen at a distance just once before.

But never really forgotten....

The words lanced into her consciousness, and remained there in spite of her efforts to dismiss them. As Alex himself had done three years before.

Yet that was hardly surprising, she told herself, considering his playboy notoriety.

The last time he'd hit the headlines had been following his thirtieth birthday party, where he'd been joined in *Selene*'s swimming pool by six beautiful girls, all naked, for what the tabloids described as 'a celebration sex romp'.

And one of them, Sharmayne Eliot, a luscious redhead who described herself as an actress and model, had later confided breathlessly to the world, 'He's sensational. Now I know why they call him Alexander the Great.'

'I wonder how many languages he needed that night,' Natasha had muttered to herself at the time, ramming the offending newspaper into the waste basket with quite unnecessary vigour.

But if I ever felt even remotely superior to Sharmayne and her companions then I'm certainly paying for it now, she thought as she stepped into the shower.

When she emerged from the bathroom, refreshed and scented, with her hair dried into a shining curve on her shoulders, she found

Josefina, fresh from her victory over the suit and ignoring all protests, waiting to give her a manicure.

Presumably Kyrios Alexandros preferred to be touched by women with soft hands, Natasha thought furiously, then was forced to endure, with gritted teeth, the additional coating of soft rose enamel that Josefina insisted on applying to her toenails.

It was mortifying to find herself being turned into some kind of clone of the smooth, pampered girls who were his usual companions.

But it was only a surface change. Some rough edges might have been removed in an attempt to make her fit the template, but it went no further than that. And it never would.

He had said she was beautiful, but Natasha knew that reasonably attractive would be a more accurate description, and that what looks she possessed would hardly compensate for her total lack of experience.

She must be the last woman in the world that any man would want as his mistress. But what did that matter when it was only Alex's desire for revenge that needed to be satisfied? she thought bitterly.

She was his trophy—that was all—a symbol of his victory in a war that had lasted far too long, and of which she'd become a civilian casualty.

But whatever he wanted from her, she would bet that it would certainly not be the resentful passivity that awaited him. When he embarked on his journey into pleasure, he'd be travelling alone, she told herself resolutely. She would make quite sure of that.

It was sunset before Alex eventually arrived on board *Selene*.

Natasha had spent the intervening hours in the saloon, restless and edgy as she listened to the bumps, bangs and shouted orders which were the prelude to the *Selene*'s departure. She couldn't really decipher what was going on, but she was aware of launches coming and going all the time, and presumed they were delivering more passengers. Perhaps other girls, in line with the yacht's reputation, she thought, flinching. But if they provided a diversion, she could hardly complain.

Kostas appeared from time to time, mainly to ask with increasing anxiety if there was anything he could get for her, but also, at one point, to convey a message from Captain Whitaker that the boat bringing Kyrios Alexandros was on its way from the marina. News, no doubt, that was supposed to prompt her to rush out on deck to welcome him.

She thought, Not a damn chance.

Aloud, she said, '*Efharisto.*' And returned to the magazine she was reading, staring at the printed words until they blurred.

She heard approaching footsteps, the sound of male voices laughing and talking just outside, and got quickly and clumsily to her feet, smoothing suddenly damp palms down the skirt of her dress, aware that she was trembling inside.

Then the door opened and Alex walked in.

Her immediate thought, which seemed to come from nowhere, was that he looked tired. He was carrying his discarded jacket and tie over his arm, his shirt was half-unbuttoned and he needed a shave.

His gaze sharpened when he saw her. He took a step towards her, and she froze into taut stillness, her hands clenching into fists at her sides. He halted instantly, his mouth twisting in sardonic acknowledgement.

When he spoke, his tone was coolly polite. '*Kalispera, Natasha mou.* I apologise for keeping you waiting, but a simple meeting suddenly became complicated.'

She kept her own voice steady. 'If you're in the mood for explanations, Kyrios Mandrakis, perhaps you'd tell me what I'm doing on this boat?'

'I thought you were looking pale, *pedhi mou*, even a little stressed,' he drawled. 'I decided some sun and sea air might restore your colour, and your spirits. And that you might find a cruise among the islands less pressured than staying in Athens.'

'You made a decision, snapped your fingers, and—this happened?'

'Pretty much,' he agreed, shrugging. 'But I spend much of my life on board the *Selene*. In many ways she has become my real home, so she is usually ready to sail when I require.'

He paused. 'I hope my people have made you comfortable.'

'Of course,' she said. 'As prisons go, this must be the lap of luxury.'

His brows lifted. 'Is that how you intend to regard me—as your jailer?'

'Even that,' she said, the words like chips of ice, 'would be too flattering.'

There was a silence, then he said quietly, 'Natasha *mou*, this has been a long and difficult day. I do not need another fight, believe me, so have a care.'

He added, 'We sail in fifteen minutes. Once I have had a shower, I will take you round the *Selene*, so you can see for yourself the opportunities for relaxation that she offers.'

'No,' she said, stonily. 'Thank you. I've already been shown the bedroom, which I imagine is the only area on this boat that directly concerns me. And I don't expect to find it particularly relaxing.

'But please don't let me keep you from your other guests,' she added. 'I'm sure they'll be dying to inspect the facilities. After all, they're world famous.'

His mouth softened into a faint grin. 'Are you referring to the guests, or the facilities, *matia mou*? If it's the guests, you are mistaken. Apart from the crew and staff, we shall be alone.'

It wasn't what she'd expected to hear at all. She said, 'But I—I thought that you always invited crowds of people.'

'The boat sleeps fifteen.' He tossed his jacket and tie across the arm of a sofa, and began to release the remaining buttons on his shirt. 'Hardly a multitude. Are you disappointed?'

She shrugged. 'What possible difference can it make to me? The *Selene*'s your yacht. You're entitled to do as you please.'

'Yes,' he said softly. 'Which is why I intend to give you my entire and undivided attention, *agapi mou*.' He paused to allow her to assimilate his words. 'Although that will not be as simple as I'd hoped,' he went on, grimacing. 'Thanks to your brothers, the affairs of my new companies are tangled beyond belief; therefore I may be forced to leave you briefly from time to time.'

He added with faint mockery, 'I trust that will not be a problem for you, *agapi mou*? Or do you wish me to issue invitations—provide company for you when I am absent, so that you can practise your skills as a hostess?'

She looked at him in horror. 'Oh, no—please. That's the last thing I want.'

'And I thought that was myself,' he murmured. 'I am encouraged.'

He paused. 'I have been considering our itinerary. You have a favourite destination among the Cyclades? Paros, perhaps, or Santorini?' He smiled at her. 'If there is somewhere you would like to revisit, you have only to say so.'

For a moment she was silent, then she said reluctantly, 'I've never been to any of the islands. Thio Basilis did not care to leave Athens, but in the real heat he used to send us down to stay near Nauplia.'

She paused again, then said slowly, 'However, I think Thia Theodosia once had a house on a place called Alyssos. Do you know it?'

'Yes,' Alex said quietly. 'I know it.'

'I remember Stavros and Andonis used to talk about holidays there when they were young boys, even before Irini was born,' Natasha continued. 'But Thio Basilis obviously preferred the Peleponnese, and she would never argue with him.'

'A jewel among women.' There was an odd harshness in his voice.

'Yes, she is,' Natasha said defiantly. 'And if you're about to be unpleasant about her for some reason, then think again, because I love her dearly.'

Also because she has a better opinion of you than you'll ever deserve...

He said drily, 'I do not have to be reminded of your affection for her, *matia mou*. It is, after all, the only reason you are here with me now. So I should be grateful to her, even if you are not.'

His smile this time was brief and almost remote. 'Now I am going to take my shower. I have asked Mac to join us for dinner,' he added. 'I hope you do not object.'

'Oh, no,' Natasha denied hurriedly. 'That's—fine.'

'Or at least more agreeable than my company alone,' Alex said smoothly. 'Until later, then, Natasha *mou*.' And he sauntered into the bedroom.

She realised she had been holding her breath, terrified that he might insist she join him. But it seemed she was temporarily off the hook.

And told herself she should be grateful for any small mercies he might be prepared to show her.

He rejoined her in the saloon some half an hour later. He was wearing narrow-legged khaki trousers and a black shirt, open at the throat, with its sleeves turned back to the elbow, and he brought with him the faint but delicious scent of the cologne she'd noticed before. And he was very obviously clean-shaven once again.

'So we are moving,' he said. 'On our way to Mykonos, to begin with. After that, who knows?'

'I see.' She sent him a swift, nervous glance. 'Are—are we going to have dinner on deck?'

'It is a beautiful evening,' he said. 'Do you have some objection to eating out of doors?'

'No, none at all.'

'I wondered,' he went on. 'Because Mac told me you had not ventured out of the suite since you came on board.'

'Perhaps I'm embarrassed,' she said tautly. 'After all, every single person on the boat must know exactly why you've brought me here. Do you realise what it's like for me to be…paraded like this?'

'If we had remained in Athens, you would have been under the scrutiny of a much larger audience,' he said, shrugging. 'You will get used to it in time, as I have been obliged to do.'

He paused. 'Would you like a drink? I am going to have ouzo,' he added, walking over to a side table with an array of bottles and glasses. 'Will you join me, or would you prefer something else?'

'Water, please,' she said. 'Non-sparkling.'

'A symbol, perhaps, of the evening ahead of us?' he enquired sardonically, uncapping one of the bottles of Loutraki water and filling a tumbler.

'Perhaps,' she returned coolly. 'However, alcohol tends to send me to sleep, and I'm sure you wouldn't want that.'

He gave her a dry look. 'You are all consideration, *agapi mou*. Yet somehow the thought of you warm and drowsy with your head on my shoulder has an appeal all its own.'

'For you, Kyrios Mandrakis,' she said. 'But not for me.'

'Let us rather say—not now, perhaps, but on some future night. At least, that is what I shall hope for.' Alex poured his own drink, and raised his glass. 'To you, *matia mou*,' he said softly. 'You are—so very beautiful.'

'You must think so,' she said. 'Or I wouldn't be here.'

The dark brows lifted. 'Am I not allowed to pay you a compliment?' he asked. 'Is that another taboo?'

She shrugged. 'You've already had me,' she said. 'So you don't need to waste time on meaningless flattery.'

She drank some of her water, aware that he was watching her, his mouth curling in faint amusement.

'Is it permitted to tell you that the dress is very becoming,' he said, 'and ask if you like it?'

'Yes,' she said. 'Of course. It—it's absolutely lovely. And all the other things too.' She added stiffly, 'You're—very generous.' Which was no more than the truth, she thought unwillingly. And this was probably the most glamorous and expensive garment she'd ever possessed. 'But I'm not really used to clothes like this.'

'I would be surprised to learn that the Papadimos family dressed you in rags, *pedhi mou*.'

'No, oh, no,' she said quickly. 'But Thia Theodosia was very strict, so I hardly ever went out in the evenings. Therefore, I didn't need dresses like this.'

'But you appeared at one social event, at least.' He drank some ouzo. 'We were once at the same embassy reception.'

Her head turned sharply. 'You remember that?'

'Why not?' It was his turn to shrug. 'Don't you?'

'You were…pointed out to me,' Natasha admitted tautly. 'Because of your companion,' she added hurriedly. 'You were with a model called Gabriella. She was incredibly famous just then. And amazingly beautiful.'

'Also very thin,' Alex said, deadpan. 'I hope you have a better appetite, *agapi mou*. It is wearying to eat with a woman who regards even a lettuce leaf with suspicion.'

Natasha took another hurried gulp of water, aware that only a couple of hours before she'd had a wild notion of going on hunger strike in order to force him into releasing her, and had abandoned the idea only because she was already so ravenous, having given up on breakfast and only picked at her lunch, that she could have eaten her own shoe.

She said, 'I think someone must have told Thio Basilis that you were there, because next day there was a row, and I wasn't allowed to accept any more invitations from Lindsay.'

'My poor Natasha,' he said softly. 'How much I have to answer for.' He paused. 'But perhaps the dress needs something more. A necklace, maybe,' he added, his dark gaze lingering on the bare hollow of her throat, then moving down with undisguised appreciation to the untrammelled thrust of her breasts against the covering silk.

'I never wear necklaces,' she said swiftly and untruthfully. 'I—I don't like them.'

'Ah,' he said, totally undeceived. 'So clothes you accept because you have no alternative, but other gifts are forbidden. Is that it?'

She said, stumbling a little, 'Not always. Because you did make me another gift this morning, when you gave me that letter. And I'm—grateful.'

'What did you do with it?' He stared into his glass, frowning a little.

'I—I tore it up.'

'And threw it away?'

She shook her head. 'Not yet. It's still in my bag. When I get the chance, I'll burn it.'

'Then fetch it,' Alex directed quietly. 'And we will dispose of it now.'

When she returned with the envelope, he was taking a metal dish and a box of matches from a cupboard. She tipped the fragments onto the dish, and watched as he set fire to them. Saw them flare up then curl into soft grey ash.

He said quietly, 'So, *pedhi mou*, it is gone. Now put it out of your mind. It is no longer between us.'

She flung back her head. Her voice was shaking. 'How—how can you possibly say such a thing? How can I forget the way you treated me because of it? Do you think—do you really imagine, Kyrios Mandrakis, that striking a match and burning a few scraps of paper could ever be sufficient recompense for what you've done to me?'

'No,' he said. 'Yet I hoped it might at least be the beginning of a new understanding.'

'Then you're fooling yourself. Because it will always be between us. Always. And if you think otherwise, you're sadly mistaken.'

'So it would seem.' His tone was almost casual. He finished his drink and put down the glass. 'But it is an error that need not spoil our dinner.' The smile he sent her did not reach his eyes. 'So, shall we go?'

To Natasha's surprise, dinner was not as much of an ordeal as she'd anticipated.

The setting, she admitted unwillingly, could hardly be faulted. The table had been set on the main deck under an awning, and shone with silver and crystal. And a few feet away the restless Aegean rippled and glittered in its own wide ribbon of moonlight.

The food was magnificent, beginning with a platter of spiced meat in filo pastry, stuffed vine leaves, fresh anchovies, tiny garlicky sausages, little cheese pastries, tomato and oregano tartlets and cubes of sharp feta cheese.

This was followed by tiny chickens simmered in wine, served with green beans and potatoes sautéed in olive oil, accompanied by a refreshingly dry white wine, while a creamy dessert fragrant with cardamom and honey completed the meal.

Admittedly, Mac Whitaker's cheerful presence helped relieve some of the tensions of the situation, although Natasha was frankly startled to find that the two men were on Christian-name terms. She could not imagine Basilis Papadimos ever allowing such familiarity from any of his own skippers, even those who'd worked for him for years.

Much of the talk between them seemed to relate to an extensive refit of the *Selene* which had not long been completed, so she wasn't required to contribute much to the conversation, which suited her just fine.

On the other hand, could the yacht possibly be old enough to warrant such expenditure? she asked herself, bewildered. It seemed unlikely. It was no wonder Alex could afford to acquire the Arianna line, along with everything else. Bucephalus Holdings, she mused, must have money to burn.

'So, Miss Kirby.' Mac Whitaker turned to her over coffee, interrupting her reverie. 'How do you feel now about Alex's moonlight goddess?'

She stared at him, sudden colour flaring in her face. 'I—I don't understand.'

'Heck, have I got it wrong?' He looked at Alex, spreading his hands in mock-dismay. 'Didn't you tell me that *Selene* was the Moon Deity in the old myths? And that you'd picked the name on purpose?'

'Yes,' Alex said, his dark eyes quizzical as he observed Natasha's blush. 'You are quite correct. And, on reflection, I think I made entirely the right choice.' He covered her hand with his. 'Don't you think so, *pedhi mou*?'

Anger warred with embarrassment, and won. 'Actually, no,' she said, her voice a chip of ice, as she removed her fingers from his clasp. 'I think Circe would have been a much more appropriate name. After all, wasn't she the goddess who turned men into swine?'

She saw a look of shock flicker across Mac Whitaker's tanned face, but Alex seemed totally unfazed.

'So the story says,' he returned softly. 'But it took just one mortal man to outwit and tame her. Something that you should perhaps remember, Natasha *mou*.'

'Which sounds like my cue to be elsewhere,' Mac remarked to no one in particular, pushing back his chair. 'I wish you both goodnight.'

When they were alone, Natasha said defiantly, 'Well, say whatever you have to say.'

Alex studied the tips of his fingers. 'You don't think you might find your situation easier, *matia mou*, if you diverted your energies into pleasing me instead of attempting to cause me irritation?'

'Easier for you, no doubt.' She lifted her chin defiantly. 'This may come as a surprise to you, Kyrios Mandrakis, but I have no plans to degrade myself by setting out to "please" you, or any other man, for that matter, because I belong to myself, and I always will, however long I may be forced to spend on that well-worn mattress of yours.

'So, you're going to have to take anything you want from me, because I don't intend to give anything.'

He shrugged. 'Then that is your choice. It does not, however, affect any of mine which were made long ago.'

He paused. 'But your description of my bed is out of date, Kyria Natasha. If you had been listening over dinner, instead of inventing ways to annoy me, you would know that the entire master suite has been involved in a complete overhaul, which was finished only a week ago. And that everything in it—every fixture and fitting, every item of furniture—is now brand-new.'

He added levelly, 'Including, of course, the bed, which I hope you will find comfortable.'

The smile he sent her was cool, even impersonal. 'So, shall we go inside—and find out?'

She had tried to make the meal last as long as possible, eating slowly and even asking for another pot of coffee. Anything to delay the moment when she would have to be alone with him.

But now it was here, she thought as she got to her feet. As she made herself walk beside him, without protest, back to the suite.

And she had no arguments to use, or trump cards to play. She never had. He wanted her, and that was all there was to it.

She heard the door close, shutting them in together, and waited rigidly for whatever was going to happen next.

He said, 'I am going to have some brandy. Do you wish to join me?'

She'd deliberately drunk sparingly during dinner, so she was stone-cold sober, as well as cold with fright, and shook her head mutely.

'Then I suggest that you retire.' His tone gave nothing away. 'I will join you presently.'

Once inside the bedroom, Natasha closed the door and leaned against it, releasing her breath in a long sigh.

Lamps had been lit on either side of the bed, and the covers turned down. In addition, a drift of white was draped across its foot.

It was a nightgown, Natasha realised incredulously as she picked it up. A simple white lawn nightgown with narrow straps, and a row of tiny satin buttons fastening its bodice.

Something she might even have chosen herself—her clothes budget permitting. And indubitably, astonishingly modest.

Josefina, she wondered with irony, making some kind of statement?

In the bathroom, she undressed, washed and cleaned her teeth, before finally dropping the nightgown over her head.

One glance in the full-length mirror beside the shower cabinet confirmed that it was indeed virtually opaque.

She emerged from the bathroom and crossed irresolutely, reluctantly to the bed, wondering if that was where he'd be expecting to find her. If there was an etiquette in such matters that she needed to learn.

As she hesitated, she heard the door open behind her and turned.

Alex was standing in the doorway, his shirt unfastened, and barefoot.

He didn't speak a word, or take a step, just remained where he was, looking across the room at her.

He probably couldn't believe his eyes, she thought, her throat tightening. The demure fabric of the nightgown must be hiding everything from his gaze—she knew that—yet in some odd way she felt more self—conscious in front of him at this moment than she'd done when she was naked the night before.

Yet how could that be? she asked herself with bewilderment. And why didn't he say something? Do something? Or was he waiting for some sign from her?

She took a breath then lifted her chin, looking back at him in an attempt to conceal this sudden and inexplicable shyness.

And a voice in her head whispered, It shouldn't be like this. It shouldn't…

But he still didn't move, just went on staring at her, the dark eyes hooded and unreadable.

When he finally spoke, his voice was abrupt, almost harsh. He said, 'Will you marry me?'

The words jolted her like a blow to the stomach, and she gasped and stepped backwards, shock rendering her mute. When she could speak, she said hoarsely, 'Is that some kind of joke?'

He said curtly, 'I am asking you to be my wife. Will you?'

'No!' She drew a trembling breath. 'My God—no. Not even if the world were going to end tomorrow. And you must be mad—or drunk—even to suggest it.'

His face was all planes and shadows. A stranger's face. His mouth was a straight line. 'May I know what makes me so unacceptable?'

'I'd have thought that was obvious—even to you.'

'If it were, I would not ask,' he said. 'So tell me. After all, you once said you were willing, and in writing too.'

'But that really was a joke,' she said unevenly. 'If not a very good one. As you well know. Because, if I had my way, I wouldn't spend another hour with you. So what on earth would ever make me tie myself to you for life?'

She drew a deep breath. 'Or did you think buying me a cupboard full of new clothes would change my attitude? Make me see you in a new and agreeable light and reconcile me to your company? If so, you can think again.

'You're rich and spoiled, Kyrios Mandrakis, and as far from good husband material as it's possible to get. I wouldn't have you if you came gift-wrapped.'

She added, 'Besides, you must be the last man alive to want to be married, so what's the purpose of this ludicrous proposition?'

He said slowly, 'I believe the correct term is "proposal". And per- haps its purpose, as you put it, is to offer the recompense you spoke of earlier today.'

He paused. 'And to ensure,' he went on levelly, 'that if we made a child together last night, it will have a legal right to my name.'

'Please don't concern yourself on that score,' Natasha threw back scornfully, aware that her pulses were hammering unevenly. 'If by some remote chance I am pregnant, I guarantee I shan't stay that way for long. Any child of mine will be born to a man I love and respect, *kyrie*, a scenario in which you couldn't even feature.

'And the only amends you could possibly make for your behavior would be to get me on the next flight to London, so that I never have to see you again. But that's probably not on offer.'

'No,' he said, very quietly. 'It is not.'

'Then let's forget all about this marriage nonsense, shall we?' she said tautly. 'And get back to what I'm really here for. Or perhaps I should jog your memory, Kyrios Mandrakis.'

Her hands went to the little buttons on her bodice, tugging them loose. She pushed the straps of the nightgown off her shoulders, and let its soft folds slip down to pool on the floor at her feet.

Then she posed, deliberately, defiantly provocative, one hand on her hip, the other raking her blonde hair back from her face.

She said, 'What you see is what you get, *kyrie*. And it's all you'll ever have of me. That was a wonderful meal tonight, so no doubt you'll be expecting your own private feast in return. I'll try to make sure you're not disappointed—this time.'

There was a silence, then Alex said icily, 'I am grateful, of course, but I find my appetite has strangely deserted me. So I will wish you goodnight.'

He went out, shutting the door behind him, and a moment later Natasha heard the sound of the saloon door closing.

Telling her with quiet finality that he would not be coming back.

CHAPTER EIGHT

WHICH was, Natasha told herself, exactly what she wanted. Wasn't it?

She suddenly realised that, in spite of the warmth of the night, she was shivering violently. She retrieved her nightgown from the floor and huddled into it, before climbing into bed and pulling the covers round her.

She had not expected to sleep. She'd imagined she would be spending the night subject to Alex's mercy—if there was such a thing. This, she thought, was a reprieve, and she'd make the most of it.

But sleep, she found, was not so easily come by. The events of the evening and their astonishing aftermath kept rolling through her mind like a video clip with far too many action replays.

She thought, I've had my first proposal of marriage, and didn't know whether to laugh or cry.

At the same time she was disturbed and bewildered by the violence of her own reactions.

I could have said a simple 'no', she thought, without screaming abuse at him like a fishwife. My God, I must have sounded like Irini on a very bad day.

Yet she'd been perfectly justified, she told herself with renewed defiance. He deserved everything she'd thrown at him, and more. She'd been hurt and insulted, therefore he needed to be hurt and insulted in his turn.

And she'd succeeded beyond her wildest dreams. The bleakness in his face as he'd walked away had told her that. So why wasn't she turning mental cartwheels? Scoring it as a direct hit?

And the answer to that was—she didn't know.

She'd just endured the most terrible twenty-four hours of her life. She couldn't deny that. But she'd also begun to discover complexities in the situation that frankly alarmed her.

Because there'd been moments when she'd almost let herself forget why she was there. Which might be because Alex Mandrakis had made her do so, she thought with a sudden thud of the heart.

Because sometimes he'd talked to her as if she was a human being instead of a mere sex object. And, although the way he'd quite often looked at her left her in no doubt that he wanted her, he hadn't attempted to make any kind of move on her.

Not even when they'd returned to the saloon together and she expected him to take her in his arms, not send her off to bed alone.

Awakening within her something dangerously like disappointment.

And wasn't that why she'd given him that tongue-lashing just now? Why she'd deliberately flaunted herself naked with a vulgarity she cringed to remember?

Because she'd been scared by her own potential weakness. By the vivid memory of his body against hers—inside hers—and how it had made her feel. By the knowledge that she'd been aroused by him, however briefly. And that the strange, fugitive yearning he'd created still lingered.

Knowing too that for one torn, impossible moment she'd wanted him to walk across the bedroom, and take her—whether it was to heaven or to hell.

She'd needed to find a defence against him and find it fast.

And that unexpected, incredible marriage proposal had supplied it.

Every instinct told her that he would not take rejection well. And that he might respond with equal scorn to her contemptuous sexual challenge.

And it had worked. Only now she needed to find some way of turning this temporary respite into permanent separation.

She'd made him angry once, she thought. Surely, she could do it again—and keep him so.

'I don't want him to be kind to me,' she whispered passionately into the darkness. 'Whatever Thia Theodosia may say, I want to judge him harshly. I need to build on dislike, and resentment—keep them permanently simmering—in order to stop me wondering, speculating on possibilities that I shouldn't even want to contemplate.

'God knows, I have so many reasons to hate him, and not the least of them is the state of confusion I'm in now. And which I don't—I can't—understand.'

Because this was not her, she thought, seizing an uncomprehending pillow and punching it fiercely into shape. The real Natasha Kirby ran her business and her life with clear-headed efficiency. She used rational judgement to solve problems, and knew that, for her, friendship, shared interests and mutual respect formed the only foundation for a relationship between a man and a woman.

You really shouldn't drink wine with him in the moonlight, she thought derisively. That's your problem, lady. And if you'd agreed to his offer of brandy, as well, you'd probably be imagining you were in love with him by now.

Besides, you're curious—of course you are—about a man who can make love in four languages, she added with savage mockery.

But how on earth had that piece of tasteless information managed to lodge in her head for the past three years? she wondered. Not to mention her total recall of the way he'd looked at her on that long-ago evening at the embassy.

An occasion he too seemed to have remembered for some obscure reason of his own.

Natasha sighed as she turned onto her side and attempted to relax. Her mind was simply going round in circles, she thought, and she needed to sleep in order to face whatever tomorrow might bring.

But it was more than a restless hour later before she finally fell asleep, and dreamed that she was running endlessly through a maze of streets, in her nightgown, as was the way in dreams, only to find that every twist and turn led to the same square with the same church, where Alex Mandrakis stood waiting for her in the sunlight, his hands filled with white roses for her bridal bouquet.

She awoke very early the next morning, and lay for a moment, totally disorientated, wondering firstly what had disturbed her and, secondly, why her bedroom was moving. Then she remembered the nightmare turn her life had taken and, groaning, buried her face in the pillow.

But at least she wasn't going to suffer any more unsettling dreams about marriage, she thought grimly.

She'd attended a number of Greek weddings, and had always

been moved by the symbolism of the exchange of crowns and the couple's slow walk, hand in hand, round the altar.

But she'd never for a moment imagined herself taking part in such a ritual, even though, as a child and to please her foster parents, she'd been baptised into the Greek Orthodox Church.

And the idea of taking such a walk with Alex Mandrakis was so far beyond belief that it was out of sight.

Especially, she thought, as it would be for all the wrong reasons.

All right, he was feeling guilty, and rightly so. But he couldn't seriously think she'd agree to marry him in order to salve what passed for his conscience—could he?

Or to protect the legitimacy of a baby who almost certainly didn't exist.

Or that was what she had to believe, she thought, pressing a questioning hand to her abdomen. Because the alternative didn't bear thinking about.

If she'd wanted an arranged marriage she could have had one three years earlier, she reminded herself. And it would have been to someone who might at least have pretended he cared for her.

Whereas, in spite of the intimacy he'd forced upon her, she and Alex Mandrakis were still virtual strangers to each other.

And that was how they must remain, she told herself. All temptation to relax—to permit herself, even fleetingly, to enjoy his company—had to be strenuously resisted.

Unless, of course, the loss of appetite she'd instigated last night became permanent, and he decided to cut his losses and send her back where she belonged.

Well, she thought, aware of an odd flicker in her heartbeat, she could always hope. And, after all, no permanent damage had been done. Whereas, if she stayed…

She stopped right there, with a little gasp. That kind of thinking was sheer madness, she told herself sternly. And she would not— *not* go there.

She glanced at the unruffled pillow beside her. With hindsight, she realised that stripping like that might not have been the best idea she'd ever had. That she was lucky he hadn't accepted her absurd challenge, otherwise she might have woken up in very different circumstances.

But it seemed she'd read him right, which was, in itself, a surprise.

She reached to the fitted night table for her watch and grimaced when she saw the time. It was hardly more than dawn, and far too early for someone, who wished to give the impression that she'd spent a tranquil and untroubled night, to be on the move.

So what had woken her? she asked herself, turning over and composing herself to sleep again. And noticed as she did so that one of the drawers in the wardrobe unit where Alex's clothing was kept was now slightly open, when last night it had been shut.

Jolted, Natasha propped herself on an elbow and stared across the room.

If the *Selene* had accommodation for fifteen people, her owner would not be short of a bed for the night, she reasoned, but clean clothes for the next day were a different matter.

Was that what had woken her—some sixth sense of his presence, here in this room, however briefly and noiselessly?

Unlikely, she told herself, when he had staff to run his errands for him. Except that she couldn't imagine Josefina, or the equally meticulous

Kostas, failing to close a drawer, or, when they departed, leaving the bedroom door ajar as it undoubtedly now was.

And if Alex had been back to the suite, the timing of his visit seemed to indicate that he might not have spent a particularly restful night, either, she thought, biting her lip. Something that would not have improved his temper in any marked degree.

Well, there was an airport on Mykonos, and she was sure she'd once heard Stavros mention enviously that the Mandrakis Corporation were now major shareholders in some airline, so he could easily be rid of her if he wanted, she told herself as she slid down into the bed again, pulling the covering sheet over her shoulders in a gesture that was almost defensive.

And she could only pray that would be exactly what he wanted, she added silently, and closed her eyes.

The next time she opened them, she found Josefina at her bedside with a breakfast tray and an expression that could only be described as disapproving. But then it was probably common knowledge by now that Kyrios Alexandros had not spent the night in his own bed, and his loyal supporters would be no doubt reeling in shock.

And they could do so with her blessing, Natasha muttered silently as she sat up. Alex might be used to living his life under a microscope, but she was not.

This morning, along with the fresh orange juice and coffee, a lidded dish contained a mound of perfectly scrambled eggs, served with grilled tomatoes and fingers of toast.

The condemned woman ate a hearty breakfast, Natasha thought wryly as she picked up her fork. But at least she was doing it alone.

At the same time, she realised that the *Selene* was no longer moving.

'Have we reached Mykonos?' she asked hopefully.

'*Ne, thespinis*. Since two hours.'

I should have woken earlier, she thought regretfully. I could be on my way by now.

Breakfast over, she showered and emerged from the bathroom in her robe just as Josefina was arranging a jade-green bikini, with a voile overshirt in jade, turquoise and gold on the bed.

She said crisply, 'I don't think so. What happened, if you please, to my suit and overnight bag?'

And when Josefina, wide-eyed, denied all knowledge of their whereabouts, Natasha walked over to the wardrobe and scanned along the rail. She'd hoped to leave as she'd arrived, without taking with her so much as a stitch that Alex had paid for, but it seemed clear she had no real choice in the matter, so she chose the plainest garment she could find, a navy linen dress in a simple shift style.

Although 'simple' did not necessarily translate as 'cheap', she realised ruefully when she saw how beautifully it was cut.

Josefina was almost wringing her hands, protesting that today would be too hot for such a dress.

Here, perhaps, Natasha returned silently. But not in England, and I'm planning ahead.

Aloud, she said, 'Please don't fuss, Josefina. This will be fine.'

Josefina subsided, but continued to mutter under her breath, and Natasha detected the words 'Kyrios Alexandros' repeated more than once.

Poor Josefina, she thought with reluctant amusement as she applied sunblock to her comparatively small areas of exposed skin. I bet none of Alex's other pillow friends ever gave half this trouble.

I expect they dressed and undressed to order, and greeted him every night with eager arms.

And they certainly wouldn't have deliberately riled him into sending them home early.

Drawing a deep breath, she went out on deck.

As she'd half expected, he was waiting for her, leaning against the rail, clad in nothing but a pair of shabby denim shorts, his eyes hidden behind dark glasses, his mouth unsmiling.

He said laconically, '*Kalimera*. Did you sleep well?'

'Thank you, yes.' She lifted her chin. 'About last night…'

He lifted a hand, halting her. 'I think it would be better if last night was forgotten. If we agreed that it did not happen.'

'But that's not possible,' Natasha said quickly. 'I—I said some pretty unpleasant things.'

He shrugged. 'That is not the worst thing that could have happened.'

'You don't think so?' she said uncertainly, nervously aware that this conversation was not going to plan.

'I know so,' he drawled. 'After all, Natasha *mou*, you might have accepted my offer of marriage and made us both wretched for the rest of our lives.'

'If you believe that,' she said, 'why did you ask me?'

'Moon madness,' he said slowly. 'A sentimental impulse, as instantly regretted as it was unexpected. Because as you so truly reminded me, *agapi mou*, I am the last man in the world who needs to burden himself with a wife. As it is…' he shrugged again… 'no harm has been done.'

'But—but you will want me to leave, surely?'

'Now why would I wish anything so foolish?' he said softly.

'Because—you're angry with me. You must be.'

'I lost my temper a little, it is true. But now I have recovered it—along with my appetite,' he added softly. 'So you are going nowhere, *matia mou*. And tonight you will make amends to me for all your harsh words, and learn to speak to me more sweetly.'

She said desperately, 'Think again about this—please. Because I'm not the only person concerned. You've been seeing someone—very recently. Can you deny that?'

'No,' he said. 'Why should I?'

'Because maybe you should give her some consideration.' Natasha swallowed. 'Think how she's going to feel when she finds out that I've…been with you.'

He said levelly, 'That is hardly your concern.'

'Then let's make it so.' She spread her hands, palms upward in the age-old gesture of pleading. 'Is she going to understand that you only took me for revenge? Because she—your girlfriend—might actually be in love with you, and be really hurt by this. Doesn't that matter to you?'

He said quietly, 'I have never encouraged any of the women who have shared my bed to fall in love with me, Natasha *mou*. It would be a waste of their time and mine. And Domenica is no exception. She knew from the start that it would never be serious between us.'

'How simple you make it sound.' Her voice shook. 'I just hope and pray, *kyrie*, that one day a woman will hurt you really badly—make you know what it's like to suffer.'

'You are several years too late, *kyria*,' he said harshly. 'Because I have already learned all the pain that a broken heart can bring. And that, eventually, it confers immunity.'

He indicated the vista of dazzling white houses and church towers roofed in blue and terracotta behind him. 'That is Mykonos. We will go ashore this evening when it is cooler, and have dinner at a favourite restaurant of mine. I hope that meets with your approval.'

She said in a low voice, 'I don't think I have a choice.'

'At last you are learning a little wisdom.' He paused. 'But for now, I have some work to do, so why don't you change into something cooler than that dress, go down to the pool and I will join you there later?'

She said defiantly, 'Because I prefer to stay where I am—and as I am.' She took a deep breath. 'Besides, won't you be bored having to share your pool with just one girl instead of the usual crowd?'

'And all of them naked,' Alex said silkily. 'You have forgotten to mention that, although I am sure it is on your mind. But I shall not miss them, *matia mou*,' he added, his mouth twisting. 'Since we met, you appear to have become so many women that you already seem like a crowd.'

And he walked away, leaving Natasha staring after him, lips parted and her hands clenched into impotent fists at her sides.

* * *

Mykonos at night was one enormous, noisy glittering party. The narrow, labyrinthine streets of the old town were so crowded that Natasha felt there was hardly room to breathe.

She'd heard it said that Mykonos was the most expensive island in the Aegean, and she could well believe it. Everywhere she looked, she saw the glitter of jewellers' shops, or the understated chic of designer boutiques. And all around her were the rich and beautiful, being...rich and beautiful.

She was definitely the fish out of water here.

But if you had to do battle with hordes like this, then Alex Mandrakis was the one you wanted on your side, she admitted reluctantly.

Casually dressed in cream trousers and a collarless grey and cream striped shirt, he looked like just another tourist. Yet everywhere his easy, long-legged stride took him, a path seemed to open up to allow him through unchecked, and Natasha, her hand firmly clasped in his, found herself almost struggling to keep up.

But then, her shoes were partly to blame. Josefina had insisted that the strapless black dress with its short, full skirt must be worn with high heels, whereas Natasha usually contented herself with rather more practical footwear.

And their unhindered progress might also have been assisted by the presence, in the rear, of Iorgos the Rottweiler.

Natasha had felt her jaw drop when she saw his burly form already ensconced in the boat waiting to take them ashore.

Forgetting the cool, impenetrable silence she'd planned, she'd turned to Alex. 'I thought he'd stayed behind in Athens.'

'Only while I did, *pedhi mou*. We came on board together, which you would have seen—had you been there.'

She ignored the implied reproach. 'Does he follow you everywhere?'

'Pretty much,' he agreed, 'since my father appointed him to watch my back a few years ago.'

She gave him a scornful look. 'To prevent you being stabbed, no doubt, by some discarded mistress.'

'If that ever becomes a problem, I shall deal with it myself,' Alex drawled. 'But I am not in the habit of discarding women, Natasha *mou*. When something is over, it's over. Isn't it better to recognise that, and part as friends?'

'Friends?' she echoed. 'Your Christmas-card list must read like a telephone directory.'

'But fortunately,' he said silkily, 'I do not have to lick the stamps myself.'

And, as she could think of no suitable response to that, she decided to keep quiet.

Strangely, talking—even to him—made her feel slightly less nervous about the night to come.

It was easy to be brave in daylight, she thought wryly. Especially when you'd been left, probably deliberately, to your own devices for most of the day. But, as sunset approached, a feeling of quiet dread had begun to build inside her to add to her physical discomfort.

Because all too soon, she'd begun to regret being quite so adamant about remaining fully dressed. As the temperature soared into the nineties the baking heat had eventually driven her indoors to the saloon again, every stitch of clothing a damp rag, her wretchedness increased by the faint sounds of splashing from the deck below, where Alex was clearly, and with total selfishness, cooling off in the pool.

Not, of course, that she was even marginally tempted to join him. And she was cross with herself for having alluded, even obliquely, to the scandal surrounding his birthday party, because it made it sound as if she'd been avidly following his erotic career through the gutter Press.

Which was the last impression she wished to give…

He, of course, had been totally shameless about the whole incident.

And his astonishing revelation that he'd once been crossed in love was no excuse at all for his treatment of either of her, or the girl most recently described by the tabloids as 'his constant companion'.

Constancy, she thought, bitterly, had nothing to do with it. He was an unrepentant serial womaniser, and his first love, whoever she was, had been lucky to escape.

She supposed she could have chilled out, calmed down her edgy restlessness with a cool shower, or even a whole series of them, but she'd been deterred by the realisation that there were no locks on any of the doors in the suite, and that Alex could walk in on her at any moment. A ludicrous attitude, probably, in view of the events of the recent past, but that was how it was. Or how she was, anyway.

So she'd waited until Josefina was around, counting on her presence as a kind of safeguard.

And, by the time Alex eventually appeared in the bedroom, she was safely zipped into the chosen dress and brushing her hair at the dressing table.

He'd paused, and she'd forced herself to sit quietly, enduring the appraisal of his dark gaze, instinct telling her that the pallor of her skin against the stark black would have an allure and a promise all its own. Reminding him of how she would look when the dress was gone.

And she'd tensed involuntarily until he'd said, 'You are very lovely, Natasha,' and continued on his way into the bathroom.

When she'd sat very still, staring at her reflection, realising that every time he came into this room in future she would wonder if he was going to take her in his arms.

And asking herself how she would bear it when it finally happened.

The Restaurant Leda was at the end of yet another alleyway. They were greeted with grave pleasure by the head waiter, and led through an intimately shadowed bar area, where Iorgos detached himself to take a seat at a corner table, into a large, brightly lit room abuzz with chatter and laughter from the crowded tables. From there, they went out into the courtyard beyond, where there were rather more secluded eating areas in vine-covered arbours.

As Alex removed the taffeta wrap from her shoulders she noted that their places had been set side by side, which involved joining him on the long cushioned seat.

He said, 'Would you like a drink?'

'Thank you,' she said, adding defiantly, 'Ouzo.'

He grinned. 'Oblivion and a hangover in preference to me, *matia mou*?'

'How clever of you to guess, *kyrie*.'

'Strangely, it did not require any particular intelligence,' Alex said drily as he gave the order.

When it arrived, he added water to the spirit in each glass, then handed her the drink, touching his glass to hers.

'To pleasure, my beautiful girl,' he said, and drank.

She murmured something incoherent in return, and took a gulp of the cloudy mixture, only to be overcome by a fit of helpless coughing as the flavour of anise caught her breath.

Alex swiftly took the ouzo from her hand, and gave her an immaculately folded linen handkerchief from his pocket to mop her streaming eyes as a concerned waiter came running with a tumbler of mineral water, which Alex took from him.

'Sip this,' he directed tersely. 'But carefully.'

She obeyed, mortified to realise that their table was now the cynosure for all eyes around the courtyard.

'Thank you,' she said, when she could speak. 'I'd forgotten how much I loathe ouzo.'

His brows lifted. 'Then why ask for it? Or did you hope to escape my attentions later tonight by choking to death? Is that not a little extreme, even for you?'

She played with the edge of his handkerchief, not looking at him. 'I suppose I thought if I got very drunk, very quickly, you wouldn't like it.'

'And if I lost my temper again, you might be left to sleep alone a second time?' There was a jeering note in his voice. He shook his head slowly. 'No, Natasha *mou*. The next time I walk away will be when it is finished between us. And that is still in the future.'

He paused. 'And now, if you are quite recovered, we shall order our food. Do you like seafood? Because the *souvlaki* with langoustines are particularly good here. And I can recommend the chicken in walnut sauce, or the beef with capers to follow.'

And how could she maintain the required façade of indifference, when it was all she could do not to lick her lips and sob in anticipation of the culinary wonders to come?

The waiter brought dishes of hummus and tzatziki with a basket of freshly baked bread, and a bottle of crisp white wine.

The skewered and grilled langoustines appeared on a bed of golden rice with a side salad, while the chicken that Natasha had asked for and Alex's choice of beef came with baby potatoes baked in their skins, okra and green beans.

Natasha ate every scrap put in front of her, and drank her share of the richly flavoured red wine which had succeeded the white, although she tried to protest at one point when the waiter arrived to refill her glass.

'Do you want me to be drunk, after all, *kyrie*?' she asked Alex, lifting her chin.

'By no means, *matia mou*.' He smiled at her. 'Just—a little more relaxed than you were when the evening began.'

But she shook her head resolutely when Alex suggested dessert, although, when his baked figs arrived, stuffed with nuts and spices and drizzled with honey, she found herself accepting the first taste he offered to her on his spoon.

Pure temptation, she thought weakly. And wondered, with sudden shock, whether she was referring to the figs or to the man beside her.

Because she had relaxed, and she knew it. Although she was sitting close beside him, he'd not attempted even a vestige of an amorous overture. In fact, there'd been times when she'd almost felt secure in his company, as if he was someone she might really want to be with. And, most astonishing of all, he'd actually made her laugh. More than once.

But of course he had, she thought dazedly. This is how he operates—the secret of his success with women.

And I, like the world's biggest fool, am making it so pathetically easy for him.

'Is something wrong?' His quiet question brought her back to the here and now.

'How could there be?' She smiled coolly at him. 'This is a place in a million, Kyrios Mandrakis. I shall remember this fabulous food when I'm back in London trying to grab a sandwich.'

'Along with many other pleasant memories, I hope,' he said sardonically, and signalled for the bill.

If he'd been playing games with her, this was the signal they were over, she thought as she rose, collecting her wrap and purse.

She was shaking inside again as she walked back through the restaurant, pausing while he responded to greetings from other diners, and shook hands with a large, calm faced man in the blue checked trousers and white tunic of the chef, who had emerged from the kitchen to speak to him.

A royal progress, she thought, gathering her fragile defences, for Alexander the Great displaying his latest conquest.

Quite apart from her choking trick, she'd been aware all evening of the attention their table was receiving and not just from the staff. Most of it had been discreet, but a few people had stared openly.

But this presumably was how her life would be lived for a while—in the public eye—and there wasn't a single thing she could do about it.

As they walked back to where the boat was moored, Natasha caught one of her ridiculous heels on an uneven paving slab, and stumbled.

In the next instant, Alex was at her side. 'Take care, *pedhi mou*,' he cautioned, lifting her off her feet and into his arms. 'A broken ankle would not suit my plans at all.'

As he carried her along the harbour, Natasha said breathlessly, 'Put me down. Put me down at once, do you hear?'

'Why should I?' he countered, laughing, before adding more huskily, 'Ah, God, but you feel so good in my arms.'

The flash seemed to come from nowhere. Natasha flinched, but Alex's stride did not even falter as he rapped out a harsh expletive.

Iorgos pounded past, his face like thunder, but came back shaking his head as they heard the departing roar of a motor cycle.

A few minutes later, as they sat in the bows, watching the *Selene* drawing ever closer, Alex said softly, 'I am sorry for that, *agapi mou*. The Leda has a blacklist of reporters and photographers to protect its clients. But I think tonight that someone sitting near us used his mobile to tip off the Press. He seemed over-busy with it at times. If so, I have just given them the picture of the year.'

'Why apologise?' She stared rigidly into the darkness. 'It will serve to establish my exact place in your life, which is exactly what you intended to happen. You told me so.'

'That is true,' he said. 'But I meant it to be in my own time, and in my own way.'

Yes, she thought bleakly. That was always how it would be, from the first moment of taking to the last, when she would be banished from his life forever.

Suddenly and shockingly, she experienced the taste of tears, thick and acrid, in her throat.

And thought, fear twisting inside her, This is madness....

CHAPTER NINE

BUT it was not the evening's only madness, Natasha thought, as she stood at the window in the saloon, staring numbly at the lights of Mykonos, glittering and sparkling in the distance.

Because, for one brief, incredible moment, while she was being carried in Alex's arms, she'd known an almost overwhelming impulse to put her arms round his neck and bury her face against the curve of his shoulder.

And, but for the unknown photographer's intervention, she might even have done so. Which would have been a disaster of untold proportions.

What's happening to me? she thought desperately. I don't seem to know myself any more. And this at a time when I need every atom of strength—of resistance—that I can summon.

That's what I should be concentrating on in these last few moments while I'm still alone—protecting myself, building a wall against him.

As they came back on board, Alex had paused for a quiet word with Mac Whitaker, but instinct told her their conversation would not be prolonged. That this might be her last fleeting opportunity for any real privacy, emotional or physical.

As she entered the saloon, she'd dropped her wrap and purse on the sofa and kicked off her shoes, before making her way barefoot into the bedroom.

The setting was exactly the same as the previous night, she noted, her heart lurching, with the bed cover turned down in invitation, the shaded lamps lit and yet another pretty nightdress laid out for her in readiness. All of it telling her plainly that she was expected to be waiting for him submissively in bed.

And only half an hour before, she might have been able to do just that. Could have managed, somehow, to lie back as planned, close her eyes and endure whatever he wanted from her, comforting herself with the reflection that nothing lasted forever.

Instead, thanks to that instant of unwelcome self-revelation, she'd found herself backing away into the saloon, and now she was standing here as if rooted to the spot, her mind whirling in a spiral of conflict that she was unable either to control, or to understand.

And she was frightened, too.

But was she more afraid of him or of herself? That was the question burning into her brain, and she was still struggling to find the answer when, although she'd heard no sound, she suddenly knew beyond question that she was no longer alone.

Once again her emotional antennae seemed to be working overtime, she thought, dry-mouthed, aware that her skin was tingling.

She saw his reflection in the window as he came silently to stand behind her. His arms slid round her waist, drawing her back against him. For a fraction of a second her body stiffened in resistance, then, in spite of herself, began to relax as the warmth, the nearness of him invaded her consciousness, dispelling the tension that seemed her only armour.

But, at the same time, forcing her to realise, with shame, how easy it would be to stay like this, resting in his embrace, her head leaning back against his chest. How, in some totally unbelievable way, she felt…almost safe….

But there was no sanctuary in Alex's arms. He was a ruthless sexual predator, and she must never forget that for a minute, she reminded herself, swallowing. Or overlook the fact that it was entirely because of him that she stood in need of a refuge in the first place.

But it was so difficult to remember all these vital factors or even start to fortify her weakening defences against him when he was turning her without haste to face him, one hand capturing her chin in order to raise her trembling mouth for his kiss.

Especially when his lips were so warm, and compellingly, insidiously gentle as they explored her own. As if, she thought dazedly, this was the first time he'd ever held her—touched her. And, even more strangely, as if her innocence were still a gift for her to bestow, and he was seeking her willing consent.

When he lifted his head, she swayed in his arms, feeling almost bereft, as the deep, powerful ache of unfulfilled desire slowly reawakened inside her. Reminding her with shaming candour that this was not the first time he had made her want him, against her will and judgement.

He was looking down at her, his eyes gravely searching hers, as if he knew and understood her inner struggle.

He said quietly, 'Shall I call Josefina to help you with your dress?'

It was the last thing she'd expected to hear. She said uncertainly, stammering a little, 'But you—d-don't you want…?'

His mouth twisted ruefully. '*Veveos, agapi mou*. Of course. But this time I am taking nothing for granted.'

For a heartbeat, she stared back at him, her eyes widening, as she realised he was telling her that surrender would not be imposed on her.

That, astonishingly, it was hers to give or to withhold.

And knew, without hesitation but also without pride, that her body had already made the choice for her. That, somehow, during the forty-eight hours between that first night in Athens and this moment, the need that he'd aroused had become frank necessity and could no longer be denied. And that she was right to be scared.

She said in a small, husky voice that she barely recognised, 'Then the answer is…no. I—I don't require her.'

She put her palms flat against his chest, absorbing the strong beat of his heart, feeling it echo in her own pulses, then, without haste, slid her hands upwards until they were resting on his shoulders, holding him, her fingers grasping folds of his shirt to steady herself, because her legs were shaking under her.

He said hoarsely, 'Ah, sweet God,' and pulled her closer, his hand in the small of her back, his kiss deepening into open yearning, as he coaxed her lips apart to admit the silken fire of his tongue into the moist inner sweetness of her mouth.

Natasha yielded, all her initial shyness and reserve overtaken and overwhelmed by her breathless, shaken response. As their mouths clung and burned she found that her small breasts were feeling strangely heavy, the nipples hardening to taut, aching peaks.

Alex's lips were caressing her forehead, her eyes and her flushed cheeks, brushing away her dishevelled hair so that he could reach the sensitive hollow beneath her ear and caress it with his tongue.

Then he framed her face in his hands and took her mouth again, in one long, sensual, draining kiss, before letting his lips travel slowly down her throat, over the frantic, crazy pulse, to move lingeringly over the slight curves of her bare shoulders.

She felt his hand unfasten the hook at the back of her dress, then tug gently at the zip so that the black taffeta slid down just far enough to release her breasts from their confinement.

Revealing them to the hunger of his eyes.

And their swell to the sensuous plunder of his hands, and mouth.

Eyes closed, Natasha lay back against his supporting arm, her breathing ragged as his fingers stroked and cupped the soft mounds, while his tongue circled and tantalised her engorged nipples, creating a pleasure so acute it was almost pain.

She had never imagined she could feel like this, she thought in some fainting corner of her mind.

Never dreamed how completely her body could melt—dissolve under the force of its own yearning.

Never believed either that sheer longing could make her moan softly and uncontrollably until she was silenced by his kiss.

His mouth still locked to hers, Alex picked her up and carried her into the next room, settling her on the bed in a tumble of black taffeta before coming to lie beside her.

He kissed her again, his tongue moving softly, beguilingly against hers, while his hand pushed back her rustling skirt to find her knee and caress it lightly, before moving upwards, his fingertips tracing patterns on the soft, vulnerable flesh inside her thighs as he enticed them into parting for him.

She was being edged quietly and inexorably towards some brink. She knew it, and feared it, suddenly aware that this time his possession of her would be very different. That he was not asking for the mere capitulation of her body but the total abandonment of her will and senses. And that nothing less would do.

She tried to say 'No' but the only sound that emerged from her throat hung between a gasp and a sigh as his hands brushed aside the lacy barrier of her briefs, to discover, with a soft murmur of satisfaction, the reality of her molten, scalding arousal.

He had spoken of pleasure, and it was here—now—in the lingering, voluptuous movement of his fingers against her secret flesh as
they explored her slowly and deeply, gliding, stroking and tantalising, seeking a response she was powerless to deny.

As he sought her tiny hidden bud and awoke it to aching, delicious excitement, Natasha was lost and drowning in a maelstrom of
sensation she had never dreamed could exist.

Alex was kissing her breasts again, taking each hardened peak
in turn between his lips and suckling them with deliberate eroticism,
every flicker of his tongue piercing her with renewed and astonished
delight, and creating tiny, tremulous quivers far, far within her.

At the same time his fingers were becoming more adventurous
and far more purposeful, questing ever more deeply, and thrusting
up into the slick wet heat of her with deliberately sensual intent.

She moaned softly and his lips returned to hers once more, passionately stifling the tiny sound. Then asking. Demanding.

The last vestiges of control were slipping away, her body writh-
ing frantically as she reached for the unknown, conscious of nothing
but his mouth possessing hers and the subtle urgency of his fingers
forcing her to the outermost margins of extremity.

The soft trembling inside her was changing—growing into a
harsh pulsation spiralling upwards. And as her body lifted towards
him in an arc of pure abandonment she heard her voice, wrenched
and hoarse, gasping, 'Alex—oh, God—*Alex…*'

In the next instant she reached the summit, and her entire being
splintered into spasm after spasm of raw, uncontrollable pleasure.

Afterwards, when a measure of sanity returned, and she could
breathe again, she found she was weeping a little—something else
she had not anticipated—and Alex wrapped her closely in his arms,
his voice a soothing murmur as she buried her flushed, damp face
against his shoulder.

She heard the faint rasp of her zip, and realised he was removing
her dress, and that even if the reality of being once again completely
naked in his arms was still a difficulty for her she felt far too languid
and boneless to protest, as Alex lifted her deftly and expertly from
the crumpled taffeta and discarded it.

He moved away slightly and she became aware that he was undressing too, rapidly shedding his clothes and tossing them to the

floor, so that when he came back to her there was only the graze of his skin, bare against her own, as he kissed her and began to caress her, his hands moving slowly, almost reverently over her body, seeking every curve, every hollow, each plane and angle as if he was learning her afresh through his fingertips.

As his mouth rediscovered her breasts, Natasha found, to her amazement, that her nipples were already hardening again under the stroke of his tongue. That her entire body, all too soon, was rousing itself from its post-orgasmic languor, her senses stirring, her flesh shivering and burning not just to answer his touch, but to actively crave it.

To crave him, she realised with shock as she felt the jutting hardness of his erection pressing at the apex of her slackened thighs, and her body clenched, fiercely, almost desperately with the need to have him inside her again. To be known completely once more—but, this time, to know in her turn.

She stretched herself against him, beneath him, her hands seeking the essential maleness of him, then, as instinct took over, holding him, cupping him, stroking his urgently responsive shaft with fingers that were shy, even hesitant at first, then increasingly confident, encouraged by his soft groan of pleasure.

'Wait.' He breathed the word unevenly, turning away from her to reach for the drawer in the night table, extracting a small packet, tearing it open and making swift, deft use of its contents.

Then he came back, pulling her close. He kissed her again, his mouth capturing hers with unconcealed yearning, before whispering huskily, 'Take me, my lovely one. Take me now.'

He slid his hands under her pliant thighs, lifting her slightly, and she obeyed, giving a faint moan as she guided him into her moist, hungry depths and felt the vital power of him filling her—making them one with a heart-stopping sense of completion.

As if, she thought wonderingly, her body had been created for this moment alone. And for this man....

Alex paused, looking down into her widening eyes. He said unsteadily,

'Ah, *Christos*, you feel so sweet, just as I always dreamed—always knew it would be...'

He began to move inside her, slowly and gently, as if he was deliberately reining back his own needs in favour of hers. Something else, she thought dazedly, that she had not expected.

And heard him add softly, 'If I hurt you again, then you must tell me.'

'And you'll do what? Stop?' Her challenge sounded strained and breathless, the words forced from her throat as her body began to melt into its own involuntary reaction to the smooth ebb and flow of his possession. Even as she tried to tell herself that it was impossible. That she couldn't be feeling like this again—not so soon...

'Yes,' he said hoarsely. 'I will stop. If you wish it. Do you?'

For answer, her hands went up to clasp his neck and draw him down to her and her waiting, trembling mouth. At the same time she raised her legs to encircle his hips, mutely inviting his deeper penetration.

His response was instant, almost explosive, as he thrust into her, all restraint gone. As he created a new and driving rhythm, which swept her away with him on a rising tide of heated, passionate delight, forcing her to give as totally, and take as fiercely.

She clung to him, the breath sobbing from her lungs, aware of nothing but the frenzy of sensation building inside her with each hard, compelling stroke from his strong loins.

Once more she could feel the throbbing deep within her as her body gathered itself for that swift, relentless ascent to rapture. And as Alex took her over the edge into the ultimate agony of culmination, and she was gripped by the first shattering convulsions of her climax, she cried out half in exultancy and half in fear, and heard his voice crack on her name as his body in turn shuddered its satiation into hers.

Then silence.

Natasha lay wrapped in Alex's arms, his head heavy on her breasts and her body still tingling voluptuously from pleasure given and received.

But, in contrast, her mind was reeling, especially as the sudden chill of reality had already begun to invade her euphoria.

Was this what everyone expected and experienced during sex? she wondered numbly. This exquisite fusion of soul and body into the moment when nothing else existed on earth or in heaven but this shared, irresistible, intolerable glory?

Was it what she'd have found with Neil, if she'd given herself to him? she asked herself, and knew that it was not. That it never could have been.

People called it 'the act of love', she thought. But, where Alex was concerned, that was a complete misnomer, and 'the act of lust' would be far more appropriate.

Because that was all it had been, or ever would be. That was what she must remember at all costs.

It was the performance that had transformed her irrevocably into Alex Mandrakis's willing mistress. Nothing more. Nothing less. In the process, dragging her down from any moral high ground remaining to her and leaving her with no room for pretence, and nowhere to hide.

All the same, Natasha was shaken by the memory of her own abandon.

Total self-betrayal in one easy lesson, she lashed herself, or, rather, a master class in sensual expertise from someone who had probably forgotten more about pleasing women than most men would ever know.

A man whom she'd allowed to discover, with paramount ease, exactly what it took to turn her into this sobbing, trembling, ecstatic *thing*, as the instrument of his pleasure. And who would expect no less from her in future.

Oh, God, she asked herself. What have I done? I must have gone crazy. But now I have to become sane again. I *have* to. Because I can't let myself simply become…his creature. Not if I'm going to survive, and walk away when he's finished with me.

Leaving—and not looking back—has to be my main, my only priority in all this.

She became aware that Alex was stirring—lifting himself away from her in order to lie beside her and look at her, a smile in his dark eyes.

'So,' he whispered, stroking her damp hair back from her face. 'Do you like me any better now, *agapi mou*?'

Natasha averted her gaze, conscious that her heartbeat had quickened, and that there was an unaccustomed tremulousness inside her which she knew, somehow, had nothing to do with sex, or the astonishing attunement that their bodies had achieved, but was concerned instead with the tenderness in his eyes and fingertips and the oddly wistful note in his voice. All of which spelled the serious danger she feared so much.

And which needed to be dealt with. Fast…

She stiffened. 'No,' she said thickly. 'Why should I?'

His caressing hand stilled. 'I hoped—because of the joy we have just shared,' he said, after a pause.

'Oh, I see,' she said. 'You wish me to congratulate you on your technique, perhaps. Well, I do, naturally.' She added tautly, 'You're living proof, *kyrie*, that practice makes perfect. In fact, you could probably get a response from a block of marble. Is that what you want to hear?'

Alex propped himself on an elbow, staring down at her, his expression incredulous.

'No,' he said slowly. 'It is not. On the contrary, I thought—I believed that our lovemaking might create a new understanding between us.' His mouth twisted ruefully. 'If nothing else, I know now how to persuade you to call me by my given name.'

Her face warmed in embarrassment as that particular circumstance invaded her memory with stinging clarity.

'Then think again,' she advised coldly. 'What happened just now has nothing to do with any kind of love. And the only thing that's changed between us, Kyrios Mandrakis, is that I now despise myself almost as much as I hate you. And I'll never forgive you for that.'

The dark brows snapped together. 'For what?' His voice was clipped. 'For showing you how to be a woman with her man?'

'You are not my man.' She stared back at him defiantly. 'And you never will be. You're merely a temporary misfortune that I hope to be rid of very soon, so that I can get on with the rest of my life.

'And when eventually I do meet someone,' she added, 'he'll be the opposite of you, Kyrios Mandrakis, because, quite apart from the other qualities you so signally lack, he'll have a sense of decency.'

He said harshly, 'And you, Natasha *mou*, on the other hand, will not be quite so naïve as you were. Tell my successor he should be grateful to me for that.' He swung himself off the bed and strode into the bathroom, slamming the door behind him.

Natasha turned onto her side and lay very still. Her ploy seemed to have been successful, she told herself unsteadily. But how many times would she need to make him angry before she became too much of an irritant, and he finally let her go?

And once she had been sent away, she wondered, how long would it take her to forget that lithe, magnificent body he used to such incredible effect?

When would the remembered touch of his hands and the taste of his mouth cease to torment her?

At the same time, it occurred to her that tonight he had used protection, so presumably he had rethought his original intention to shame the Papadimos name by making her pregnant.

And for that, she supposed, she should be grateful. Yet gratitude did not appear to be a major priority at the moment.

She sat up slowly, retrieved the fresh nightgown from the floor, put it on, then pulled the covering sheet up over her body and switched off the lamp in an attempt to settle herself for sleep, although her mind was still wide-awake and teeming with questions she didn't understand, and certainly couldn't answer.

Because, with every day, every hour she spent with Alex, her mental and emotional confusion seemed to be growing. Spiralling out of control in some strange and disturbing way.

Therefore, she'd done absolutely the right thing, said the right words just now. She couldn't afford the slightest temptation to weaken, even if she was haunted by the bleakness in his face as he'd left her.

But nor could she escape the realisation that when he came back to bed he would, in all probability, still be angry with her, so that any further sexual contact he instigated between them might be more punishment than passion. A thought with the power to make her shiver.

Yet I had to protect myself, she argued silently. I had no choice. And tensed as she heard him come back into the bedroom.

She felt the mattress dip slightly as he lay down beside her, and, as his lamp was extinguished in its turn, waited, heart thudding, for him to reach for her.

Only he didn't do so. And as the minutes passed, lengthened, she realised that there was going to be no further contact between them that night—physical or even verbal.

It was a long while before she eventually risked a glance over her shoulder, to find that he was lying on the far side of the bed, his back turned to her and his soft, regular breathing indicating that he was already asleep.

She told herself she should be thankful she'd been spared the possible repercussions from her outburst, and closed her own eyes with determination, trying to ignore the deep, sensuous ache within her which informed her with unwelcome candour that if Alex had decided to take her in his arms again he would once more have found her much more than willing.

It also emphasised that, for her, sleep was not going to be an option—not then, or for some considerable time to come.

And that it would be uncomfortably easy for her to burst into tears instead.

When she opened reluctant eyes the next morning, Natasha made two discoveries.

Firstly, that the *Selene* was moving, and secondly that Alex had gone, leaving her in sole occupation of the big bed and totally unaware of his departure.

She sat up slowly, looking round her, wondering when they'd sailed—and where he was.

Because this was not the way she'd planned this new day to begin as she'd lain beside him last night, staring with aching eyes into the darkness.

Naturally she would not—could not apologise for what she'd said, because that would involve her in some kind of explanation, and she certainly couldn't let him know that her attack on him had been pure self-defence, in case he asked himself why she felt she needed to take such stringent measures.

But there'd been no reason at all not to simply...slide across the bed to where he was lying, and offer a silent attempt to defuse the situation by some form of reconciliation.

Only he wasn't there to be coaxed into lovemaking. The very fact that he'd left her to sleep without a word was almost certainly a sign of his ongoing displeasure with her, she thought, biting her lip, as she threw back the sheet and slid out of bed. So she would just have to change to Plan B, which, as yet, did not exist.

He'd used the bathroom earlier, she realised when she padded in, barefoot, because there was a damp towel in the linen basket and a tang of soap and aftershave still lingering faintly in the air. For a moment it was like being in his arms again, breathing the scent of his skin, and Natasha stood, her eyes closed, her body warming as she allowed herself to remember….

As she heard herself say his name softly, yearningly into the stillness.

Her eyes flew open, and her hand went to her throat as she realised what she'd done, and exactly what she was thinking and feeling.

No, she thought shakily. This is not true. It is not happening to me.

She was feeling…overwhelmed, that was all. Knocked sideways by her incredible physical reaction to Alex as he'd initiated her into the mysteries of sex. Nothing more.

Because how could she possibly want a man who'd overturned her life with such ruthless cynicism? she asked herself. Someone, moreover, who only three days ago had been a complete stranger to her.

But was that really the truth?

Had she ever managed to get Alex Mandrakis out of her mind since she'd seen him on the night of that embassy reception three years before?

It was a crush, she told herself desperately. That's all. I was little more than a child then, for God's sake. And he was older, glamorous, and totally out of my league for all sorts of reasons besides the feud. The utterly seductive appeal of forbidden fruit by the cartload.

It should have been over and done with as soon as it began, but I—I kept it alive somehow. Allowed that awareness of him to be continually sparked by all the stories featuring him in the newspapers, whether they were in the business pages or the gossip columns.

In fact, she thought, swallowing, if she was being honest at last, she'd gone looking for them. Had devoured, avidly, every word written about him, only to discover painfully in the process that many of them had the power to affect her personally. To matter, and even—in some ridiculous way—to hurt her.

That was when she'd tried to stop, telling herself that, for her own peace of mind, she had to end this dangerous obsession with her family's enemy, because he was nothing but a despicable, loathsome, womaniser—not worth a second thought.

He was not Romeo, she'd told herself with determination. And she was definitely not Juliet. End of story.

Except that it wasn't the end. Not then. And certainly not now.

Instead she was being forced to deal with the extraordinary sense that a door had suddenly opened into a new and different world, and Alex had been there waiting for her, as she'd always known, somehow, that he would be.

No, she thought frantically, that—*that* is a complete delusion. It has to be. Anything else is totally impossible. It's sheer insanity to let myself think that I might ever have been in love with him. Or—even worse—that I still could be.

Because until Stavros and Andonis intervened with that disastrous marriage scheme, I'd managed to put him out of my mind. Convinced myself that my fixation with him was finally over. I'm sure of it.

And if I'd stayed safely in England, I'd have kept it that way. A sweet, silly memory to smile about sometimes in the far future when I was safe and happy with someone else.

But instead I found myself trapped, facing him in his bedroom. Discovering what it meant to belong to him in bed. And if ever there was a time when I needed to hate him, it was then—as he touched me for the first time…

So I tried to hate him. Heaven help me, I tried. Only to find that nothing had changed. That, although I might have buried the old feelings for him, they were still alive, simply waiting for resurrection.

That I wanted him still. And, more than that, I loved him.

She sank down onto the tiled floor, kneeling with her arms wrapped defensively round her body, staring blindly into space.

God, she thought, what a fool she was. But at least she'd retained enough common-sense to understand that the feeling of warmth and safety she'd experienced in his arms was and always would be an illusion.

I have never encouraged any of the women who have shared my bed to fall in love with me. It would be a waste of their time, and mine.

Alex's own words, so she could not say she hadn't been warned, she thought, rocked by a pain so fierce she almost cried out.

He'd taken her for revenge at the beginning, as a trophy attained in the war with her brothers. But he'd kept her for her novelty value—his still unconquered conquest, she told herself, a sob rising in her throat.

And that was what she would continue to be, from this moment until the day he told her she was free to go.

With the secret of her true feelings, she whispered silently, hers to keep hidden then—and for the rest of her life without him.

CHAPTER TEN

IT WAS the fear of being discovered there, weeping silently as she whispered his name under her breath, that eventually prompted her to move. To drag herself to her feet and begin the essential preparations to face him again.

She showered rapidly, and then found the jade bikini, and its pretty overshirt that she'd rejected the previous day, and pulled them on. Readying herself for his eyes—his pleasure—she thought wryly. Accepting the role imposed upon her, because that was all she could hope for, and she had to believe that it was better than nothing. Had to…

She brushed her hair loose, applied mascara to her lashes and a touch of soft coral to her lips, then stood for a long moment, studying her reflection, searching for some betraying sign of the emotional storm that had gripped her earlier, and the aching emptiness that was left in its place, as she silently rehearsed the part she had to play.

Then, bracing herself, she went up on deck.

One glance told her that Mykonos was fast becoming a memory on the horizon.

More to the point, there was still no sign of Alex, either.

As she paused uncertainly, Kostas came to meet her. 'You will take breakfast, *thespinis*?'

'Please.' She forced a smile, as she saw the table under the awning was set just for one. 'Has Kyrios Mandrakis already eaten?'

He looked astonished. 'Hours ago, *thespinis*. Before he leave to go to Athens.'

Natasha was very still. 'You mean—he's not on board?' She steadied her voice. 'He's—gone?'

'*Ne, thespinis.* He take the early plane from Mykonos.' He paused, clearly embarrassed. 'You did not know this?'

She managed to shrug. Even to smile. 'I knew he'd be returning there some time. I hadn't realised it would be quite so soon.'

Or that it would be without a word of goodbye....

She found herself remembering what he had said only last night: 'The next time I walk away will be when it is finished between us.' And thought with swift anguish, *I may never see him again.*

From now on, her only contact with him would be the ongoing stories in the newspapers. And if they'd hurt her before, they would now have the power to wound her to her very soul.

'You wish coffee, *thespinis*?' Kostas asked.

'Yes, please.' Natasha lifted her chin resolutely. 'Plus an omelette with cheese and ham, hot rolls, yoghurt and fruit.'

She wasn't sure how much of it she'd be able to eat, but at least it would seem as if Alex's decision wasn't causing her to pine away, she told herself with a brave attempt at defiance as she went to the table and sat, staring across the water with eyes that saw nothing.

So this time she'd really inflicted lasting damage, she thought, pain twisting inside her. But if that was the case, why had she not been taken ashore to the airport herself and sent on her way? After all, there must be any number of direct flights from Mykonos to the U.K., as well as Athens, giving every opportunity for Alex to wash his hands of her for good and all.

Unless, of course, he wished to punish her by keeping her hanging around, her entire future still in question. Waiting—and wondering. If so, she thought wryly, he was succeeding beyond his wildest dreams—but not for the reasons he imagined. When—if—he returned, it would be the necessity to hide her true feelings from him which would cause her the real agony.

But at least he couldn't expect them to part as friends, because that was something they'd never been. There had never been the opportunity, and now, like so much else, it was all too late.

She heard a quiet tread approaching and snatched at her disintegrating self-control as she realised that Mac Whitaker was crossing the deck towards her.

'G'day, Miss Kirby.' His greeting was civil rather than cordial. He glanced up at the cloudless sky. 'It seems we have ourselves another beauty.'

'It does.' Natasha paused. 'They're bringing me coffee. May I offer you some?'

He hesitated, then thanked her and took the seat opposite.

'So, it's goodbye to Mykonos,' Natasha went on, over-brightly. 'What a pity. I was looking forward to seeing the famous pelicans.'

'I'm sure there'll be plenty of future opportunities,' Captain Whitaker returned as Kostas appeared with the coffee and a jug of chilled orange juice. 'When Alex has less on his plate.'

Her heart missed a questioning beat. 'Yes,' she said. 'Perhaps so.' She hesitated. 'I presume that Iorgos the guard dog has gone with him?'

'Yes,' he said, 'but that's only to keep his Dad happy. The old man worries about him.'

Natasha filled a cup with the dark, strong brew and handed it to him. 'Has he any reason to do so?'

'There've been threats,' he said laconically, 'in the past.'

And she could guess the source, she thought, grimacing inwardly. She said with deliberate lightness, 'You mean—apart from angry husbands?'

'With Alex? You must be joking.' He shook his head. 'Married ladies have always been strictly off-limits where he's concerned.'

'I bow to your superior knowledge.' She took a deep breath. 'May—may I know where we're going?'

'Didn't Alex tell you? We're heading off to Alyssos.'

'Alyssos?' Natasha repeated almost mechanically, her mind going into overdrive as she told herself that Alex's choice of destination might suggest that he hadn't simply walked away after all.

'I presume you've heard of it.'

'Well, yes,' she said slowly, still faintly bewildered. 'Someone I know used to spend a lot of time there.'

'Then they must have been loaded,' Mac Whitaker said. 'The island's a mini-paradise for millionaires, with tourism strictly discouraged. Just a couple of pleasant villages, some olive groves and a few houses owned by some very rich people, Alex's father being among them. In fact, Alex was born there. Or didn't he mention that, either?'

'No,' she said. 'No, he didn't.' But she could understand, she thought, why the island had suddenly become out of bounds for Thia Theodosia. And it was just one more thing to blame on that bloody feud.

Aloud, she said, 'I thought Alex was an Athenian through and through.'

Mac Whitaker shrugged. 'Maybe Alyssos is no big deal as far as he's concerned,' he said. 'I don't think either he or his father have spent much time there in past years, although I know Alex had a load of work done to the place a while ago, as if he was planning to use it again at some point. And I guess that point's now been reached.'

His smile was polite. 'Perhaps he's intending it as a surprise for you.'

'Yes,' she said. 'He's—good at surprises.' She paused. 'Has he issued you with any other instructions—about me?'

'Not as such, Miss Kirby.' He took a reflective sip of coffee. 'Naturally he'll expect us all to make sure you're comfortable, and I dare say he'll be grateful if I can stop you falling overboard, seeing as you don't swim. But apart from that…'

'Don't swim?' Natasha set down her cup. 'What gave you that idea?'

Surely not Alex, she thought, her face warming. Not when he'd stood in the shadows of the Villa Demeter watching her water-nymph act.

Mac Whitaker shrugged again. 'I guess I assumed it,' he returned. 'After all, you haven't been near the pool since you came on board.'

'Unlike Alex's previous companions, who couldn't get enough of it—or of him?' she queried coolly, and saw him flush in his turn. 'Perhaps I simply don't care for its…associations, Captain Whitaker.'

'I guess that's a reference to the famous birthday party.' His pleasant mouth curled in open distaste. 'Which means I'm not the only one under a misapprehension, Miss Kirby.'

Natasha lifted her chin. 'Are you trying to say that Alex wasn't in the pool that night with six naked girls?'

He shrugged again. 'For a moment or two, yeah—after they pushed him in fully dressed,' he added grimly. 'But he guessed he was being set up, even before they stripped off and dived in. I was there, Miss Kirby, and I can tell you that all Alex took off was his dinner jacket, and that he was out of the water well before they got anywhere near him. End of story.

'The girls were fished out, given their clothes and sent back to shore on Rhodes, together with a flea in the ear for the idiot who'd let himself be talked into inviting them on board.

'It was all over in minutes. Half the guests didn't even know anything had happened, until the ringleader decided to make a name for herself with the tabloids.'

'But if she was lying,' Natasha argued, 'why didn't Kyrios Mandrakis issue a denial? Say what really happened?'

Mac Whitaker's mouth tightened. 'Maybe because he has his fair share of pride, and felt it was beneath his dignity to take any notice of such garbage,' he retorted. 'Surely you, of all people, must realise that he simply doesn't go in for stuff like that.'

Natasha stared past him. 'Or not quite so publicly perhaps,' she suggested woodenly.

'Not at all as far as I'm aware.' His tone was blunt. 'As it was, do you really imagine he'd have insulted his friends, not to mention their wives and partners—Linda, my own fiancée among them—with behaviour like that?' He shook his head. 'No way, especially in *Selene*'s pool,' he added drily.

'What do you mean?'

'It's a sea-water pool,' he said shortly. 'Sea equals salt. Not the friendliest environment for that kind of cavorting.'

'Oh.' Natasha's colour rose. 'I—I didn't realise.'

'So I gathered.' He paused. 'Forgive me for speaking out of turn, Miss Kirby, but I can't figure you out at all. Here you are, living with Alex, yet you don't seem to have one good thought in your head about him.'

What do you want me to say? Natasha asked in silent anguish. Do you want me to tell you the truth—that for the last three years there've been times when he's been the only thought in my head, good or bad?

But that I've just realised that I love him with everything that's in me?

Love him against my will, my principles and my better judgement, and that being without him now is like suffering an amputation?

And that, living with him again, knowing that our time together has strict limits, promises to be a thousand times worse?

Aloud, she said quietly, 'Whatever may have happened at the

party, his playboy reputation is hardly a secret. I can't pretend to be oblivious.'

'Yeah, he likes to relax in female company,' Mac Whitaker agreed. 'I don't deny that. He's a single bloke, and I guess he's entitled to enjoy himself. But it's a great pity the fact that he works like a dog doesn't get mentioned quite as often.'

She looked back at him. 'You're very loyal to your employer, Captain Whitaker.'

'I have reason,' he said shortly. 'Alex isn't just a boss, Miss Kirby, he's a good mate from way back, and my family owe him big-time.'

'I didn't realise.' She was genuinely surprised. 'How—how did the two of you meet, if I may ask?'

'The Mandrakis Corporation has major holdings in the Oz wine trade,' Mac Whitaker told her. 'Dad's in charge of one of their vineyards, and Alex came to stay with us when he was very much younger, in order to learn the ropes.'

He grinned reminiscently. 'I have three sisters and a younger brother, so it was his first encounter with family life on that scale. His mother died when he was six, and his father never married again, so he stayed an only child, and a pretty isolated one at that.

'But Mum's a genius with shy kids, and she soon coaxed him out of his shell.'

Something in Natasha's heart twisted at the thought of a withdrawn and lonely boy finding comfort with strangers on the other side of the world.

'Once he went back to Greece, we didn't really expect to see him again,' Mac Whitaker went on. 'But we were so wrong. He became a regular visitor.' He sighed. 'To be honest, I think he was glad to have a place where he could escape some of the tensions at home.'

Natasha said constrictedly, 'I can understand that.' She could remember when even some minor clash involving his Mandrakis opponent could throw Basilis Papadimos into a black temper for days, and they had all walked warily. Then, almost as if a page had turned, his mood would lift, and the sun would come out again. Until the next time...

And perhaps Petros Mandrakis had been the same.

She hesitated. 'Presumably, then, you know about the feud?'

'Some of it.' His mouth twisted wryly. 'I certainly realised how much Alex hated it and how desperately he wanted it to end.' His brows lifted. 'How did you find out about it?'

'I lived in Athens myself for a time.' Relieved that he didn't know the actual connection between them or how she'd come to be with Alex, Natasha decided on a half-truth. 'Where it was common knowledge, of course. Except for how it started. Did—did Alex ever mention that?'

Mac Whitaker shook his head. 'Not to me. I gathered it was all a bit of a taboo subject. But, if he'd confided in anyone, I guess it would have been Mum. And she's totally discreet, besides adoring Alex for what he did for Eddie.'

Natasha's head was whirling. 'Eddie?'

'The young brother I mentioned. The brains of the family. Went off to university, expected to graduate with first-class honours. Only he blew it. Got in with a seriously bad crowd in the city, ended up on drugs and in debt to nasty people.

'Alex paid him a visit out of the blue, realised what was going on and rescued him. Saved his bloody life, if you must know.' He counted off on his fingers. 'Paid off what he owed, put him in rehab and gave him the tongue-lashing of the century. Ed told me later that he'd been far more scared of Alex when he was mad than he'd been of any of the crooks who'd been after him. Result, he's now clean and got to finish his degree course with a respectable result.'

He paused. 'And it didn't do Alex any harm, either. He was in a really bad way himself at the time—chewed up over some love affair that had gone horribly wrong. Taking stupid risks with fast cars, faster boats and dodgy polo ponies as if he didn't care what happened, and it didn't matter whether he lived or died. Ed gave him something else to think about, instead of some foolish girl who didn't know a good thing when it was offered to her.'

He stopped suddenly, reddening, as if belatedly aware this might not be a favoured topic with the current lady facing him across the table.

'But that's long in the past,' he added hurriedly. 'All forgotten now.'

She said quietly, 'Are you absolutely sure about that?'

'Hundred per cent.' He looked past her. 'And here comes your breakfast, which I'll leave you to eat in peace.'

Peace, Natasha thought, forcing herself to eat the deliciously fluffy omelette set in front of her as if she still had an appetite, was hardly the word she would have chosen.

Not when she'd just had it confirmed that Alex had been devastated—almost destroyed—by his failed love affair, and left feeling as if he had nothing left to live for.

She wondered if Gabriella, the exquisitely elfin model who'd accompanied him to the embassy party, had been the woman he'd wanted so badly, and if she'd turned him down as a husband in order to pursue her admittedly star-studded career.

If so, it was small wonder, she thought unhappily, that he'd evolved into this…serial monogamist, using women to satisfy his physical needs, yet denying them any deeper, closer share in his life.

It explained, too, why he might have been prepared, however briefly, to consider the arranged marriage that Stavros and Andonis had offered.

It had only been pretence on their side, of course, yet it had prompted Alex into refreshing his memory about a girl he'd once seen for a few minutes on the other side of a room.

A girl with no reason to want him who therefore, might have proved a suitable partner in a marriage of convenience, she thought, pain tightening her throat. Which he would see as a cynical business contract, with love neither given nor received, its sole advantage being a means for ending that damaging and dangerous feud.

The idea must have seemed definitely tempting to a man with no desire for commitment.

Prompting him to take a second look at his potential bride, she reasoned, if only to make sure hers was a face he could endure to see on the adjoining pillow on those rare nights that he'd spend at home, so that the occasional performance of his marital duties would not prove too onerous a task.

All of which, with the connivance of the venal Stelios, had led to that covert night-time visit.

Even so, she told herself, he'd taken one hell of a risk.

He'd have assumed, of course, at that hour she'd be deeply and peacefully asleep, not lying awake fretting over her brothers' gleefully revealed schemes.

A moment or two on either side, she mused, and they'd probably have met on the staircase leading up to her balcony, with Alex making an undignified dash for safety before her screams alerted the entire household.

Because she would have screamed—wouldn't she?

And he would have run.

Unless, of course, he'd stood his ground and survived the inevitable fallout by pretending he'd acted on some wild, romantic whim. And if he'd also added that, having seen her again, he was prepared for the wedding to take place at once, Stavros and Andonis would have been left without a leg to stand on.

Because, ostensibly, that was what they wanted too, and they would not have dared to say otherwise.

It would have been down to her, instead, to flatly repudiate any notion of marriage between them, and make it clear she was returning to England without delay.

Which would have been the end of it, she thought, sighing silently. No fatally damaging letters sent, and all subsequent recriminations thankfully settled in her absence. Her life her own again.

But it didn't happen like that, she reminded herself flatly. Because he didn't get as far as the stairs to your room. He didn't have to when you were there at the pool, with your clothes off. Driven there because, once again, you couldn't sleep for thinking of him, even if you tried to pretend it was nothing of the kind. That he was no longer a problem.

And nothing else happened, either. Remember that. Because he didn't walk forward into the moonlight, take the towel from your hands, dry you slowly and gently, then kiss you as he did the other night.

And felt her nipples harden swiftly and involuntarily against the fabric that draped them as she recalled the unlooked-for sweetness of his hands and mouth.

At the same time, it occurred to her that it was not very wise to fantasise about her lover's caresses when she'd been left alone with no idea when she would see him again, or if he would even want to touch her when he did return.

She needed to re-focus her attention, she thought with a kind of desperation. And maybe this was the time for a belated tour of the *Selene*—surely a better option than spending more time cooped up in the suite, brooding.

'My real home,' Alex had once said, and maybe it would give her some further clue into this other identity of his that was slowly being revealed to her. A man who was 'a good mate' and went the extra mile for friendship's sake, as opposed to being merely the casual playboy of the Press stories.

Someone who'd once been lonely and shy, and was still capable of being vulnerable instead of merely a vengeful, uncaring predator.

A lover whose undoubted expertise had been mingled with heart-stopping tenderness.

And a man who had once loved a woman to the point of desperation without the return he'd longed for.

'You may find him kinder than you think.' Thia Theodosia's words, dismissed at the time but now stinging at her memory. Provoking more questions for which she desperately needed answers.

Accordingly, when she'd finished breakfast, she sought out Mac Whitaker on the bridge.

'I was wondering,' she said diffidently, 'if you could spare some-one to show me round the boat. Or shall I ask Kostas?'

He swung himself out of his chair. 'No need for that, Miss Kirby.' His smile was suddenly much warmer. 'I'll go with you my-self. Be glad to.'

They started on the main deck in the vast saloon, which he told her was used principally for entertaining, with its graceful fluted columns supporting the corniced ceiling, and the adjoining formal dining room.

Looking at the long, polished table under the elaborate chande-lier, Natasha found she was remembering Alex's sardonic offer to let her practise being a hostess and winced inwardly at the thought of having to sit facing him at the other end of that expanse of gleam-ing wood.

She was glad to turn away and concentrate instead on the nearby conference room, sited next door to Alex's private office, which was the only place where she was not permitted access.

'More than my life is worth,' Mac informed her cheerfully. 'And it's locked anyway.'

She gasped when she saw the small but comfortable cinema, and was entirely lost for words when she realised that another room had been fitted out as a children's play area.

'A lot of Alex's friends have kids,' Mac said as she turned to him, her eyes widening incredulously. 'He's godfather to quite a few of them. And sometimes his business contacts are invited to bring their families too. He reckons it makes for a more relaxed atmosphere outside working hours when the meetings are over.'

Natasha tried to imagine Stavros and Andonis and their wives, not to mention Irini, as the *Selene*'s guests, enjoying all this laid-back luxury, but failed totally.

Each of the elegant staterooms and their glamorous bathrooms had been individually designed, and obvious thought had gone into the provision of the crew's quarters, while the galleys, where she'd been greeted by Yannis, the beaming chef, were an immaculate and efficient dazzle of stainless steel.

An hour later as they sat beside the swimming pool, sipping the iced lemonade Kostas had brought them, he said, 'So, what do you think?'

Natasha drew a deep breath. 'Amazing,' she said. 'And also stunningly beautiful. A floating palace.'

But not exactly a home perhaps, she thought, although that might partly account for Alex's restlessness, and his reluctance to settle down. It was just too simple for him to up anchor and sail away when the mood took him.

She hesitated. 'It's strange that his father's remained a widower all this time. You'd have thought he'd have remarried and provided Alex with a more stable background and some brothers and sisters.'

'Well, Kyrios Petros isn't exactly in the best of health,' Mac said slowly. 'Years ago he was involved in a bad car accident and ended pretty smashed up. He's had a few operations since then, particularly on his back, but he still walks with a stick.'

'Oh.' Natasha's brows lifted. 'I—I had no idea.' And that was no more than the truth, she thought in bewilderment. There'd never been the least mention of any past accident, or injury to Basilis's hated rival. The perceived wisdom at the Villa Demeter had always represented Petros Mandrakis as the devil incarnate, the strong, all-powerful enemy.

Certainly not with the human face of a man no longer young, perhaps living his life in pain, who needed to lean on a cane when he walked.

'Alex doesn't talk about it much,' Mac was saying. 'But I guess that's why he persuaded Kyrios Petros to let him take the strain over the companies earlier than he wanted, maybe, in order to give the old man a chance to get some rest, and more treatment. In fact, he's in Switzerland seeing a new specialist right now.'

She said quietly, 'It must be worrying for Alex.'

'Sure,' he said. 'He and his dad have become pretty close these past few years. If the Papadimos bunch want to keep the feud going, they'll find they have a real fight on their hands.'

'Yes,' she said. 'I'm sure they will.' She took a deep breath, then smiled at him brightly. 'You mentioned earlier that you were engaged. Please tell me about your fiancée.'

He was clearly delighted to do so, producing a photograph of a pretty brunette with candid eyes and a curving mouth.

'We're planning to get married next year,' he told her, 'and settle down in Oz.'

'You're giving up the sea?'

'Hell, no. We're planning to start our own boat-charter service.' He looked around him. 'I'll miss the *Selene*, of course, but there's no guarantee she'll be around for much longer—not if Alex finally decides to please his dad and bite the bullet by settling down too, once a suitable heiress appears.'

She said steadily, 'Is that likely?'

He looked uncomfortable, clearly regretting his frankness. 'Pretty inevitable, I'd say. Kyrios Petros wants the dynasty made secure, and now Alex is heading up the Mandrakis business empire, he'll have less time anyway for—for…'

'Diversions like me?' Natasha supplied. 'It's all right,' she added reassuringly as his face reddened even further in embarrassment. 'I'm under no illusions about my place in his life, and when the time comes, I'll go quietly.'

She paused. 'So, what time will we get to Alyssos?'

'Around mid-afternoon.' He snatched with relief at the change of topic. 'Josefina's started packing for you now. And she'll be going ashore with you too. So you'll have a familiar face about you from day one.'

'Oh.' Natasha digested this. 'Doesn't she mind?'

'Far from it. It's a bit of a homecoming for her as her dad, Zeno, is major-domo at the villa, and her mother, Toula, is the house-keeper.' He added, still with faint awkwardness, 'You'll be well looked after, Miss Kirby. Alex has seen to that.'

After he'd excused himself, and gone back to the bridge, Natasha sat for a long time, lost in thought, as ideas, questions, impressions and snatches of conversation jostled each other in her mind.

She felt as if she'd been presented with an inextricably knotted skein of wool to disentangle, or a jigsaw with innumerable missing pieces. That the past, present and future were somehow a jumble of events that could make sense if only she knew where to begin.

But maybe it would be simpler if that was all she had to deal with, she thought with irony.

Instead, she found her thoughts dominated—haunted—by the prospect of Alex, the dutiful son. Alex, the husband. Alex, the father.

And could only hope that when it—the inevitable, the unbearable—happened, some merciful providence would ensure that she was long gone and far away.

CHAPTER ELEVEN

THE beach below the house on Alyssos wasn't large—just a crescent of pale sand shelving gently into the Aegean, reduced even further by a large boathouse and a wooden jetty on one side—but it had become Natasha's chosen refuge during the long days she'd spent waiting for Alex.

She was not, she thought drily, the only one. The whole household seemed aquiver with anticipation, waiting almost on tiptoe for the master's return. Although he seemed in no hurry to oblige them. Or herself.

In his absence, she seemed to have entered a kind of limbo, trapped there between unease and loneliness, as one baking day succeeded another. And the nights were worse, as she lay in the darkness, tense and shivering with a need that only Alex could satisfy.

Not that there was any guarantee that he intended to do so. This time her clothes and belongings had not been placed with his in the master bedroom, but taken to a guest room at the far end of a long corridor, and when Josefina, surprised into indiscretion, had queried the arrangement she had been quickly silenced by a look from her father.

Zeno was a tall, grizzled man whose behaviour, while totally correct, was nevertheless faintly aloof, an attitude echoed by his plump, bustling wife. In addition, neither of them seemed to speak much English, which made her all the more glad of Josefina's generally uncomplicated cheerfulness. And she could not deny that the food and service at the villa were impeccable. All the same there was—something.

And when Natasha, puzzled, asked Josefina if she hadn't been expected, the Greek girl admitted with some embarrassment that her parents had always believed that the first girl brought by Kyrios Alexandros to his Alyssos home would be his bride.

Making me a very downmarket substitute, Natasha told herself in self-derision. No wonder they don't approve. And it's my own fault. He asked me about islands. I happened to mention this one.

And she could understand why Thia Theodosia had loved Alyssos, having always suspected that her foster mother found the noise and hurly-burly of Athens oppressive.

At the same time, she found herself wondering where Madame Papdimos's house was situated and who occupied it now. And how much it had cost her to give it up—a sacrifice, she supposed, to the god of marriage.

And another reason, she thought, why I decided to leave three years ago—in case I became another one.

Although if I'd stayed and done what Thio Basilis saw as my duty, I wouldn't be in this mess now.

She toyed briefly with the idea of asking Zeno, but soon abandoned it. He was a Mandrakis man, she acknowledged ruefully. Any mention of the name Papadimos would probably be like waving a red rag in front of a bull.

In the meantime, she decided it would be good to touch base with Molly. Find out how business was going, and assure her that she'd be back soon. Try and resume something approaching normality, she thought drily, in preparation for her eventual return to London and the real world.

But her request for the use of a telephone or access to a computer had been politely parried. Such facilities, she was given to understand, were in the remit of Kyrios Alexandros only, who would no doubt be glad to assist her on his return.

What did they imagine she was planning? she wondered as she turned away, defeated. To send a scream for help so that the SAS would drop out of the sky and snatch her away?

Being denied contact with the outside world really did make her feel like a prisoner, yet she could not pretend she was completely unhappy in her surroundings.

Alyssos was indeed a very small island, with a rocky interior that made no attempt to aspire to be a mountain. It possessed a tiny port bearing the same name, where the chief excitement, it seemed, was the daily arrival of the one ferry.

Not that she was allowed to observe it at first-hand in case, she supposed, she decided to hop on board, and be gone. But how far would she get without her passport, which she'd discovered was missing the first day on the *Selene*? And which was still, presumably, in Alex's possession. Which meant she was going nowhere.

And, apart from the ferry, it seemed that watching the olives and other fruit ripen appeared to be the island's main pastime. And, in different circumstances, probably a perfect way to de-stress.

As was lying in the shallows of the Aegean, letting slow gentle wavelets wash slowly over her body as tiny fish darted unafraid among the fronds of weed around her.

It could, she thought, be paradise. If only…

The Villa Elena itself, named, Josefina told her, for Kyrios Alexandros's late mother, was a large single-storey residence, painted white with a green-tiled roof. Its rather stark lines were softened by the masses of pink and purple bougainvillea sprawling over its walls. There were two substantial wings jutting out like strong arms reaching to the sea, one containing the lavish bedroom accommodation, and the other holding the kitchens, store rooms and staff quarters.

The floors were pale marble, the décor muted and the furniture sleek and modern, apart from the deeply cushioned and gloriously comfortable sofas and chairs in the *saloni*.

And all of it, according to the all-knowing Josefina, designed by Kyrios Alexandros himself.

In the lawned gardens there was a large freshwater swimming pool, surrounded by a tiled sunbathing terrace with changing cabins, and screened by tall hibiscus hedges.

Natasha found it a little daunting for solitary use and preferred the simple privacy of the beach two hundred yards away. And once this had been established, unseen hands set out a sun lounger and parasol for her use each morning together with a cold box containing bottled water.

There was a small dinghy moored at the jetty and further out in the bay an elderly caique painted brown, its tan sails neatly furled, rode sedately at anchor.

The *Selene*, however, had sailed almost as soon as Natasha had come ashore, giving her the uncomfortable feeling that she'd been marooned. It also meant that Mac, the one person who might have been privy to Alex's plans, had gone too. Nor could she ask him any of the questions still teeming in her brain.

Now, as she finished her careful application of sunblock to her exposed skin, and stretched out on her lounger for another solitary day, she found herself wondering once more why and where the yacht had gone. Certainly not to fetch Alex because, according to the helpful Josefina, he invariably flew in by helicopter.

She had even been shown the area at the side of the villa where he would land. So she could be waiting, no doubt, with a posy of flowers and a curtsy for the visiting celebrity, she thought with faint bitterness, then paused with an impatient sigh. What was the earthly use in pretending she wasn't living for the moment when she would see him again?

Not that he appeared to share her sentiments. Not when ten whole days had now passed without a solitary word from him. *Ten!* And her pride would not allow her to enquire if anyone at all knew when he would be arriving.

Nor could she prevent herself from speculating where he might be. And, more damagingly, with whom…

Not that it took much working out, she thought, a fist clenching in her chest. He'd even mentioned her rival's name. Domenica.

'His latest squeeze', she recalled, had been Molly's description just before she'd set off for Athens, but Domenica was far more than that. She was the Italian rock chick whose first album sizzling with dark sexuality had taken the charts by storm only a few months before, helped along by the inevitable demands that it should be banned.

And the album cover, where only that beautiful, sultry little face had been highlighted, leaving the rest of her obviously naked body in shadow, had been advertised everywhere.

My rival, Natasha told herself, grimacing. And another golden opportunity for Alex to practise his language skills.

And stopped abruptly, knowing that such flippancy was out of place. That she must not let herself think like that ever again, even for a moment, because it hurt her to the point of destruction.

She could only hope that by the time she did return to London, there would be some new sensation in the music world, so she wouldn't be haunted by the image of all that sensual allure purring her pleasure in Alex's bed.

Sighing, she picked up the book she was reading, one from the box of recent bestsellers which Mac had arranged to be sent ashore with her, and tried to revive her interest in the story, knowing just the same that she was too restless and on edge today to allow it the concentration it deserved.

If and when Alex returned he would probably find her on the verge of a nervous breakdown, she thought wryly, and paused as she heard in the distance the unmistakable sound of an approaching helicopter.

She sat up abruptly, shading her eyes as she looked up into the cloudless sky, peering to see the direction it was coming from. It might not be Alex, she reminded herself. After all, there were other millionaires with hideaways on Alyssos, who probably used similar forms of transport.

But that would not explain why, in spite of the heat, she was suddenly shivering with excitement. With desire. And—with fear. That possibly most of all when she remembered how they'd parted, and the fact that there'd been silence between them ever since, she thought, sinking back on her cushions.

The helicopter appeared, flying low over the adjoining headland, then turning inland.

Natasha stared down at her book, the printed words swimming before her gaze, as she told herself that she would not—*not*—under any circumstances look up.

Neither look up, get up, nor walk to the house. Instead, she would stay exactly where she was and wait until he sent for her.

It turned out to be a very long wait, and she spent much of it in the sea, trying to ease her tension and frustration by swimming up and down as if she were practising for the next Olympics.

In the end, her summons came only from the prosaic and distant beating of the gong with which Zeno announced mealtimes.

Lunch, it seemed, was served.

She picked up her sarong and tied it over her damp bikini, then stood for a moment running her fingers through her tangled, salty hair to loosen it a little. God forbid that she should look as if she was trying too hard, she thought with irony as she found a colourless lip salve in her beach bag and applied a little to her mouth. Then, swallowing past the hard knot in her throat, she started up the track back to the villa.

She usually ate outside on the wide paved terrace, and saw that the table had been set as usual under the awning outside the *saloni*.

But for one place only.

Her steps faltered, and she was suddenly far more breathless than could be justified by that relatively gentle climb up from the beach.

As she reached the terrace, Zeno emerged through the double glass doors, carrying a carafe of water and a plate of salad.

Natasha couldn't pretend indifference any longer. She said, 'I—I thought Kyrios Mandrakis would be here.'

'He has a meeting of business, *thespinis*,' Zeno informed her with faint hauteur. 'Therefore he eats in his dining room with his guests.'

She said, 'I see.' And so she did. She was being quietly but definitely shown her place in the scheme of things. And that was not as any kind of hostess. At best, her role would be as the provider of his after-hours amusement.

So she sat alone and ate her salad, and the grilled lamb chops that followed, and told herself she should be glad that Alex had no longer any wish to exhibit his trophy mistress to his visitors.

But the real shock came with the coffee, when Zeno placed an envelope on the table beside her cup and silently departed.

She picked it up with fingers that shook.

What's this? she wondered, feeling a bubble of hysteria rising inside her. Dismissal? A month's salary in lieu of notice?

But instead she found another envelope with her name scrawled across it in Molly's distinctive writing.

She tore it open, and began scanning the letter inside.

'Nat, darling,' it began.

'I hate to drop this on you when you clearly have problems of your own, but I don't have much choice, because my life is about to change hugely. You see, Craig has had a terrific offer to stay on in Seattle for the next two years, and he wants us to bring the wedding forward so that I move out there as his wife. And obviously I want this too, although it's the last thing I expected. I thought we'd settle in the UK and life would go on as usual.

However I need to know what your plans are. Although I'm not the only one, as Neil keeps calling to ask when you're coming home too.

On top of all this, right out of the blue we've had a really good offer to buy Helping Out from The Home Service, which under the circumstances—you in Greece, me in America— we should consider.'

The figure she mentioned made Natasha gasp before she hastily read on.

'I planned to write to your Athens address,' the letter continued, 'but Mr Stanopoulos, your lovely Greek lawyer, who's been overseeing everything this end, tells me you're travelling, and he'll see my letter's delivered. He also thinks The Home Service's offer is too good to miss.

I just hope it's not all a horrible shock, especially when you've had to cope with the shipping lines being sold off.

Let me know what you think, and also that you're all right. In spite of assurances from Mr Stanopoulos, I'm starting to worry. And pretty soon I'm going to need a bridesmaid too.

And the letter was signed, 'From Molly, with love.'

Natasha went back to the beginning and reread the whole thing, feeling her first confusion turning to suspicion. Closely followed by anger.

Although she wasn't angry with Molly. She and Craig were made for each other, so of course she'd want to be with him, and Natasha wished them both nothing but everlasting happiness.

The Home Service, and its offer, was a different matter. It was a very large network of companies, offering every aspect of household maintenance, repairs, plumbing, electrics, small building works, decoration and design, and domestic cleaning. And now, apparently, it wanted to extend its activities into the kind of individual care and support that Helping Out provided.

And with Molly going to America and herself temporarily out of the picture, they'd certainly picked the right moment to step in.

As if, she thought, her heart thudding, they'd known...

My entire life—just signed away.

As her own words came back to her, she pushed her coffee away so abruptly that it spilled across the white tablecloth.

Because she'd spoken them, she thought angrily, to that same Mr Stanopoulos who was apparently in London, purporting to act on her behalf. And, in spite of his past assurances, this was exactly what was happening.

If she allowed this, she'd be going home to nothing. No job, an empty flat, and an uncertain future to add to the inevitable heartbreak of being Alex's discarded mistress.

The edifice of her existence totally dismantled, forcing her to start again—somehow—completely from scratch.

Well, it wasn't going to happen. She had to have something to provide a diversion from the desperation of love and loss.

This is my business, she thought stormily, pushing back her chair and rising, the letter clutched in her hand. My livelihood and my future. All I'm going to have in the world. And I won't let it go. I can't…

She marched into the house, making straight for the dining room. Iorgos was standing outside in faithful sentinel mode, and he gave her a startled look. 'Kyrios Mandrakis does not wish to be disturbed, *thespinis*.'

'Tough,' said Natasha, and ducked under the arm intended to bar her way. She flung open the door and walked into the room beyond.

The meal had been cleared away, and the coffee and brandy stage had been reached, the table littered with paperwork and cigar smoke heavy in the air.

As Natasha walked in, six heads swivelled to look at her in silent astonishment. Then, as their eyes absorbed her bikini-clad figure under its thin veiling of black and silver, she saw the growing smiles, and the amused murmurs of, '*Po,po,po,*' from all of them except Ari Stanopoulos, who looked faintly anguished, and Alex, whose face wore no expression whatsoever.

He rose to his feet, and the other men followed suit.

He said quietly, 'Natasha *mou*. I am involved in a business meeting.'

'So I was told,' she retorted. 'And I too have business to discuss.' She faced him, her chin lifted, her eyes glittering as she tossed her letter onto the table in front of him.

'I'd like you and your henchman here to understand one thing. I am not selling my company. So if this is your idea, forget it. When

I return to the UK, I intend to pick up my old life where I left off. Do I make myself clear?'

'I think this is something we need to talk over in private,' Alex said calmly. He turned to the rest of the company. 'Perhaps you would excuse me for a few minutes, gentlemen.'

One of the men said something quietly in Greek that was greeted with a ribald shout of laughter from the rest. Alex grinned, shrugged ruefully and picked up the letter before walking round the table to Natasha. His hand gripped her bare shoulder, propelling her from the room in a way that brooked no argument.

He walked her swiftly past the stricken Iorgos and down the corridor to his private office, and took her inside, slamming the door behind them.

Leaning against the big desk which dominated the centre of the room, he looked her up and down.

'So,' he said with a certain grimness, 'I see that you are still seeking ways in which to try my patience, Natasha.' He flicked the letter he was holding with irritable fingers. 'What is so urgent about this that you need to disrupt an important meeting? Burst in half-naked like a crazy woman?'

She said defiantly, 'You've never seemed troubled in the past over how little I was wearing. The less, the better, in fact.'

'Yes—when we are alone,' he said, 'but not if I am in conference with male colleagues.' He paused. 'You realise what they imagine is now happening between us.'

Her colour rose. Her Greek might have lost much of its fluency but thanks to Stavros and Andonis, she'd recognised one particularly graphic word from that muttered comment just now.

She said with a touch of breathlessness, 'Then they'll be wrong—won't they?'

'Yes,' he said. 'But that will not prevent the kind of speculation I was anxious to avoid.'

Natasha lifted her chin. 'Haven't you left it rather late in the day to decide you want to keep your personal life private?'

'No,' he said shortly. 'But let us waste no more time.' He glanced through the letter, his mouth tightening. 'You are being asked to consider a generous offer to buy your company, Natasha. What is the problem?'

'There is no problem,' she said. 'I'm not going to sell, that's all.'

'So you say,' he said slowly. 'But perhaps it is not that simple.'

Her voice was suddenly husky. 'Please don't tell me that your lawyer has agreed to this in my absence.'

'No,' he said. 'He has not.'

'And you're not behind it—in some mysterious way?'

He said flatly, 'Until Ari mentioned this proposal, I had never heard of the company. Does that content you?'

Natasha paused, then gave an unwilling nod.

'We make progress.' He paused. 'Now, tell me something. Is Kyria Blake just a friend who works for you, and shares your living accommodation?'

'No, of course not,' she said hotly. 'Molly's an equal partner in the firm.' She punched a fist into the palm of her other hand. 'Oh, God, if I was there in London, if you hadn't tricked me into leaving, all this would never have happened. I'd have put a stop to it at once.'

He said coldly, 'You are being irrational, Natasha *mou*. Could you have prevented your friend's fiancé taking a job on the other side of the world, or talked her out of joining the man she loves?' He shook his head. 'I think not. So what will happen when the partnership ends, as it must?'

'I began Helping Out by myself,' Natasha said. 'I can run it alone in the future.'

'Can you?' he asked softly. 'And what of Kyria Blakes's wishes?'

She said quickly, 'Molly doesn't want to sell, any more than I do.'

'Are you so sure?' He glanced down at the letter, his mouth twisting. 'Now, I would say she is undecided.' He gave her a level look. 'So let us be practical. If you refuse this offer, Natasha *mou*, can you afford to buy her out? She is entitled to expect fifty per cent of your company's new market value.'

She felt hollow inside. She said, 'Molly—Molly wouldn't do that.'

'Then she is either a fool or a saint,' Alex returned sardonically. 'And her future husband may take a different view of the situation. He may feel that her efforts deserve their just reward.'

She said in a stifled voice, 'Of course, and I'll deal with it. Get a bank loan for her share of the money if necessary.'

'As the Papadimos brothers attempted to do with much better collateral?' He shook his head slowly. 'I doubt your success.' He added drily, 'Unless, of course, you intend to offer your charming body as part of the deal once again. But I think most banks prefer their repayments in cash rather than kind.'

Anguished colour flooded her face. She said hoarsely, 'That is—so unfair.'

'You insisted on this interview,' he said. 'I did not. And perhaps I am not in the mood to be fair.'

He handed back the letter. 'When you are calmer, I recommend that you give the matter careful thought, and let your head rule your heart when you make your decision.' His tone was curt. 'Now I must return to my meeting.'

As he went past her he paused suddenly and turned, his hands reaching for her shoulders. He jerked her towards him, into his arms, and his mouth came down hard on hers in a kiss that seemed to hold more anger than tenderness or passion.

For one endless moment she could not think—she could not breathe. Then, with equal abruptness, he let her go and walked to the door without looking back.

Natasha was left standing alone, staring after him, one hand pressed to her bruised mouth and the crumpled letter crushed in the other.

So this—this was the moment she'd longed for, she thought, trembling inside.

To be in Alex's arms again. To feel his mouth on hers.

But their reunion was far from how she'd dreamed—how she'd planned it might be. And was it really so bad that she'd interrupted his meeting, inappropriately dressed?

Didn't he understand that Molly's letter had knocked her sideways? And that it wasn't just the potential loss of her business, either, that had devastated her, but the fact that her best friend was going away, and she was going to be alone at a time when she needed help and support as never before?

Alex must surely realise that her company was her one remaining scrap of stability in a world that he himself had set reeling, and make allowances.

Except that he did not seem prepared to do so, she thought, swallowing. It was only her body that mattered to him, not her feelings. And it was clear that he had neither forgiven nor forgotten their previous parting.

Well, tonight when they were alone together, and she went into his arms, she could atone for that at least by offering him, without reservation, the physical response he required from her.

At the same time making absolutely certain that he did not guess even for a moment what her true feelings for him might be.

And in spite of everything else going on in her life, Natasha knew that would be the greatest difficulty she would ever have to face.

To love—to give—and to be silent.

CHAPTER TWELVE

WRITING to Molly wasn't the easiest task Natasha had ever undertaken.

But after numerous false starts, during an endless afternoon, she eventually managed a version which sounded positive, even upbeat, about the deal with The Home Service and, at the same time, hid that, with her entire future in the melting pot, she was scared.

'So we'll both be making an entirely fresh start with our lives,' she ended. 'With my share, I'll be able to go where I want, and do something completely different, if I please. And how exciting is that?' She added, 'And I'll make sure I'm back in plenty of time for your great day.' She signed it with her love, then folded the sheet and put it in the envelope, which she left open.

At some point she'd heard the helicopter take off, presumably to transport Alex's visitors back to wherever they'd come from, and wondered suddenly and with dismay if Alex had left with them.

Suddenly there were no certainties any more, she thought, touching a rueful finger to her lips and wondering if, with that brief, harsh contact a couple of hours earlier, he'd been kissing her goodbye.

At sunset Josefina came tapping on the door, bubbling with excitement over the return of Kyrios Alexandros, and keen to help the *thespinis* to choose something suitably glamorous to welcome him home. Proving that he was still around, after all.

But to the other girl's disappointment, Natasha gently but firmly sent her away. Tonight she would get ready for dinner alone. Dress in order to be undressed later, she told herself with a quiver along her senses that mingled anticipation and fear.

And, while doing so, she needed to think.

She'd already decided on her dress, simple and sleeveless with a brief swirl of a skirt, in a dark green silky fabric that clung to her slender curves in overt enticement.

But then, after that botched reunion, she needed all the help she could get, she thought as she showered, then dried her damp hair into a silken cloud on her shoulders as Alex liked to see it. She moisturised and scented her skin, then darkened her lashes with mascara and accentuated her mouth in a soft shade of coral. Then, taking a deep breath, she went to find him.

He was in the *saloni* with Ari Stanopoulos, and they talking quietly together over their ouzo. At her entrance he turned, his face unsmiling as he watched her approach, his dark eyes scanning her body under its green veiling with a frankness he made no effort to hide.

And if they'd been alone, she thought, aware that her nipples were hardening involuntarily under his almost clinical regard, she would probably have walked straight into his arms, lifting her mouth to his in mute invitation, instead of halting at a discreet distance.

And perhaps it was just as well that Mr Stanopoulos was present, too, or she might also have blundered into some serious act of self-betrayal—like breathing *'S'agapo—I love you'* against Alex's lips.

As it was, she was able to say lightly, 'You'll be relieved to hear, *kyrie*, that common sense has finally prevailed,' and hand him the unsealed envelope.

His brows lifted with faint irony. 'You are sure you want me to see this?'

She shrugged. 'I've taken your advice. There's nothing secret about it.'

He read the letter through expressionlessly, then handed it to the lawyer. 'Do you wish Ari to act for you in the transaction?'

She forced a smile. 'That—might be best.'

'I will prepare the necessary authority.' Mr Stanopoulos looked at her kindly. 'This cannot have been an easy decision for you, Kyria Kirby.'

Natasha flushed, recalling her stormy descent on the dining room.

'No,' she said. 'I was—a little thrown to begin with.' She paused. 'But, once again, I seem to have been made an offer I can't refuse.'

There was a tingling silence. She saw Alex's lips tighten momentarily, and wished the words unspoken.

But all he said in response, his voice coolly courteous, was, 'May I pour you a drink?'

'Thank you. Some orange juice would be good.' She took the glass he handed her, and walked to one of the sofas, picking up a magazine and studying its contents with feigned absorption as she watched Alex covertly beneath her lashes.

He'd changed into light chinos that accentuated his long legs and lean hips, and against the short-sleeved blue shirt his skin was bronze. Merely looking at him made her mouth dry, and her heartbeat quicken uncontrollably.

Ari Stanopoulos had said something which amused him, and as his mouth curved she began to tremble as she recalled how his smile had felt against her skin. That—dear God—and the slow, arousing glide of his hands...

Maybe tonight, she thought breathlessly, she would turn the tables by undressing him, before giving full rein to all the fantasies that had kept her awake at night during his absence.

My turn, she told herself, to make amends—if he'll let me.

When dinner was served she was nervous beyond belief, fumbling with the cutlery and almost knocking over her wineglass. She was far too aware of him—of the lithe strength of his body, lounging in the chair at the head of the table, of every gesture, every note in his voice—to be able to relax. She had to force herself to eat, even though the food was wonderful, as always, and knew that her contributions to the conversation at the table were few and stilted.

As coffee was being served, she found that Ari Stanopoulos was asking her kindly how she liked the island.

'What I've seen of it seems lovely.' She made herself smile. 'But so far I've spent most of my time here on the beach.'

'Now that will all change,' he said. 'Kyrios Mandrakis knows every square metre of Alyssos from his childhood. You could not ask for a better guide. There are no ancient ruins, alas, but the interior has rugged charm.' He turned to Alex. 'You must take Kyria Kirby up into the hills, my friend.'

Alex's own smile did not reach his eyes. 'Of course,' he said. 'I came back for no other purpose.'

There was an awkward silence which Natasha hurried to fill, addressing the lawyer again. 'Maybe you can tell me where my foster mother, Madame Papadimos, used to live. I'd like to visit the place she loved so much.'

There was another, even deeper silence as the two men exchanged glances, then Alex said curtly, 'I do not advise it. There is nothing to see.'

'But there's the house, surely.' She looked at him in bewilderment. 'Stavros and Andonis said it was surrounded by olive groves, with a path through the trees leading down to the sea.'

She paused. 'I realise it belongs to someone else now, and naturally I wouldn't dream of intruding. I just want to tell Thia Theodosia that I've seen it—even at a distance.'

Ari Stanopoulos leaned forward as if to speak, but Alex halted him, his hand raised. He said quietly and coldly, 'If that is what you wish, Natasha, then I will take you there. One day.'

He didn't add 'Before you leave', but he didn't have to. It was implicit in his tone, and the finality of those two chilling words.

Natasha lifted her chin as inner pain lanced her. 'Then that will be something to look forward to,' she returned brightly, and rose, cup and saucer in hand. 'I'm sure you have things to discuss,' she added, 'so I'll take my coffee to the *saloni*.'

But if she was expecting a denial or for them to conclude their business quickly and join her, she was due for serious disappointment. When the two men left the dining room, it was only to adjourn to Alex's study and close the door behind them.

Left to herself once more, Natasha tried again to read, but couldn't concentrate. Switched on some music, and found it irritating. Attempted to watch television, only to find the channels dominated by sport played by teams she'd never heard of.

Eventually, after more than an hour and a half had passed, and she'd been reduced to walking up and down the room, her arms wrapped defensively round her body, Zeno appeared.

'Kyrios Mandrakis wishes more coffee, *thespinis*,' he announced. 'May I bring also for you?'

'Thank you, no,' she returned politely, even though her heart was sinking. She paused. 'Actually, I'm rather tired, so I'm going to my room. Perhaps you would inform Kyrios Mandrakis.'

He inclined his head austerely, clearly disapproving of the intimate implications her message conveyed, but the damage to his sensibilities was nothing when compared to the aching emptiness of her own, she told herself rebelliously, caught between anger and wretchedness.

What a fool she'd been to think that anything Mac Whitaker had told her could possibly make any difference, she brooded as she walked to her bedroom. Alex was a law unto himself and always would be, so why should he care if her judgement of him had been so fundamentally revised?

In her room, the lamps had been lit on either side of the bed and her nightdress put ready for her as usual. She replaced it in the drawer, then slowly undressed and got into bed, adjusting the sheet to cover her naked body to her shoulders.

Willing, she thought, her mouth twisting, but not too blatantly so.

Then, extinguishing the lights, she lay back against the mounded pillows and waited. At her request, the sliding glass doors to the terrace were again slightly open, allowing the slight breeze to stir the filmy drapes, while in the distance she could hear the faint sound of the sea.

A beautiful night she thought, with a little yearning sigh. And a night when she would heal any breach between them. When she would do anything he wanted. Be everything he wanted. When somehow she would banish the coldness from his eyes, and return the husky passion to his voice. Telling him with her body all that she dared not put into words.

A night that would perhaps make him remember her when they were no longer together. And for all the right reasons too, she told herself wryly.

After a while, she found her mind beginning to drift and her eyelids getting heavy, and had to force herself back to wakefulness. This wasn't the plan at all, she thought with faint bewilderment. Surely Alex's discussions with Mr Stanopoulos couldn't last much longer.

And, however deplorable he might find it, Zeno would remember to pass on her message—wouldn't he?

She said Alex's name under her breath, her need for him throbbing inside her like a harsh pulse, her body moving restlessly in the loneliness of the wide bed.

As the time passed, she shook off another light doze to discover that the darkness and stillness in her room had somehow spread to the entire house. That there wasn't a sound anywhere or a movement, except in this bed, where she had turned onto her side at some point, her hand reaching across the empty space beside her, seeking him.

Only to realise that her quest was totally in vain, and that she was destined to spend another night in solitude. And that she'd woken to find her face wet with tears of loneliness.

The next time she opened her eyes, the room was bathed in sunlight.

Josefina had been in to wake her earlier, because she could remember returning her greeting in a voice still drowned in sleep. Besides, there was a tray of cold coffee on the bedside table as mute evidence of the girl's visit.

And there was also the noise which had finally invaded her fleeting uncomfortable dreams, and brought her back to harsh reality. The busy sound of a helicopter departing.

She sat up abruptly, her heart thudding, a voice inside her whispering, Oh, no. Please—no.

Then she flung back the sheet and scrambled out of bed, going through drawers and cupboards, grabbing a handful of lingerie, together with a pair of white shorts and a turquoise top.

And as she walked to the main part of the house, a little while later, her hands were clenched into nervous fists at her sides.

She found Zeno on the terrace, clearing away used cups and plates from the table.

'May I bring you breakfast, *thespinis*?'

His tone held its usual formality, but was she imagining a flash of pity in his eyes as he looked at her? Presumably the entire household knew by now that she'd not been favoured by Kyrios Alexandros last night. And that her days on Alyssos were already numbered.

'I'm not very hungry, thank you.' She squared her shoulders. 'I heard the helicopter earlier. Has—has Kyrios Mandrakis gone back to Athens?'

He looked at her in open astonishment. 'He goes nowhere, *thespinis*. He works. It is Kyrios Stanopoulos who leaves.'

'Oh—I see.' It took a supreme effort to keep her voice casual, disguising her sheer joy and relief at the news, and she had a shrewd suspicion that he wasn't in the least deceived anyway.

Also, in view of the fact that Alex hadn't come near her last night, that it was far too soon to feel relieved.

I have to see him, she told herself. I have to know—one way or the other.

She turned back into the house and went straight to the study before her courage failed her. Iorgos wasn't on sentry duty for once, so she tapped on the door and entered on Alex's quiet summons.

He was seated behind his desk, a sheaf of papers in front of him, and he glanced up, his brows lifting as he registered her presence.

'*Kalimera*.' He made a note on the margin of the document he was reading. 'Did you wish to speak to Ari? If so I regret that he has already left.'

Caught on the wrong foot, Natasha stared at him. 'Why should I want to do that?'

He shrugged. 'I thought you might have other more private messages for him to convey to London in addition to your letter. Some—afterthought perhaps. But it seems not.' He paused. 'I hope you slept well.'

'I suppose I did—eventually.' Natasha swallowed. 'Not at first, though.' She took a deep breath. 'You see, I—I stayed awake, waiting for you.'

'I am flattered.' He put a line through an entire paragraph. So easily done, she thought. So quickly removed from some equation by a stroke of the pen. Like a girl, perhaps, who no longer held his interest.

'But now I'm wondering why I'm still here,' she went on bravely. 'Why you didn't send me away with Mr Stanopoulos just now—if you no longer want me.'

'I have not said so.' His frowning attention remained on his paperwork.

'Then what is it?' She swallowed. 'Are you still angry about my interruption of your meeting yesterday?'

'No.' Alex put down his pen and leaned back in his chair. 'Maybe what I require, Natasha *mou*, is some evidence that you want me.' He added drily, 'There has been little enough in our dealings together so far.'

'I don't understand…'

He shrugged. 'It is not so difficult,' he said. 'You knew where I was last night. You admit you found it difficult to sleep, yet still you chose to remain by yourself.'

She stared at him. 'You mean, you expected—you wanted me to come to you? To ask…?' She shook her head. 'But you can't have done. Besides, I—couldn't…' she added, biting her lip.

He resumed his study of the papers in front of him. He said almost casually, 'Then sleeping alone will become a habit for both of us.'

In spite of his tone, Natasha could recognise an ultimatum when she heard one. And it seemed that nothing but complete capitulation would do.

Her throat tightened. From some far distance, she heard herself say, 'I—I'm here now.'

'I am aware of that.' He did not look up. 'Sadly, I must soon leave for a lunch engagement on the other side of the island. You must forgive me.'

'I see.' She was very still for a moment, absorbing his rejection and wincing inwardly at the pain of it. She forced a smile. 'I take it that, once again, I won't be going with you?'

'My host is a friend of my father's, Natasha,' Alex told her levelly. 'A good man, but strictly conventional in his views, as is his wife. They would not approve of your presence on the island, let alone here at the Mandrakis house.'

'I see.' She bent her head. 'I think Zeno shares his views.'

'Probably.' He sounded faintly amused. 'He too is a traditionalist.' He paused, suddenly frowning. 'However, I will speak to him.'

'No, please. I—I wasn't complaining.' She drew a breath. 'But, knowing what people would think, I'm wondering why you had me brought here.'

'For the sake of peace and privacy, Natasha *mou*,' he drawled. 'There are strict controls at the port. No prowling photographers or gossip writers are allowed on Alyssos. Whereas the *Selene,* regrettably, is a magnet for such vermin whenever she puts into harbour. Wherever we had gone, they would have been waiting for us.'

She said, 'I can understand why you don't like newspapers. Mac—Captain Whitaker—told me what really happened at your birthday party.'

His brows lifted. 'That was…good of him.'

'So I'm sorry for the things I thought—and said about it,' she added in a little, desperate rush.

'It is not important.' He shrugged. 'And at least there were no photographers there that night. The man who saw you in my arms on Mykonos must have made a fortune from the picture he snatched of us. It has appeared everywhere.'

She said tautly, 'Yet—isn't that what you wanted, as your revenge? For all the world to know that I belonged to you?'

'Perhaps,' he said. 'But I have discovered since that revenge is not as sweet as I had hoped.' He added quietly, 'Now, if you will excuse me, I must finish what I am doing.'

'Yes,' she said. 'Yes, of course.' She paused. 'Then, I'll see you later.'

She stood for a moment outside his closed door, feeling the uneven race of her heart.

She didn't have to do as he asked, of course. She could stay in her room, and he could remain in his, until he became bored with this stalemate between them and decided to send her back to England.

That would be the safe—the sensible course of action.

Except that she had no guarantee he would also see it that way. After all, he'd once told her that she was a challenge. Maybe his demand for her unequivocal surrender was simply the next move in this convoluted game of revenge he was playing. A game he would be determined to win, in spite of any belated regrets he might be having.

Unconditional surrender, after which, his victory achieved, he would be free to go on to his next conquest, business or personal, she thought, moving aimlessly away from his door, her arms wrapped defensively round her body.

However, there was another course of action she could choose instead of fighting him.

Because he'd also said on that first night together that he would keep her until she no longer wished to leave, and only she knew that particular stage in their relationship was already past and gone.

I wouldn't even have to pretend, she told herself unhappily. Just— turn to him, cling to him day and night as if he was every hope of heaven I'd ever had. And wait for him to get bored, which shouldn't take too long—once he realises what's happened, and that I could become a serious nuisance.

But before that, she thought, at least I will have tonight.

It was a very long afternoon, which eventually, with mind-numbing slowness, turned into evening. But Alex still did not return.

By the time Zeno came to her to tell her with faint awkwardness that Kyrios Alexandros would be dining at the port with friends and sent his regrets, Natasha had already prepared herself for disappointment and heard the news with a smiling calm that amazed her.

It was not a defeat, but a test of her resolve, she told herself. Later was simply going to be—much later. That was all.

When she had eaten, she watched a film from the DVD collection in the saloni without absorbing one word of the dialogue or one twist of the plot, then went quietly to her room.

She took a long, warm scented bath, put on the silver robe that Alex had given her and lay on top of the bed to wait.

No sleep, she told herself. Not tonight. No second thoughts, either.

She allowed midnight to pass, before making her way barefoot down the long passage to the master bedroom, wondering if she would find it empty, and if so what her next course of action should be.

If she would ever be brave enough to do this again.

As she twisted the handle the door opened noiselessly, and she slipped inside. The room was lit by the moonlight streaming in through its open glass doors, where Alex was standing, staring out into the night, a dark figure in his dressing gown, his back turned towards her.

She said his name, then repeated shyly, 'Alex—*mou.*'

He turned slowly and looked at her, his brows drawing together as if he did not really believe what he was seeing.

She said, 'I'm here now,' deliberately repeating the words she'd used in his study hours before, then reached for the sash of her robe, untied it and shrugged the garment from her shoulders. Praying that this time he would not turn away.

He strode to her across the marble floor, sweeping her up into his embrace, his mouth fastening on hers in almost savage yearning, and her arms went round his neck, her fingers twining in his hair, holding him to her.

He carried her to the bed, threw off his own robe and entered her in what seemed like one agonised movement.

She came at once, taken unawares by the force of her own necessity, her body convulsing round him in spasm after spasm of unbearable delight, her voice crying out in shaken ecstasy against his shoulder, and he remained still, lying with her—within her—murmuring huskily to her in his own language, a hand smoothing her tumbled hair as he waited for her to recover.

But, as reality returned, shame at her own greed came with it and she closed her eyes, shielding her embarrassed face in the warm muscularity of his chest. He'd wanted her to want him, she thought, her mind reeling. And she'd given him incontrovertible proof that she did. But what else had she betrayed by her helpless, desperate response to him?

He said huskily, '*Matia mou*, my sweet one. Don't try to hide from me. Your joy is mine.'

He began to kiss her slowly, his mouth paying sensuous homage to her eyes, her burning cheekbones and her parted lips, before moving down to her breasts, his tongue circling the excited rosy peaks in a leisurely, devastating caress, making her moan softly—helplessly—her head thrown back on the pillow.

And, because there was no longer any cause to pretend indifference or hold back in any way, she began to touch him in her turn, running her fingers through his dishevelled hair, still damp from the shower, then stroking her hands along the hard, muscular shoulders and down the strong back to the powerful male buttocks and long thighs, his skin like warm satin under her fingertips.

Exploring his body—enjoying him with a delight that went beyond any fantasy.

And finding herself aroused anew, not just by her roving touch of him, and the heaven of his hands and mouth on her own body, but also by the overwhelming sensation created by the heated strength of him sheathed, waiting inside her.

By the knowledge that her desire for him had only been temporarily assuaged by his initial possession, and certainly not sated.

Because she was already stirring, slowly, restlessly beneath him, every nerve-ending in her flesh a tiny, separate flame. Arching towards him as she offered herself mutely for his satisfaction. And once more, it seemed, for hers…

Alex muttered something hoarse in his throat and began to move in his turn, his body thrusting deeply into her moist and trembling heat, establishing the powerful, irresistible rhythm that she remembered so well from the last time they'd made love.

Except that it wasn't love, she thought from the small, sane corner of her brain that still remained, even as her body lifted to him—joined him in a rapturous and all-too-willing response. Or not love in the way she wanted—that she longed for with her entire soul. However passionate and heart-stopping, it was just an exchange of physical pleasure.

And then his mouth closed hungrily on hers and his hands were caressing her everywhere, stroking her thighs, her belly, her breasts, his fingertips teasing her aching nipples, and, for Natasha, all coherent thought ceased.

They were straining together faster now and ever more intensely, blind and deaf to everything but the wild spiral of their approaching consummation.

Both taken utterly by storm as the savage, pulsating ecstasy had its way with them, flinging them out together into some matchless void, their voices breaking as they cried out.

Afterwards they lay, still joined, their bodies slick with sweat, in a profound and shaking silence.

She thought, Don't leave me, and did not realise she had spoken the words aloud until he said on a breath of husky laughter, 'I am going nowhere, my beautiful one.'

A long time later, he said, 'Dare I ask if you have missed me a little?'

She lifted her head from its pillow on his chest. 'I think you know the answer to that already.'

'Yes,' he said. 'But perhaps I need to hear you say it.'

'Then—yes, *kyrie*. I missed you.'

And you, my darling. If I asked you the same thing, what would you say? Could you reply 'Yes', or would you hesitate, knowing that you'd found consolation with Domenica or someone else while we were apart, then tell me a kind lie?

Alex sighed softly, contentedly, and rolled over, imprisoning her beneath him.

'At last,' he whispered. 'Now tell me again, but this time without words, *agapi mou*.'

CHAPTER THIRTEEN

I AM going nowhere…

Natasha found Alex's words tingling in her mind as soon as she opened her eyes the next morning.

It was still very early, the pale sky hardly tinged with the pink of sunrise, and she lay quietly, assimilating her surroundings and the sweet, lingering ache of physical delight. Remembering…

And as she did so, she felt her body warm and her mouth curve gently in utter contentment.

As she took this moment—waking in Alex's arms, with her head on his shoulder and his cheek against her hair—captured and hid it deep in her consciousness. A fragment of sheer happiness to be treasured and enjoyed in the inevitable loneliness ahead of her.

Although she would not think of that now. Not allow herself any sad thoughts when she had the rapture of last night's lovemaking to savour—the total mastery of his body, his hands and mouth taking her to new heights, urging her into new responses, new demands that she would never have believed possible.

Quite—irresistible, she told herself languorously. And she had not even attempted to resist.

They had finally fallen asleep, still entwined, in sheer exhaustion, although she'd been drowsily aware at some point of Alex moving, taking the crumpled sheet and arranging it over their damp bodies, before drawing her close again.

All the same, she thought, it was now day—and time she wasn't here.

She eased herself out of his embrace, infinitely careful not to disturb him, knowing that if he woke and drew her down to him again she would make no protest.

She hadn't really noticed her surroundings last night. She had seen only him, but she looked round her now as she retrieved her robe and fastened it round her. It was a very big room, but the bed she'd just left dominated the space—king-size going on emperor, she thought—its massive carved headboard giving it dignity to the point of grandeur. An important bed.

On the wall opposite a large unframed picture of a wild sea dashing itself over rocks. The Aegean raging in a storm, and she shivered suddenly as if she could feel the spray on her warm skin.

An imposing mirrored dressing table in the same dark wood as the bed, and, by the window, a couch and a table. Two doors leading, she guessed, to the bathroom and his dressing room. Nothing else.

She trod back to the bed and looked down at him tenderly, longing to bend and kiss him, but telling herself that would be an indulgence. And that later there would be plenty of time for kisses and other pleasures too.

Then crept quietly out of the room.

She was having breakfast on the terrace when she heard his voice from the *saloni* aiming a sharp question at Zeno.

He came to join her, his hair still wet from the shower, and a thin shirt open over a pair of dark swimming trunks.

'*Kalimera.*' He bent and kissed her, rubbing his freshly shaven cheek gently against her face. 'I woke without you, *matia mou*. Why?'

'I thought it would be better if I went back to my own room,' she said, suddenly shy as her body stirred involuntarily in answer to his brief caress.

'Not better for me.' He sat down, pulling the coffeepot towards him. 'And from now on, you share my bedroom. I will arrange to have your clothes and belongings transferred at once.'

'No,' she said. 'Please—Alex, don't do that.'

He stared at her, dark brows drawing together. 'Why not?'

She hesitated. 'Perhaps,' she said haltingly, 'for the same reason that I didn't have lunch with your father's friends. For the sake of appearances.' She forced a smile. 'I gather your household isn't altogether accustomed to having your…female guests here.'

'No,' he said, after a pause. 'They are not.'

They thought the first would be your wife—because Josefina told me so. And they will still believe that your bride alone should have the right to share the master bedroom with you.

And they would be right, she thought. I shouldn't sleep there, because that amazing bed is a marriage bed, not a place for a transient love affair, and I—I turned you down when you asked me. Even then, in my subconscious mind, I must have known that I loved you. But that I couldn't bear to be married simply because your honour demanded it—because you'd taken my virginity and spoiled me for any other marriage.

I knew that being tied to me in such a way could only lead to indifference, with resentment not far behind. And having to live with you on those terms would have been a real fate worse than death. Far more so than any seduction.

She hurried back into speech. 'Therefore,' she said, 'it might make things easier all round if we were…discreet.'

Alex took one of the fresh rolls from the napkin-covered basket on the table, and began to butter it.

He said drily, 'I hoped for discretion too, *pedhi mou*. But I think your arrival in the dining room the other day damaged any lasting hope of that. By this time the world will know I am not alone here. And I assure you that no one in the house will be even slightly deceived over where we spend our nights. But let it be as you wish.'

He sent her a sudden wicked grin. 'So, do I whisper "My place or yours?" over dinner?'

She tried not to smile back, and failed completely. 'I'm being serious,' she protested.

'I know,' he said. 'And please believe I am entranced at this belated effort to establish my unswerving morality.' He refilled her coffee cup. 'And in future I shall come to you at night, although I do not guarantee to wait until everyone else in the house is asleep, or leave at dawn.

'I shall have also to think up all kinds of reasons to be alone with you, Natasha *mou*, in the daytime, as well,' he went on. 'And I think that today we will go sailing.'

She said rather wistfully, 'That would be lovely. But are you sure you can spare the time? I know how busy you always are.'

'Yes,' he said. 'And lately I have been working extra-hard trying to clear my desk in order to be with you, my beautiful one, and give you all the attention you deserve, instead of snatched moments.

'So for a while at least, we can put the world at a distance,' he added quietly.

For a while at least…

Yes, she thought as he reached across the table and took her hand in his. And for that time, however long, however short, he would be hers. She would hope for nothing more.

It was a day captured from heaven. Aboard the caique *Mariam* they sailed all the way around the island, eventually anchoring off a deserted beach where they went ashore in the dinghy and Alex cooked the fish he'd caught a short while before over a driftwood fire on the sand.

'You're full of surprises, *kyrie*,' Natasha commented from the rug he'd spread in the shade of an ancient olive tree at the edge of the beach, as she watched him deftly prepare their food.

He looked at her across the fire, his eyes paying tribute to the slender curves revealed by her bikini.

'And when we have eaten, *kyria*, I intend to surprise you in a different way,' he promised softly, and she threw back her head laughing, because there was sunlight, food and wine, and the anticipation of her lover's arms around her and his kisses on her lips.

One glorious sun-filled day seamlessly became another. Turned into a week that slipped into a second, then a third.

I am going nowhere…

He'd said that, and it seemed he'd meant it.

When they were not aboard *Mariam* they were often beside the pool, Alex taking full advantage of its seclusion to swim and sunbathe naked, and to encourage her to do the same.

They'd been in the water together the first time he'd swiftly stripped her of her bikini before discarding his own trunks, and tossing them onto the tiled rim.

'Alex—no,' she'd protested desperately, trying unsuccessfully to hold him off. 'Someone might see us.'

'No, *agapi mou*,' he whispered. 'I promise that we will not be disturbed.' And pulled her close.

Much later, she said breathlessly, 'I thought you didn't approve of naked girls in swimming pools.'

He laughed, kissing her softly. 'I approve of you naked anywhere and at any time, Natasha *mou*,' he told her.

His behaviour on the beach below the villa was rather more decorous, however, and, to her own astonishment, Natasha found herself being swiftly initiated into the thrills and spills of waterskiing and windsurfing, at both of which Alex was effortlessly expert, and, more unexpectedly, a remarkably patient teacher, and as her fledgling skills developed and improved under his careful tuition she felt almost triumphant.

Iorgos was at the wheel of the speedboat when she attained sufficient prowess to ski beside Alex and, while he remained taciturn, there were times when he bestowed on Natasha a faint smile that was almost approving.

She realised she was learning other lessons too. Making discoveries all the time about the man she loved, seeing a younger and altogether more carefree side to the powerful controller of his business empire.

Someone, she thought, who sang softly under his breath, and held her hand as she walked beside him. Someone who seemed to know intuitively the occasions when she was tired enough to wish just to sleep in his arms.

Someone who talked to her, argued with her, teased her. Who encouraged her to revive the Greek language skills of her younger years. Who challenged her in the evenings to play the wickedly fast Greek form of backgammon that she'd learned with Thio Basilis, and sometimes allowed her to win. Who was teaching her chess.

Someone who fulfilled every dream she'd ever had. Except for the most important one…

He spoke of his desire for her so frankly that it still had the power to make her blush, but he never spoke of love.

Sometimes, when she lay drifting in the exquisite euphoria of her climax, she imagined him whispering, *'M'agapas?'* 'Do you love me?'

And was thankful she was not forced to lie—to deny her most secret, most precious feelings, and have to suffer the subsequent pain.

Because Alyssos was such a small island, it was hardly worth using the Jeep, so she and Alex spent a lot of time walking, and she guessed that quite often they were visiting places that had been his favourites in childhood.

He didn't say much at these times, just looked around him with hooded, reflective eyes.

She remembered that Mac Whitaker had hinted that Alex and his father had more or less given up on the island, just as Thia Theodosia had done, and wondered why this should have been, as it clearly meant so much to him.

But when she asked him, he merely shrugged and drawled, 'Things change, *matia mou*.' Which left her none the wiser, and reluctant to put the real question hovering in her mind—to ask him how the feud between their families had begun.

Because it never, she thought ruefully, seemed to be the right moment. And now the opportunity might have gone altogether.

'The world at a distance.' At the time that had sounded like a promise, but suddenly it was nudging closer again, working its way insidiously back into their lives, like a latter-day snake in Eden, and it seemed to Natasha that Alex's words had been more of a warning.

Very much like—'Things change...'

Because they had already done so, almost before she was aware.

And the major change was in Alex himself. The light-hearted lover was becoming unsmiling and introspective, his movements and manner almost abrupt. Sometimes when she woke in the night, it was to find him standing at the window, his face brooding as he stared into the darkness.

She longed to ask what the matter was—if she could help in any way—then reminded herself just in time that she was there solely to share his bed for a while, not his thoughts.

He was once again spending part of each day in his study, and their mealtimes together were often interrupted for phone calls which needed to be taken in private. Nor was there any more relaxed and sensuous nudity beside the pool in case a member of staff brought down a message for him, while the lingering, breathless siestas in her bedroom with the shutters closed were also becoming a thing of the past.

As, it occurred to her, she might well be herself.

And when, for the first time, he did not come to her room at night, she knew with aching certainty that it was the beginning of the end, and that she must prepare for it.

Her heart was thudding when he joined her for breakfast the following morning. Waiting, she realised, for the axe to fall.

He said without preamble, 'Natasha, I have to go away later today. There are matters I must attend to that can be put off no longer.' He looked up frowningly at the hazy sky. 'Would you like to go out on the boat this morning—before the weather breaks?'

She did not think she could bear the boat, where she'd spent so many happy hours with him. Not when it could be the last time...

She steadied her voice. 'That would be nice, but you did promise once that you'd show me where Thia Theodosia used to live.'

He hesitated, his frown deepening. 'Very well,' he said quietly. 'If you are sure that is what you want.'

This time they took the Jeep, Natasha realising at once that they were heading to a part of the island they had not visited before. For a while they followed the main highway, then Alex turned off abruptly onto a much narrower road, its surface scarred and pitted, showing how little it was used.

The new owners clearly didn't mind being jolted, Natasha thought breathlessly as the Jeep made another turn onto a steep and rocky track down into the promised shade of the olive trees with their silver, shivering leaves, and, as they finally emerged into the open, directly ahead of them was the subdued glimmer of the sea.

But that was all.

Natasha turned in her seat, staring round her. She said half to herself, 'But this can't be the place. There's nothing here.'

'As I told you.' His confirmation was harsh.

'But there was a house once.' She pointed. 'Some of the foundations are still there—see?' She scrambled out of the Jeep and went over to examine the remains of the concrete platform.

'So, what happened?' Alex had followed her, and she turned to him, spreading her hands in bewilderment. 'Was there an earthquake? If so, it must have been pretty selective.'

'No earthquake,' he said. 'The house was demolished in another way.'

She stared at him, her throat tightening. 'Tell me how.'

'With explosives first,' he said. 'Then the rubble itself was removed.' He shrugged, his mouth hard. 'Until everything had gone. As you see.'

'Yes,' she said thickly. 'I—see. Only too well.'

She shook her head. 'How could you do this?' Her eyes searched his, trying and failing to find some trace of the warmth and tenderness of the past weeks. 'Does Thia Theodosia know about this?'

'Yes,' he said. 'She has always known.'

'That's awful,' Natasha whispered. 'Because she's so kind, so lovely. She wouldn't deliberately hurt a living soul. So how could you destroy an innocent woman's home—something which meant so much to her? What kind of people are you?'

'Human beings,' he said harshly. 'With all the faults and failings of that condition. Capable of hatred, jealousy and vengeance. Did I ever pretend otherwise?'

'But why this? It makes no sense.'

'That is something I am not qualified to answer,' he said, after a pause. 'Nor, Natasha, did I light the fuse or move the stones. I was too young. Now, shall we go? If you have seen enough?'

There were tears in her throat, burning, acrid. She could only nod, then sit beside him, staring at nothing as they returned to the villa in silence.

As she made to leave the Jeep, he said quietly, 'Natasha—it was an empty building. Worse things have happened since this feud began, believe me.'

'You'll never convince me of that,' she said shakily.

This was more than two proud and arrogant men locking horns in enmity over their commercial dealings. It went far beyond cruel and spiteful, or a desire to win—to beat a rival a down, she thought. There'd been real hatred in this act of destruction.

She swung back to face him. 'Oh, God, how long will this vile thing be allowed to go on—poisoning people's lives? Why can't you do something to make it stop?'

He said slowly, 'Perhaps I can. But it might be something you would hate even more.'

'No,' she said. 'Never in this world.' She looked past him. 'I—I can't stay here any longer.'

'In this house?' he said. 'Or anywhere on the island?'

'Anywhere.' She shuddered. 'I thought it was so peaceful here. So beautiful.'

You made it beautiful, and now it seems uglier than any nightmare.

She said, 'But—knowing about this mindless violence—I can't think of it in the same way ever again.' *Or of you—your father's son...* 'And I want to leave. You have to let me go.'

'Go where?' he demanded roughly.

'To England,' she said. 'To London. Back to road rage, muggings and football hooligans. They'll all seem like a walk in the park compared with Alyssos.'

She swallowed. 'There'll be a helicopter coming for you, won't there? Will you let me go with you to Athens? My plane ticket might still be valid.'

'I regret that I am not going to Athens,' he said. 'Not immediately. But I will send the *Selene* for you, and instruct Mac to take you wherever you wish.'

'Thank you,' she said. 'How soon can he get here?'

'I will tell him it is a matter of urgency.'

They were talking like strangers, she thought. As if they had not spent all these past nights in total intimacy, drowning in pleasure in each other's arms. She had given herself to him utterly—heart, mind, body and soul. Given herself to a man she did not know.

'Urgency,' she said. 'Yes.'

He was beside her as she walked into the house. He said, 'Natasha *mou*,' and put a hand on her arm, which she shook off.

'Don't touch me.' She heard the note of panic in her voice, and took a deep, calming breath. 'You said once you liked to part from your...women...as friends. But that can't happen with us. Not now. Probably it never could.'

'No,' he said, quietly and bleakly. 'I think you are right.' He paused. 'Has it really been so bad, *matia mou*, being with me?'

She did not look at him. Her voice was stifled. 'No,' she said. 'Not—bad. Unbearable.'

And walked away from him to her room without looking back.

It was the sound of the helicopter that woke her, and she sat bolt upright, clothes sticking to her and her eyelashes gummed together with weeping as she listened to it fading into the distance.

Too late now, she realised, to run to Alex and say, I love you. Nothing matters but that, so please—please take me with you.

Which was one humiliation at least that she'd been spared, she thought, catching sight of herself in the mirror across the room, her face streaky, her eyes swollen and her hair plastered to her damp face. No man in his right mind would have taken her to the end of the street looking as she did.

Even a man who still desired her....

As Alex no longer did. And who had also warned he did not require love.

I knew I would only be with him for a little while, she thought. That he has a low boredom threshold with women. But I fell into the trap of being happy.

But even if their brief affair had not come to its end, she would have wanted to leave.

Because what Alex had done did matter. As a boy, he could not have been responsible for the destruction of Thia Theodosia's beloved house, but as a man he'd kept the feud going, totally and relentlessly, until he'd achieved a different kind of ruin for the Papadimos clan. Herself, included.

And now she at least had to put herself back together again—and survive.

Starting, she decided wearily, with a shower and a change of clothes. But as she swung herself off the bed she saw her passport lying on the night table beside her, and knew that he must have put it there, and seen her asleep, flushed and worn out with heartbreak.

So she'd been spared nothing after all, she thought bitterly, wrapping her arms round her body and bending her head in total defeat, because she had no more secrets to hide.

The next forty-eight hours were a living nightmare, made infinitely worse by the attitude of the rest of the household, who were universally and hideously kind to her.

Zeno the aloof was suddenly never far away, watching her like a benevolent hawk. His wife, her plump face a sympathetic mask, saw to it that small, delicious offerings were sent out from the kitchen to tempt Natasha's non-existent appetite.

And Josefina was in and out of her room, anxiously packing and re-packing all the lovely things hanging in the wardrobes and folded in the drawers, because Natasha did not have the heart to tell her she was wasting her time. That she would be taking nothing but what she stood up in and a change of underwear.

Oh, God, she thought, why had she agreed to wait for the *Selene*, when she could have told Alex, Forget Athens. Just put the helicopter down at the nearest airport and send me on my way. I'll cope.

Anything would be better than this…limbo.

She spent most of her waking hours on the beach, her eyes fixed painfully on the horizon, straining for the first sight of *Selene*.

But when on the third day she heard, instead, the noise of an approaching helicopter, she thought for a moment it was another bad dream like all those others that had put sleepless, unhappy shadows under her eyes.

But they had all featured departures, not arrivals, and she scrambled off her lounger, reaching for the gauzy blue and gold caftan which matched her azure bikini, and slipping it over her head, her heart thudding wildly.

Halfway back to the house she met Zeno coming in search of her. 'Kyrios Mandrakis is here, *thespinis*.' He sounded wary, his eyes concerned. 'He waits for you in the *saloni*.'

As she reached the lawns, she heard the rotors and saw the helicopter rise over the house and turn away inland. Which meant he was staying, if only for a little while.

She almost skimmed across the terrace and through the tall glass doors into the *saloni*, then stopped, her smile fading and her throat closing nervously as she saw the man waiting for her.

He was tall and white-haired, his features strongly marked, especially the beak of a nose that he'd passed on to his only son, and he was standing leaning lightly on an ebony cane with a silver top.

For the first time, Natasha was face to face with Petros Mandrakis.

CHAPTER FOURTEEN

'SO,' HE said, his dark eyes studying her as if she was an interesting specimen displayed in a glass case. 'You are the girl who turned my clever son's head, and made him forget all he owes to his family name. I am…surprised.'

She said crisply, 'No more than I was myself, *kyrie*, and please believe it's an episode I am eager to forget.'

He inclined his head unsmilingly. 'Then we can agree on that. And at least he had the sense to conduct his liaison with you in comparative privacy,' he added grimly. 'So it is to be hoped an open scandal can be avoided.'

He paused. 'But you cannot, of course, remain here.'

'I know that. I thought I'd already have left by now.' Her mouth felt dry. 'He—Kyrios Alexandros—said he would send his boat to fetch me. I—I've been waiting…'

'There has had to be a change of plan,' he said. 'The *Selene* is required for another purpose.' He paused, as if considering his words carefully. 'She is bringing some special guests to Alyssos, *thespinis*.'

He paused. 'You must understand that Alexandros has at last convinced me to bring this feud to an end with a properly contracted marriage between our families.'

Natasha was suddenly very still. She had the curious impression that the tall man standing in front of her had suddenly receded to some far distance.

But his voice reached her with total clarity. 'I have therefore invited Madame Theodosia Papadimos to visit me here on Alyssos, and to bring her daughter with her. We hope that Kyria Irini may be persuaded into acceptance of this new relationship, and maybe welcome it, once she has recovered from the initial shock.'

She was freezing cold, burning up, and sick to her stomach all at the same time, while a voice in her head was moaning, No—oh, God—no.

She stared at Petros Mandrakis, her mind spinning out of control.

Alex, she thought, trembling. Alex and Irini, locked together in a dynastic marriage of convenience, her dislike matched with his indifference. How could that possibly happen?

She'd always known that Alex would marry one day. 'A suitable heiress', as Mac Whitaker had said, who would give him a son and she'd thought, when it happened, time would have passed, and she'd have found some way of steeling herself to the inevitable.

But she'd never envisaged him taking Irini as his wife—even in her worst nightmares.

Yet when she'd stormed at him to end the feud, he'd warned her that she might find the solution worse than the problem. But she'd never guessed he intended this cynical piece of expediency.

And how could Thia Theodosia even consider it?

She wanted me to be a cherished wife and a happy mother, she thought. Surely she must have the same ambition for Irini. And found herself wincing away from a swift inner vision of Irini with Alex's baby in her arms.

She squared her shoulders. Steadied her voice. 'Madame Papadimos returning here, *kyrie*, after all that's happened? You amaze me.'

'Ah, yes. Alexandros told me you had insisted on seeing the house,' he said, his tone reflective. 'What happened there was—unfortunate. But not all Kyria Theodosia's memories of Alyssos are so painful.'

'Am I allowed to see her—just for a moment or two?'

'That will not be possible.' He shook his head. 'Your presence here, under the circumstances, would not be appropriate, as Alexandros was the first to point out. Negotiations are still at a most delicate stage, but I hope and believe they will be finalised during this visit.'

She said numbly, 'Yes. Yes, of course.'

'I have therefore arranged for you to stay for a while with my friend Dimitris Phillipos and his wife at their house on the other side of the port,' he continued. He frowned a little. 'Alexandros assures me they are unaware of his…irregular dealings with you, so I hope you will be good enough to maintain the pretence that you are merely a friend of the family whom they are entertaining as a favour to me.'

He added blandly, 'It may be some time before my son will be able to visit you. He must help reconcile Kyria Irini to her new circumstances, and cannot afford distractions, however charming.'

What was he saying? Natasha asked herself in disbelief. Did he think that she was still involved with Alex, and would be willing to remain his mistress throughout his courtship and marriage? Be—his bit on the side?

She felt a stab of sympathy for Irini, who had never had the affection she craved from her father, and looked to be equally unfortunate in her husband.

But I won't be causing her a minute's grief, she swore silently. When Alex starts playing away, I shall be long gone.

And she found herself praying inwardly that Irini would never suspect that her hated foster sister had spent even a minute sharing the master's bed in the master bedroom.

She said quietly, 'You are under a misapprehension, *kyrie*. Any dealings I have had with your son are at an end, and I have no plans to meet him again.'

His mouth twisted in frank scepticism. He reached into an inside pocket of his linen jacket and produced an envelope.

'I think Alexandros has a different viewpoint,' he remarked. 'He has asked me to give you this letter. Perhaps you should read it before reaching so definite a conclusion.'

She took it without further argument. Her troubles had begun with a letter, she thought. They would end with another.

After that, things moved fast. Almost before she knew it, her luggage was being piled into the Jeep, she had changed into a cream linen skirt, and a black sleeveless top, in order to be driven to the Phillipos house by Zeno. As the Jeep moved off, she could see Petros Mandrakis watching her frowningly from the main doorway.

Making sure I'm safely off the premises before his guests arrive, she thought, biting her lip.

Zeno was speaking to her with halting concern, asking if she had a hat, and she made herself smile back and say she was fine. It was certainly very hot, but the port was little more than fifteen minutes away, and the house she was going to would not be much further. She'd survive, even though she felt as if she'd been torn apart and discarded.

And the fact that Thia Theodosia didn't want to see her added to her sense of utter desolation.

They were just driving into the small town when she heard three steady blasts on a hooter and realised it was the warning that the ferry was about to leave.

According to Josefina, it wound its way among the islands, calling first at Naxos, where the myths said Ariadne had been abandoned by Theseus.

And in pre-history, that could have happened. These days, Ariadne would probably have shrugged and caught a flight from Naxos Airport to Athens and the UK to find a more reliable man.

And she could do exactly the same.

She sat up straight, clutching the strap of her bag. She had her wallet, her passport and the unused portion of her ticket. All she had to do was get down to the quayside before the ferry sailed.

She stole a sideways glance at Zeno, who was muttering because their way down the narrow street was blocked by a donkey and a cart laden with flowers.

She said, 'The sun's given me a headache. I see a chemist's sign a little further on. I'll walk up there, and buy some painkillers.'

She was out of the Jeep before he could object, and walking rapidly towards the pharmacy. She went in, and stood for a moment scanning a rack of toiletries, then peeped back into the street.

The donkey's owner had returned, and he and Zeno were fully engaged in a fiery altercation.

No one was looking at her, so Natasha put her head down and ran like a hare down one of the twisting alleys that led to the harbour.

Two men were just about to remove the gangplank, but she shouted 'Wait' in breathless Greek, and they paused, grinning broadly as she flew past them, calling, '*Efharisto,*' over her shoulder.

She went up to the bow and sat on one of the benches, recovering her breath. And as the ferry nosed its way into the open sea towards Naxos, she took Alex's unread letter from her bag, tore it up and tossed the pieces overboard.

'It's done,' she whispered under her breath. 'Finished. Over. And now my life can begin again—without him.'

* * *

'So,' Neil said with ominous calm. 'Exactly how did you become "The Mandrakis mystery girl"?'

Natasha looked down at the garish magazine he'd just slapped on the table in front of her. Ever since her arrival back in London a week ago, she'd known that sooner or later he'd be round and there'd be some kind of confrontation, but she'd not expected it to be like this.

Not that he'd just turn up unannounced and clearly furious, catching her in her old bathrobe, her wet hair wrapped in a towel, and Molly out for the evening.

And she'd certainly never thought she would find herself staring at the blaring headline above the cover photograph—her unmistakable self in a welter of black taffeta being carried in Alex's arms as he smiled down at her, and she looked back at him, her heart in her eyes. The ultimate giveaway.

They might as well, she thought, have drawn a balloon coming out of her mouth saying, 'I love you. Take me, I'm yours.'

She marshalled every atom of control she possessed. 'That,' she returned steadily, 'was quite some time ago.'

'Not that long.' His finger stabbed accusingly at the date. 'Melanie, one of the PAs, picked it up at the hairdresser's only last week. When she brought it into the office, I felt a complete fool.'

Well, please don't ask how I feel, she thought, or I might start crying again, and I cannot afford to revert to being a sodden heap in the corner of the sofa, or on the bed. Not when I have the rest of my life to pull together.

'You were supposed to be in Athens, signing papers,' he went on angrily. 'Not—cavorting on Mykonos with a notorious playboy like Alexander Mandrakis. What the hell was going on, Natasha?'

She was going to say, 'You're an adult male. Work it out for yourself.' But she stopped herself just in time. Because she'd pretty much given him the right to think better of her than that, and he'd be hurting too.

She looked away. 'There's nothing I can say,' she told him dully. 'Except—I'm sorry.'

Sorrier than I ever thought it was possible to be, and in as much pain as you could ever wish.

'But it was going to be...us,' Neil persisted. 'You and me together—wasn't it?'

'Things change.' *Had she really said that?* 'I—I have no other excuse to offer.'

He called her a bitch then, and other words besides, and she let them rage over her because she deserved them all.

'And now he's dumped you, and you're back here on your own.' Neil paused at the door, face flushed, his gaze inimical to deliver his valedictory. 'Not exactly hung with diamonds, are you? Maybe he didn't think you were worth it.'

When he'd gone, she sank down on the sofa because her legs were shaking under her.

He thought she'd gone to Greece and had an affair. And neither he nor anyone else could ever know the truth.

Even Molly, who'd welcomed her back, unsuccessfully concealing her dismay at Natasha's white strained face and dazed, shadowed eyes, had only had a strictly edited version.

'I fell in love,' Natasha had told her. 'And had a brief, crazy fling. But it's over, and I'm sane again.'

'You look like hell,' Molly said, concern making her brutal. Then her eyes widened, and she gasped, 'Oh, God, Nat. He hasn't... You're not...'

'No,' Natasha said quietly. 'I'm not.'

She'd stayed on Naxos for two nights, shopping for a basic change of clothing and a canvas holdall to stow it in, then hiring a room above a small, cheap taverna while she waited for a flight. On the first night there she'd received irrefutable evidence that she was not having Alex's baby, and knew that she should be thankful.

And, instead, had curled herself into the foetal position on the hard bed and wept herself to sleep, tears of loss and loneliness soaking the pillow.

Knowing that she'd secretly hoped for a child, because, even though he could never know of its existence, it would still be his. Something of Alex that would belong to her alone, she thought, to love and cherish.

And Molly had read the bleakness in her eyes and said more gently, 'You should have kept to Thia Theodosia's rules, my love. I don't think you're the type for flings.'

She'd made herself smile and say, 'Don't worry about me. I'll be back fighting my corner before you know it.' And tried not to be glad that Molly was rushing around making arrangements for the wedding, and had no idea how often Natasha yielded to the despair inside her when she was alone.

When the door buzzer sounded, she flinched.

Neil, she thought. Again. Either to apologise, or to hand out more of the same, and whichever it was, she didn't want to know. She was tempted not to answer the door, but then the buzzer went again, imperatively, and he might well be prepared to stand there for the duration unless she let him in.

She sighed, tightened the belt of her robe, and trailed down the short passage to the door.

'*Kalispera*,' Alex said shortly, and walked past her into the flat.

Gasping, she went after him into the living room. 'What do you think you're doing? What do you want?'

'You,' he said. 'And I have crossed Europe to find you.' He added with steely emphasis, 'It has been an inconvenience.'

'Then you could have saved yourself the trouble,' Natasha retorted. 'Because I came back here to get away from you.' She wrapped her arms defensively round her body. 'So will you go, please?'

'Why? Are you expecting your previous visitor to return?' There was a harsh note in his voice, and the dark eyes raked her, as if he'd reached out and dragged the robe from her body. 'If so, I think you will be disappointed, *agapi mou*. He seemed in no mood to do so as he left.'

'Can you blame him?' she queried tautly. She held up the magazine. 'Discovering that his girlfriend had been tagged as your Mystery Mistress?'

'But you were never his, *matia mou*,' Alex reminded her softly. 'Only mine.'

'Not any longer.' She took a deep breath. 'As we both know. So why are you here?'

'To talk.' He took off the jacket of the dark suit he was wearing, and tossed it across the arm of the sofa, before loosening his tie, and unfastening a couple of shirt buttons. 'May I sit down?'

'If you haven't the decency to leave,' she said. 'How can I stop you?'

'Will you sit with me?' He patted the sofa cushion, and she winced inwardly with by mute anguish as she remembered all the evenings in the *saloni* curled up on his lap or beside him, her head on his shoulder.

'No.' The denial emerged more fiercely than she'd intended, and elicited a wry smile.

'Even if I tell you there is nothing to fear,' he asked. 'That I have given my word of honour not to…molest you in any way.'

She answered him with silence, taking the small chair with wooden arms as far from the sofa as the room allowed, and tucking the skirts of her robe around her bare feet and ankles.

The silence lengthened, then he said quietly, 'Why did you run away, *matia mou*? My father's friends are kind people. They would have welcomed you. I told you so in my letter.'

Natasha bit her lip. 'Not if they'd known what I really was,' she returned. 'I preferred to return to my own friends.'

'Leaving poor Zeno distraught,' he commented. 'When you were not at the pharmacy, he called at every shop in town, searching for you. He even went to the hospital in case your headache had become heatstroke. It was only then that he remembered the ferry.

'I had just disembarked from *Selene* with our visitors when he returned and told me you had gone.'

His mouth tightened. 'And there was nothing I could do—not immediately. Having placated my father over our affair and promised my support for his future plans, I could not desert him just when I was most needed.

'I could only pull a few strings and arrange for someone at Naxos Airport to contact me if you tried to get a plane.' He added quietly, 'The next forty-eight hours of silence were the worst of my life. I began to think you had gone for ever.'

'A good thought,' Natasha said stonily. 'Hang on to it.' *Because you have no right to talk to me like this.* 'But I didn't intend to distress Zeno. Please offer him my abject apologies when you see him next.'

'Abject?' Alex's mouth twisted. 'Not you. But why didn't you wait until I could come to you? You knew the difficulties.'

'Yes,' she said. 'Those tricky negotiations. I hope they've been successfully completed.'

His shrug, his smile were rueful. 'To some extent at least. And that is one of the reasons I am here, *agapi mou*—to invite you to a wedding.'

For a moment, Natasha was stunned into silence. Then she said hoarsely, 'That is—unbearably cruel.'

'Ah,' he said quietly. 'But you should be accustomed to that, according to our last meeting. So, may I have an answer, if you please?'

'I already have a wedding to go to,' she said. 'I think one's enough for the time being. So the answer is—no.'

He gave her a reflective look. 'Kyria Theodosia will be much grieved if you stay away.'

'I hardly think so. She wanted me out of the way while the marriage was being set up.' She glared at him, glad that she could fight her pain with anger. 'She and everyone else. Of course, there were Irini's feelings to consider,' she added raggedly. 'But if you think she'll have forgiven and forgotten anything that's happened if I turn up at the wedding, think again. Because I can guarantee she won't.'

She lifted her chin. 'And on whose side would I sit? Or do they have a special corner in the church for the groom's discarded mistresses? If so, I think it will be quite crowded enough without my presence.'

He said harshly, 'You are being unfair, Natasha. My father has loved two women in his life. One was my mother, and the other is Theodosia Papadimos, the lady he intends to marry on Alyssos next month. As you well know.'

He saw her stunned expression, and his eyes narrowed. 'What is wrong? My father gave you my letter, didn't he?'

'Yes.' Her voice was almost inaudible. 'But I didn't read it. I—I threw it away.'

'In the name of God, why?' His tone was incredulous.

'Because you were going to marry Irini. I heard it from your father, but—I couldn't bear to see it in black and white.' She was on her feet suddenly, white-faced, her voice raw. 'I needed somehow to pretend it wasn't happening. Is that what you wanted to hear? Are you satisfied now?'

'Natasha *mou*,' he said gently. 'Even you must know that marriage between brother and sister is illegal.'

'Brother and sister.' She pronounced the words slowly and carefully as if she'd never heard them before. 'What are you talking about?'

He held out a hand. 'Sit with me,' he invited quietly, 'while I tell you what was in my letter—how the feud began.'

She walked slowly to the sofa, and sat beside him. Careful to keep her distance.

The dark eyes held hers. 'Think of a man and a woman,' he said. 'Already friends. He, a widower, she, a neglected and lonely wife. They fall in love in a place that has become a sanctuary for them both, and wish to spend the rest of their lives together, if her husband, with whom she shares little but a roof, will give her a divorce.

'But he refuses, telling her, among other threats, she will never see her two young sons again if she humiliates him by leaving.

'Instead, he demands that she return to him, even though she is carrying her lover's child.'

Natasha whispered, 'Oh, God, this can't be true. It can't…'

'Believe it,' he said. 'She refuses, saying that her lover will fight beside her for the custody of her children. But on his way to her, her man's car is involved in a serious collision with a hit-and-run driver, and he is badly injured.

'At the same time, the house where she knew happiness is totally destroyed, as if it never existed. Leaving her with little choice but to return to what passed for a home.'

She said in a stifled voice, 'You mean—you're saying it was Thio Basilis who did…all that? Those terrible things? Oh, no. Please—no. It—it's too horrible.'

He said levelly, 'If you doubt me, *matia mou*, Madame Papadimos herself will confirm all that I have told you.'

Natasha was silent, staring down at her fists clenched in her lap. At last, she sighed. 'I—I don't need to do that. Everything you've told me explains so much that I didn't understand. Things that I felt were wrong, but didn't examine too deeply, because he—Thio Basilis—was so kind to me.'

'You took the place of a daughter he could not love, *pedhi mou*.'

She said bitterly, 'No wonder Irini hates me.'

'She will not always do so.' He took her hands in his, gently stroking her fingers. 'Although the truth has been a great shock to her, and her immediate reaction was everything we had most feared. And that is why, having witnessed her past behaviour to you, I needed to get you away. I told my father I would not allow you to be subjected again to that kind of abuse or worse.'

He added drily, 'Papa now fully understands my caution. At one point she was like a wild thing, threatening violence—to herself and everyone around her. Even her mother. But she is already becoming calmer, as she comes to realise that she now has a father who loves and wants her.'

She said quietly, 'Also a brother who will be kind to her. And your father and Thia Theodosia have found each other again too. Which is—wonderful.' She swallowed. 'Do Stavros and Andonis know the truth—about the feud?'

'Kyria Theodosia says her husband spared her that final humiliation, and they still believe it was a business quarrel, as I did myself until a few years ago.'

He paused. 'Irini will keep their family name, and, to the world, Papa will be no more than a caring and affectionate stepfather.'

He smiled a little. 'When Irini has learned to control her temper and her tongue, he will find her a good man to warm her bed and her heart.'

She withdrew her hand from his clasp. 'So her fate is already sealed.' She tried to speak lightly. 'And, unlike me, she has no means of escape.'

'Is that what you want, *pedhi mou*? To escape?' There was an odd note in his voice.

'Of course. That's why I'm here, back to my own life, and my real world.'

'But not to your boyfriend, it seems,' he said. 'Or your best friend, either. Won't you find it lonely?'

Not as lonely, she wanted to cry out, as loving you, without hope of return.

She shrugged. 'Independence has other advantages.'

'If Iorgos had been driving you,' he said softly, 'you might not have found escape so easy.'

It was not easy now, when he'd moved closer, making her aware of the warm, evocative scent of his skin. When she'd only have to reach out a hand to free the remaining buttons on his shirt.

She hurried back into speech. 'Is he waiting outside for you now?'

'No, he is in Athens, with a new job at one of our companies. I have managed at last to persuade my father that I no longer needed a watchdog.'

She looked away. 'Mac said you'd received threats at one time.'

'Yes,' he said. 'It was three years ago, just after I had seen you at an embassy party, and defied my father's anger by writing to Kyrios Papadimos requesting his permission to call on you formally to court you as my wife.'

She stared at him, her eyes widening. 'You—asked Thio Basilis—for me?' She shook her head. 'But why?'

'Because I looked at you, *agapi mou*, and fell in love. It was that incredible—that simple—and I was lost forever.

'I went home after the party in a daze, and told Papa I had found the only girl in the world I would ever want to marry, and he smiled. I told him who you were, and he stopped smiling, and forbade me to think of you again.

'We—quarrelled, but I wrote my letter anyway, and the reply came back the following day. I have it still. Kyrios Papadimos warned me that if I—the womanising scum my father had spawned—ever turned my degraded eyes in the direction of his innocent child again, he, Basilis, would ensure that I would first be beaten unconscious, and then damaged so badly that I would never again be able to satisfy a woman in bed or father children.'

'He said that?' Natasha repeated numbly. 'Oh, God, how could he?'

Alex grimaced. 'There was worse. He also added that what had happened to my father would be nothing by comparison. Letting me know that Papa's car crash had been no accident, and that he had been deliberately driven off the road. Taunting me with it.'

Natasha pressed a hand to her trembling mouth. She said again, 'Oh, God...'

'It was clear there was more to this than mere business rivalry,' Alex went on. 'So I showed my father the letter, and it was then that he confessed to me about his affair with Theodosia Papadimos, and told me there had been a child—a daughter he had never seen. And in telling me, he made it clear that you were lost to me forever. That no girl was worth such a risk, and I must forget you.'

He shook his head. 'I went a little crazy, I think. I could think only that he had robbed me of my one chance of happiness with the girl I loved. I told him that I hated him—that I would never forgive him.

'And he looked at me with tears in his eyes, and said, "Do you think I shall ever forgive myself, Alexandros *mou*?"'

He paused. 'Since that time, Iorgos has been my shadow. It was only after Kyrios Papadimos died that I allowed myself to think of you again. To wonder. I knew that you had gone back to England, but had a nominal place on the Papadimos board. As your brothers were already experiencing commercial and financial difficulties, it seemed possible that I might see you again.

'When it was suggested that any deal between our organisations should be sealed by marriage, I felt as if I had been given the world. I wanted you so badly, I forgot to be cautious. I ordered an immediate refit of *Selene* for our honeymoon, and extended the work already being done at the house on Alyssos. I told myself we could spend our weekends there, at first, and extend our visits once our children came.

'I could think of nothing but the dream of my heart which was coming true at last. My dream of you, Natasha *mou*, my moonlight goddess.'

He paused, then added flatly, 'Then I received the second letter, and all dreaming stopped. I was destroyed—sick to my stomach. It was as if I'd lost you a second time, and this time it would be forever.

'I also knew by then that your brothers intended to renege on any deal made between us, so I was angry, as well as hurt. I thought of you naked by the pool, and decided to take the sexual favours you were offering, and enjoy them for as long as it suited me.

'Instead I found innocence, and, though I hated myself for what I had done, I could not let you go. And when I came to you that first night on *Selene* and found you waiting for me, all in white, I could only think of the adorable bride on our wedding night I had longed for. It was like coming home. As if an empty space in my life had been filled at last. So, what could I do but ask you to be my wife?'

'But you didn't say that.' Her voice shook. 'You just talked about…making amends, and the possibility I could be pregnant. And you told me later you didn't want me or any of your other women to fall in love with you.'

His smile was wry. 'Self-protection, *pedhi mou*. I thought you hated me. Every time I tried to get close, you pushed me away. Even when we were so happy on the island, I thought it was just my lovemaking that you wanted, and not my love. And when you said that being with me had been unbearable, I almost gave up all hope.'

She said huskily, 'For three years, I remembered the way you'd looked at me. Thought of you, and dreamed too, but never knew why.

I was so afraid that I would never be more to you than another willing body in bed. Just one more among so many. That's what I couldn't bear.'

'I am no saint, *matia mou*,' Alex said gently. 'But I can swear I have been more selective than you might think.'

He slipped off the sofa and knelt beside her. He said slowly, 'I was yours since that first night, Natasha, and you have always been mine. My woman, my wife and the only love of my heart. Now, and for all time.' His hands trembled as they closed round hers. The dark eyes pleaded. 'So, will you take me as your husband, my dearest one, and let us heal the hurt of the past?'

'Alex,' she whispered. 'Oh, darling, I've been so unhappy without you. And I love you so much—more than you could ever believe.'

He got to his feet, pulling her up with him, holding her for one endless moment. He said softly, 'You will find I have infinite faith, my sweet one.' Then kissed her, his mouth warm and ineffably tender as it caressed hers.

At last he put her from him, sighing reluctantly. 'And now you must get dressed, *agapi mou*. I have promised Madame Papadimos that I would take you to her.'

She gasped. 'Thia Theodosia's here in London?'

'She is here to buy her wedding dress, and, if God was good, to help you choose yours too. Also to act as your chaperone,' he added pensively. 'She and my father are prepared to forgive my past behaviour with you, only on condition that I now behave with suitable restraint until our wedding night. So you will have your formal wooing after all, *agapi mou*.'

She stood up on tiptoe and kissed him on the lips, swiftly and mischievously. 'Formal, and very short, I hope, Kyrios Alexandros.'

He laughed. 'Shamefully brief, Kyria Natasha, I give you my word. And once I have you,' he added with sudden fierceness, 'I shall keep you safe forever.'

'I know,' she said, and her smile was misty. 'My dearest love—I know.'